NOBILITY

BY

CORINA ZURCHER

NeverMore Publications, LLC

Library of Congress Cataloging-in-Publication Data Available

Library of Congress Control Number: 2017907807

ISBN: 0991172485
ISBN-13: 978-0-9911724-8-1

Printed in the U.S.A.
First American edition, June 2017

"The true soldier fights not because he hates what is in front of him, but because he loves what is behind him."

— G.K. Chesterton

I

He walked with footsteps of fury. The burnt-out path he pursued was branded with the signet of the storm that would soon be coming. The rage within his heart rivaled the fire of the burning sun as his eyes roamed the abandoned roads that once led to the sea — the lifeline of the realm — the domain he claimed as his own. He tilted his head to the side, listening for the sound he longed to hear: the song of beauty being sung from the trees, rising up from the rainbow of blooms adorning the hills, decorating its borders, marking the landscape with signs of terrestrial change as one travelled from one side of the realm to the other.

But there was nothing.

No echo of sound.

No sign of life.

Only the markings of death.

He had reached the banks of what was once Mariner Sea and stopped dead in his tracks. His heart stilled at what he was seeing before him. The brutal suddenness of his halt caused even the air to grow still under his stance.

Gone. The people. The fluid waters. All of it…gone!

And as his turquoise-colored eyes stared out at the lifeless sea, the muscles in his body tightened like a noose, constricting his movements like a vice as the rage and the hate twisted and wove around him like ivy, binding and shielding any love, hope or empathy he had left from breaking free and pouring out over those remaining inside the realm.

He dropped to his knees, driving his fists into the ground as he tried to keep the agony he felt at bay. He was answered with a shower of ash and dust exploding up from the soil, covering him with the bones of the dead, the tears of the forgotten, and the rubble of war.

The horror of the nightmare before him was more than he could bear. But just before he erupted into a tornado of fury to unleash his wrath over those of the living, he felt the earth move slowly beneath him. He quickly shifted his eyes to the ground and saw the soil swirling and weaving between his clenched fists, gently, consolingly.

That was when the noose loosened and the vice lost its grip, hinting at the tone of oncoming virtue — but only just a bit.

His shoulders suddenly dropped as the tension seemed to dissolve from his body as the soil continued to caress his skin. He spread his fingers wide, filling his hands with the dirt as it moved coolly over his palms, caressing him with a whispered message all too dear.

He sighed, "Ah, sister..." He closed his eyes to feel her movement, to understand what she was trying to say. He felt a low rumble rising from beneath his feet in reply; it was a groan and a yearning, pleading with him to move with her.

And so he did.

He stood and followed her path as she lamented over the earth and out across the realm. Through the woods of hollowed-out trees he followed, past the haunted desert, up the thirst-starved hills he walked as the land trembled and quaked, beckoning him to follow.

And as he reached the top of a forlorn hilltop in Bull Valley, he knew exactly where she had led. He stood there overlooking the fortress his sister had guarded, the queen he helped protect. Begrudgingly, he knew what she was trying to tell him; even as she wove her vines around his legs and feet, rooting him to the spot she wanted him to see, binding him to the moment she wanted him to understand. And she knew that he would. Whatever her will desired, he would do — even this.

He looked down at the pleading vines wound around his legs and reluctantly nodded his comply. Her grip squeezed tightly around his ankles, her answer filled with gratitude and relief, before unraveling around his legs and sinking rapidly back into the ground. The rumble of her movement continued down the hilltop heralding the sound of a small avalanche, and out toward the massive gates she had constructed fifty years ago.

It was there that he saw a young man and his cheetah warrior standing outside the enormous iron gate.

The noble heart.

It was then he felt the heat of the sun radiating down over him.

Looking up at its crimson hue, he understood what was about to happen. The moment had finally come. It was time. And as the wind

blew across his shoulders and out toward the kingdom below, he knew they were all in agreement. Their sister had summoned them all, for the time had come to unleash one last moment of hope.

The woman they had guarded for the time when creation needed a light to shine through would get one last chance to let the flame of mercy burn bright through the darkness; one last moment to allow what was meant to be from the beginning be again. He knew that if this final act did not change the hearts of men in this realm, there would be no other chances. No more opportunity to fix what had been broken. And as he stood there with the wind on his back, the sun shining down from above, and the earth moving beneath his feet, he vowed that he would destroy those who scoffed at this last gift of mercy, those who tried to extinguish the flame.

He watched as his sister's vines gathered the lion prince and cheetah warrior within the bird queen's gates, yet he did not celebrate the moment. He did not dance to the tap beat of grace, for although he bent to his sister's will and would hold back the storm of rage that quelled in his heart, he believed this last effort would be in vain. The dust of ash and bone adorning his footsteps was evidence that the realm did not understand the gift of beauty or the blessing of life. Instead, it tore down the banner of peace and wove a flag of violence and abuse in the name of power — a power that was never their own. Mariner Sea was the only argument he needed to remind them all if anyone disagreed with his perspective again.

The sea…

How his heart ached for the massive sea.

He had watched the hearts of men across this realm for centuries — and it was all the same. Nothing ever changed. And for that reason, he knew that even this promise finally kept would turn to tragedy; and in that knowledge he did not weep, for he knew that vengeance was coming with or without his influence. For there was another being slumbering beside the queen whose mind was a mirror of his own. This being could see the darkness inside the hearts of men — just as he could. And as the Lord of the Sea stood on the hilltop overlooking Bird Kingdom down below, the warm breeze blowing across the land suddenly turned cold.

II

Queen Rebekah whirled around as the wind blew wildly all throughout the ballroom. Her charcoal-colored eyes roamed the marble floor, scanning every column, every nook, searching behind every shadow, seeking the one who had awakened her. She knew whomever it was had to be a man, for it was Man that had set the stage for her demise, and it was Man who needed to be redeemed.

As she continued to search the large ballroom, she saw only darkness. Yet as she shifted her eyes to the shadows, she could feel his eyes on her — the stranger hiding in the dark. Rebekah took a step forward toward one corner in particular when the room suddenly began to spin. She halted mid-step, trying to center herself, when she heard a voice inside her head, *"Queen…"*

She looked down at the floor, using all of her energy to shut out the voice just as another one called to her.

"My queen…"

She lifted her eyes, finally finding her center. The room stopped spinning the moment she looked at the eagle.

"Kenuen!" The eagle warrior bowed his head to his queen. "You are alive!" Rebekah looked all around her, forgetting all about the intruder inside the room, finding that all that mattered at this moment were the birds standing before her. "All of you!" She took in the sight of her warriors, examining the strength of their limbs, feeling the fullness of their wings. Her face radiated joy and relief as they stretched their limbs wide, ruffling their feathers, standing on their own two feet.

Alive.

Rebekah's heart was pounding in exhilaration as they circled around her: the falcons, the hawks, the crows, owls, eagles and woodpeckers.

"Let me look at you!" She reached out to them and cupped their faces in her palms: her children, her family, her clan. They were healthy, vibrant. Rebekah was completely overcome as she took in each and every one of their faces, caressing them as they gathered around her. Lowering their heads, relishing in her touch, the bird queen realized what she was witnessing in her flock — a new birth.

Tears streamed down her face as she tried to find the words, "In all my days as your queen, I have never been as happy as I am at this moment." She lowered her head. "It was my fault that we almost perished. It was my blindness to my desires that got in the way of my duty to you as your queen. For that, I beg you for your forgiveness."

Daniel and Cheetah hid in the shadows in the corner of the room, watching as the bird queen turned to face her warriors. Cheetah grabbed hold of Daniel and hissed in his ear as he tried to pull him to safety, "My prince! We must go!"

"No!" Daniel tore himself free from Cheetah's grasp and gripped the marble column tight as he tried to get a better view of the scene that was laying itself out before him. He was mesmerized by what he had just done and by what he was now seeing as the painted images and frozen beings had suddenly come to life. Daniel was overcome with a deep sense of joy, for he had done it. He had awakened the queen who would feed the clans. She would send the rain and end the famine, and the realm would thrive once more. There was hope now standing before him, wiping out the idea of hopelessness.

"I promise you, all of you, that for the rest of my days, I will *never* allow my heart to stand in the way of my head when it comes to you, my clan. *Your* lives are all that matter now. Yours alone. "

She lifted her head, and it was then that Daniel saw them — *her eyes*. They were darkening from what appeared to be a shining gray to a cold black. The moment he saw the darkness behind them, he froze, confused by her sudden shift in emotion. Her face, gentle and loving moments before, was now filled with a coldness that made his whole body shudder. He looked at his guardian and saw Cheetah's fur sticking straight up as he digested her vow; he too could not hide his sense of dread.

Daniel remained hidden, trying to decipher what all of this meant. This was not the queen he had remembered Reginald telling him about. She was good and kind. The one he thought he saw just moments before. The one that was now standing before him was…

"If she is awakened, there's no telling what she'll do! Vengeance or mercy…she could annihilate us all with her army of birds!"

His uncle's warning suddenly thundered in his ears. What was she?

Daniel's eyes roamed over the powerful warriors that filled the room. They were strong, untouched by the devastation of the famine that had weakened and crippled his clan…and all the others.

"Stay away from that kingdom! Stay away from the queen!"

"My queen, what of the other clans? Now that we have awakened, would they not try to march upon us once again?"

"If they do, Kenuen…attack."

Daniel could not believe it. This was not the way it was supposed to be. This was not the way *she* was supposed to be. He knew, however, that he had to get out of here. *Now.* Daniel released his grasp on the marble column and began to back away from the scene before him, knowing that they needed to escape unseen, but all he kept thinking was, What have I done? He had just awoken what appeared to be the most powerful clan in the entire realm. One that appeared to be unstoppable. One that was focused. One…that had suffered. And that's when it him like a punch to the gut: his clan…*they* were the ones responsible for the bird clan's failed annihilation. *They* were the ones who had tried to kill the queen so long ago. *The lions.* And here he was, a lion prince hiding in the shadows of the bird queen's kingdom. What would they do to him if they found him? And even worse: what would they do to members of the den if any of the Lion's Den warriors came looking for him?

He suddenly thought of his grandfather. He and members of the den would surely come looking for him. Knowing his king, he was already on his way. He had to warn him to stay away. He had to warn them all.

Get out of here. Get out! Now!

Daniel's mind screamed the silent command as the flow of fear pumped through his veins. He nodded to Cheetah as the warrior pulled him back toward the open doorway they had entered through; they fled without notice out to the grounds beyond.

Cheetah and Daniel raced through the gardens, running the fastest they had ever run. The wind was blowing wildly all around them — and it was freezing.

"What did I do, Cheetah?"

Cheetah hissed, "I don't know. Just run!"

They ran even faster.

Her words were like chains bound around his heart, *"When it comes to you, my clan….your lives are all that matter now. Yours alone."*

Why? Why had he come here! Why had the vines pulled him through?

Cursing himself, they were almost to the gate when Daniel noticed a gigantic shadow on the ground hovering over them. It was keeping pace with them seeming to swallow them whole as they continued running down the hill. He looked up just as a large being slammed down in front of them.

Cheetah jumped in front of Daniel, shielding him from the darkened creature that had crashed down before them. Daniel fell back against Cheetah's force as his guardian growled and hissed ferociously at the beast that had just descended. The lion prince looked closer at the cloaked, seven-foot-tall being that towered over them, and what he saw before him was the most lethal and malicious-looking clan warrior he had ever seen.

It was his eyes.

"Tok...tok...tok..."

The warrior's eyes glowed and matched the scarlet-colored armor that adorned his muscular form. The creature lowered his ebony head and stared the prince down. *"Lionsss are not to be trusted..."*

It was the raven from his dream.

Images flashed across his mind as the eagle and the raven emerged from the fire: *Rising from the shadows on her right and on her left there came an eagle and a raven, whose eyes glowed red, red like the sun. The bird warriors turned away from the fire — one faced east while the other faced west. Upon their movement, the flames grew higher as the woman swayed before the flames...*

It was his dream that had driven him here.

And before Daniel could react, Cheetah was thrown like a ragdoll down the hill. The raven turned and lunged at Daniel, driving his two black talons deep into the prince's shoulders. Daniel roared in pain as the raven ripped him off of the ground and into the sky. He shouted in fear, *"CHEETAH!!!"*

His cries echoed across Bird Kingdom, and the only being to hear them was the Watcher in the Sea still standing on the hilltop in Bull Valley. The moment he saw the raven rip the lion prince into the sky with cries for help answered by none, it only made him smile.

III

Nathan and members of the den were making their way swiftly across the plains when a warm breeze blew all across the land. That was when he heard it: a voice crying out in pain. He knew that voice, for it was the voice of the one being he cherished above all; the one he had been trying to protect all these years.

"DANIEL!!!"

He shouted so loud, that the earth beneath him seemed to shake as he and a small band of Lion's Den warriors raced toward Bird Kingdom. He knew that's where Daniel had gone. And he knew that if the prince was there, shouting in pain, the queen must have awakened.

For all the years he had waited for the moment for Rebekah to rise, he did not anticipate a day like today. How did Daniel even get out of the den? How had he found his way to Bird Kingdom? He was going to find Daniel and bring him home and lock him inside the den for all eternity. Then he was going to strangle Cheetah for not doing his job in keeping Daniel safe. But even as all these thoughts and emotions swirled through his head as he ran toward her gates, they were dominated by one simple plea, *Please, Rebekah, do not harm him. Do not destroy the last piece of me that has held me together all these years. Not him. Hurt me instead. Only me.*

Nathan's heart trembled in agony as the mirrors of the faces of the dead flashed across his mind: the body of his dead son Matthew, the lifeless form of his daughter-in-law Tara, the woeful sobs of his short-lived queen Lara…on and on it went as the agonizing cry of his grandson thundered in his ears. Daniel was in pain. It was that single sound of suffering that drove him onward at a pace not even his warriors could keep up with.

The lion warriors raced behind their king as they ran as one toward the dead kingdom that had now come to life. They were almost to the border when, out of nowhere, a panther warrior cried out as he was suddenly knocked to the ground. A tiger suddenly hit the ground, followed by a lynx and a cheetah. All around Nathan his warriors fell one by one until he slowed his step, coming to a complete stop. He looked all around only to find that he was the only one still standing. That was when he saw the mounds of dirt shift and move until a multitude of large-winged birds rose up from the rubble like new hatchlings. Nathan's eyes slit to a cat as the ostrich warriors rose from the ground, their eyes blazing with fear and rage. They had risen from the holes in the rubble around them and had attacked his warriors. They continued to rise until Nathan and his warriors were completely outnumbered twenty to one.

"*LIONS!!!*" Their long necks snapped at them like an army of whips. Their screeching cries pierced the lions' ears as the ostriches kept the lions at bay. They circled the lion warriors, moving in rapidly as more rose up from the ground all around them. Nathan knew they were about to attack at any moment, which meant only one thing: it was going to get bloody.

"*STOP!!!!*"

The ostrich warriors suddenly stopped their whipping motions and stood as still as statues, halting in mid-movement, immediately attuned to the voice of their chief. Racing forward, weaving between the army of ostrich warriors that now covered the ground, having risen like weeds over the course of this race, Nathan watched the ostrich chief storming toward him.

The moment he saw Nathan come into view, the ostrich warrior's bulbous eyes seemed to grow even larger. His head dipped back and forth as he surveyed the scene before him. The chief began to pace rapidly, as if he was weighing his choices. It appeared to Nathan that he was moving so swiftly back and forth that he just might be gathering enough momentum behind his neck to strike his beak down hard and fast if need be.

"Ume."

"King…you are still alive…"

Nathan gripped his sword debating his next move. All eyes from the den were on him.

The ostrich chief surveyed the lion warriors alongside Nathan, taking in their number and their form.

"Your den looks weak. Malnourished. Fading…" His eyes darted back to Nathan. "And yet you charge."

"My grandson, the lion prince, has awakened your queen." Ume's pupils dilated rapidly as he took in the news. "I've come to ensure that he is returned to the den safely. I heard him shouting from the sky. Where is he?" Nathan's eyes were wild with fury. It was taking every ounce of his strength to remain calm.

Ume extended his long neck to the side as if surprised that the lion king would dare speak to him in such a tone, considering the fact that he and his warriors were outnumbered. "No doubt with my queen. If he cries in agony, then he deserves to be in it." The lion guard Chester growled lowly behind his king.

"Not if he is the Noble Heart, *bird*. Take me to your queen before I give the command for my guards to attack."

"Attack? You are outnumbered, *king*."

"Numbers matter not when the life of a lion prince is at stake. You may have just awoken, but eternal slumber is just around the corner if the prince is not returned to me...alive and whole."

Ume began to pace again, this time slowly, never taking his eyes off of the lion king. He screeched loudly and a warrior trotted over to him. The chief spoke in whispers to the warrior as Nathan and everyone else waited. The warrior dipped his head and raced toward Bird Kingdom.

"We shall wait, lion king, to see what my queen commands. Your grandson's fate is in her hands." He screeched a loud cry that caused the den warriors to flinch as the ostrich warriors gathered around them. Ume looked directly at the lion king. "As is yours..."

Chief Ume turned and raced back toward the mountains on the footsteps of his soldier, leaving Nathan and his warriors with nothing to do but count the time...and pray.

IV

"How much time has passed?"

Queen Rebekah and her birds were gathered around the woodpecker guard named Wek-Wek as he finished hacking away at one of the two trees that stood on either side of where the queen had stood frozen in time. The tree collapsed and all gathered around its trunk as Wek-Wek examined the rings.

"Fifty years, my queen."

The warriors watched their queen's face as she deciphered this news. Part of Rebekah was shocked that so little time had passed, and yet it seemed like an eternity since she was last among the living.

She stood there thinking, Was there anybody left? Alexander, Ivan, Tatiana…Nathan. And then it happened. It hit her so violently and savagely, she did not see it coming. The air seemed to leave her lungs as a wave of sorrow and anguish constricted her diaphragm. That last moment of her life flashed before her eyes and poured out over her like an avalanche of pain: her clan on the verge of extinction, the ravens slaughtered, its lone remnant lying broken in her arms barely clinging to life, the armies of the lesser clans marching upon her gates followed by the gorilla clan. More memories poured out as the room spun violently all around her as the memories kept coming. Rebekah keeled over, sickened all at once as the memories engulfed her mind. It was then that the voices from those last moments came flooding back to her.

"Your lion lied to you…Nathan didn't love you at all."

"It is a relic. It belongs with my clan."

The room was a cyclone of memories and haunted voices, twisting and turning all around her. The queen could barely stand as the words hammered away at her.

"Don't…don't you cry, Rebekah, not in front of me and not over this. I told you. I told you to stay away from the lions…you…are a disgrace to your clan!"

The queen dropped to her knees trying to center herself, but the memories would not stop their moving pictures.

"Fire. Wind. Ice. Earth. Protect my clan…"

She could barely breathe; her body temperature rose as the memory recreated itself as her body reacted to the light striking through her body, electrifying it — until her last memory came forth and all went black and cold.

The queen crouched low to the floor, her body trembling; her fists were clenched into tight balls. She did not even realize that her birds were on the ground beside her. When she looked up, she saw them all around her, breathing hard, feeling her pain.

It was Kenuen who spoke through heavy breaths, "My queen, it's all right. They are nightmares of the past that to us are memories of yesterday. Our scars have yet to toughen."

She shook her head, trying to slow the pounding in her ears, "I am…" She looked at her birds, trying to find the words.

Kenuen interrupted her thought, "There is no one like you, queen; you remembered us in all your grief, you protected us when there was no way out, and we have lived on because of you. Our allegiance will never die. No weapon shall ever touch your head. And we, the clan, will rise from the ash heap on the dawn of this new day to set the world right. We march with the footsteps of the faithful. And where the wicked have thrived, under my watch and your command, they will not prevail. Not this day or any other day under the burning sun." He stared into the eyes of his beloved queen, "Though we have walked through the valley of the shadow of death, we fear no evil, nor do we fear this pain. For it is in the suffering that we become."

The pounding in her ears began to lessen until only a dull thud remained, pulsating with the slow beat of her heart. She breathed in long and deep. His words had calmed something deep inside her that could not be reached by any other words but the ones he had just spoken.

She nodded to him in gratitude and respect. It was then that the sun's rays slowly crept through the ballroom windows and shone down brightly over the queen and her clan. The bird queen turned her head and lifted her eyes to the light, closing them as she drank in the warmth of the sun. Breathing in the sunlight, she was consumed by a sense of overwhelming peace. And just as fast as the sun appeared, it faded away behind a cluster of clouds…and a cold wind followed.

"Tok…tok…tok…"

Rebekah's eyes burst open at the sound of his toggle. She whirled around and immediately stood as her raven assassin flew through the ballroom doors. She walked slowly toward him as he approached carrying a young man in his blackened talons. The moment Rebekah saw the man, her eyes swirled to sheer black as her raven descended. All the warriors were on their feet, their weapons were drawn; their pupils shrunk to the size of pins as the raven chief threw the young man down on the floor at his queen's feet.

"Poe."

Without a word, he swiveled his large head and peered at his queen, reading her mind without a spoken word.

"He wasss running back to hisss den…"

Rebekah's heart thundered inside her chest as she looked down at the young man.

A lion.

The young man stared at the surrounding birds with a look of both dread and terror. The clothing around his shoulders was stained with blood where Poe's talons had gripped him tight.

"The noble heart." Her words were barely a whisper but he had heard them.

Daniel turned his head and stared up at the queen. Her body stilled as she took in the features of his face. They were one and the same, and she knew they were *his*. She stared at the lion prince for a long time, siphoning the memories and emotions of the one who promised to love her forever — and did not.

Nathan.

She could see Nathan's face behind those aqua-colored eyes. And someone else…it was their color. The color of the Mariner Sea.

"He was married to Princess Lara this morning."

She immediately shut her eyes, feeling a sharp stab to her chest. She winced at its sudden impact and grabbed hold of her breast as she flinched in pain. She felt dizzy again. Kenuen was immediately behind her, holding her upright. She opened her eyes, centering herself just as two crow warriors dragged a cheetah warrior inside the room. They threw him down beside the young man as it growled and hissed. The cheetah immediately hovered around the young man as it bore its fangs and claws in a protective stance around the man. The crows had disarmed the den warrior and held his sword in their talons.

She breathed in deep, finally speaking, "So it is you…the noble heart."

The man turned his head.

"For one so noble, you have a coward's heart. Why do you run?" Cheetah hissed at her. She shifted her darkened eyes to the warrior. "Quiet, *cat*. For this one to awaken me, I would bring him no harm." She looked at Daniel. "I know your face. What is your name?"

He answered in a deep, confident tone, "Daniel."

Cheetah corrected him, *"Prince* Daniel."

"Prince Daniel. Why have you come here?"

Daniel was deadly silent, unsure of what to do next. He could not think of a single answer to her question, although he had a thousand reasons why. He looked at Cheetah's wild eyes and fur standing on end, knowing that the next words he spoke would either help them or hurt them. And then he remembered the book — *Reginald's* book. His journal filled with all of the queen's thoughts written down and remembered by the wisest member of her clan. He heard Reginald's voice sounding in his ears, *"She was a good queen…"*

Gaining confidence off of that single thought, Daniel pushed himself up off the floor and faced the queen. He bowed his head to her in respect. "Queen, I came here this day to awaken you." He lifted his head and looked deep into her eyes. "The clans in the five kingdoms are dying. They're starving."

The warrior birds swiveled their heads in unison the moment the lion prince spoke the words. Rebekah's eyes narrowed. "*Five* kingdoms. There are seven."

Daniel felt every single eye on him. He felt the heat of the bird warriors' bodies as they slowly gathered around him to hear the news of the status of the realm. All were silent as they waited in anticipation of his words. He swallowed hard as he said, "No, queen. There are five."

Her eyes, already black, seemed to grow even darker.

"Go on."

"There's been war. There's been plague. Famine is everywhere. As a result, two of the clans perished long ago." He saw the slightest tightening around Rebekah's jaw. She moved slowly toward the far end of the room and looked out at the sun. She could not see it. It had suddenly been covered by clouds, shutting the light out completely. Rebekah inhaled deeply but dared not ask which two. She was not ready to hear his answer. She knew that she would not be able to bear it if it were one in particular. "What made you come here after all this time?"

He chose his words carefully. "Your eagle — Reginald." She turned and looked at him. Tears filled her eyes as her they rapidly began to brighten.

At the sound of Reginald's name, the bird warriors cried out. The color behind Rebekah's eyes began to shift to a softer hue. Poe, however, remained as still as a statue, silent amongst the shouts. Cheetah continued to watch his every move, disturbed by the fact he showed no sign of emotion at the great eagle captain's name. If anything, his appearance seemed to darken even more. It was then that a chill ran down his spine. There was someone else in the room; they were watching from the shadows. *Not human.* A ghost perhaps? Cheetah turned his head toward the darkness but saw nothing there. When he looked back, the raven was staring right at him. He lowered his black head like a bull, his scarlet eyes glowing blood red. The raven knew he had sensed the presence in the darkness — and he wasn't happy about it. Cheetah knew they needed to get out of this place as fast as possible. But how? He turned his attention back to his prince.

"You know of my eagle."

Daniel nodded. "He has come to the den to visit me often."

Poe's body twitched, as if an electric shock shot down his spine.

"He has told me much about you. His memories of you know no bounds. Which is why I came here. I believed him. I believed every word he ever said about you. And now that I'm here, my only hope is that my belief in his words is true."

Rebekah looked at all the birds surrounding her, looking for his face amongst the flock. She had forgotten all about Reginald. And out of nowhere, the room began to spin once more. Rebekah suddenly had a hard time breathing as she tried to talk.

"Reginald...I need you to do something for me."

The memories came flooding back.

"I will not go down this day. Not for any man. Not for any reason."

Daniel watched as the colors behind Rebekah's eyes continued to swirl.

Where was Reginald?

Rebekah desperately tried to feel for him, to sense him like she always had before. Yet there was nothing. Nothing but Poe. She tried to stop the overwhelming feeling of anger and grief from overcoming her entirely by focusing on her bird warriors surrounding her instead.

"Queen Rebekah..."

She turned her attention back to the prince, trying to focus on him to center herself, but the room kept spinning.

"I've come here on the hope that you will help the clans in their darkest hour."

That was when the spinning suddenly stopped. Whatever softness was trying to penetrate the queen's heart was suddenly defeated at the moment by the prince's words.

"Their darkest hour..." Rebekah could not quite swallow those

simple words as she thought of her own. How she admired this young prince for daring to come to her doors to plead for her help after all that had happened, but something in her refused to feel the impact of what he was saying. Her heart was a distant thread that had severed itself from her connection to a realm she loved so long ago when she had travelled to the lion's den; there was no way to feel the sympathy the young prince was trying to convey. And without looking at him, she simply replied, "I will not help the clans."

Daniel swallowed hard, remembering her words moments before where she vowed to help only her own clan. He moved in front of her, hoping to stir her heart once more. He could not leave this place without laying it all to bear. "But the people...my people...they..."

Rebekah's eyes swirled to sheer black, "The *people* of this land, noble prince, wished to destroy me and my kingdom! Look me in the eye, lion, and tell me if these people were part of the reason the realm has now become five!"

The birds reacted with loud caws as she shouted her words. Daniel stepped back, taken off guard at the ferocious tone upon which she had suddenly spoken. Cheetah tensed as his cat eyes shifted to the raven. The assassin stood absolutely still, memorizing every movement and word spoken by his queen.

"The people I knew wanted my lands for their own wanton desires! They all wanted me dead! And they almost accomplished it. Are those the people you are referring to...*your* people?"

Seeing the rage behind Rebekah's eyes, Daniel knew it would be futile to answer.

Rebekah continued, "Tell me, lion, tell me why I should care. Tell me why my heart should bleed and weep for such a cry. Your people did not want me. They only loved me that I seemed to die — especially you lions."

Daniel could clearly see the pain behind the young queen's eyes. He knew her pain was just, he knew her logic was right, but he refused to allow the past to drag down the idea of a brighter future.

His voice was gentle yet strong. "No, queen. Those are not my people. You speak of the generations before me who lived behind the idea that it was better to live behind what you fear rather than challenge the idea that fear was meant to be overcome."

Poe slowly turned his head and zeroed in on the prince; even he had been struck by the wisdom of the young man.

"The people I speak of are the members of my den. The ones beyond it, I do not know, but I have heard their cry of pain. It echoes the cries of my own kind. It was your eagle, Reginald, who told me such stories of you. Your dreams, your desire to help our clans when you came to the den long ago. That is what I have counted on all these years as I came to your door. His memory of you...his most awesome queen."

Rebekah sat back against the trunk of the tree. She suddenly looked exhausted. And for the first time, Daniel noticed one other thing: she looked tremendously sad. Several moments passed before she finally spoke, "You are noble indeed, to come to my kingdom to turn the tide, young prince. I once rioted over such courage — change for the better. It was once the passion of my own heart."

Daniel could not help but notice she was using the past tense. For all the truth the lion prince had just spoken, it was too much for Rebekah to hear just then. She could barely breathe, let alone think. She needed time to adjust to being awakened in order to deal with the pain of being alive. She looked up at the Thunderbird Guard and issued the command, "Kenuen, take the prince and his protector back to his den."

The Thunderbirds moved in.

Daniel cried out, "Wait! I...you *must* help us or we will all die!"

His words reminded her of King Mar's words from long ago, *"Everyone knows what we want and what we need. Now it's up to Queen Rebekah to decide what it is that she wants...should she choose to help us and keep her word in doing so — or we all die."*

"You asked me why I came here! It was you! *You* were in my dreams! You were calling to me. And I answered!"

Rebekah did not understand what he was saying as he struggled in her guard's grip. He began to fight with one of the birds as they tried to grab him. *"Queen!!!"* Prince Daniel tried one last time, "Queen! The lion king...my grandfather...Nathan! He said you were best of them all! He loves you! He loves you still..."

At the sound of Nathan's name, the raven assassin's feathers stood straight up and Rebekah's entire body froze. She closed her eyes as the room shifted like a cyclone. It spun so rapidly she could see nothing but blurred images as she tried to stop the images from rushing through her mind. She could not breathe. "Kenuen, get him out..."

She was breathing hard, trying to control the pain.

Daniel shouted, *"Queen Rebekah!"*

She felt the stabbing pain in her chest once more. She could not control her pain as she gripped the trunk of the tree. She shouted, *"GET HIM OUT! GET HIM OUT OF HERE!!!!"*

The Thunderbirds lifted Daniel and Cheetah off of the ground and carried them out and into the sky as Rebekah continued to shout. More memories and words came rushing at her.

"I've given many things away, but the one thing I've never given anyone is my heart. I'm giving it to you. It will never belong to any other woman as long as I live. That is my promise to you, should you want it, but say you'll have it. Take it...because it's yours. Marry me, Rebekah..."

"GET...HIM...OUT!!!!" She shouted across the realm of time and space.

And as the eagles soared through the night sky, a being emerged from the shadows in the room and slowly came forth. He extended his hand to Rebekah, reaching for her as she fell to the ground. She recognized the strong features and dark eyes of the dead king.

"Queen..."

That was when the sky turned dark and the eagles went down and fell from the sky.

V

The bird king looked out over his balcony and onto the magnificent garden below. Nothing in the entire realm stirred his heart more than seeing his clan thrive, for down below was the pulse and the lifeline of the seven kingdoms, their seed to longevity. It was not the Mariner Sea like all had come to believe. It was the bird clan itself, as King Palimus himself had come to know. No other kingdom cultivated the land like the birds in the north.

Not the lions.

Not the gorillas.

Not even the wolves.

And there was no other king like Palimus.

No other king had thought to venture past their own borders beyond their own kingdom to see what lay beyond. But Palimus had — many times. He had seen rivers and mountains and footprints of creatures that were different than the clan beasts residing within the Seven Kingdoms. It excited him, it angered him, it motivated him. For it was proof that there were others in this world that would find them. Others that could overpower them. Others who could enslave them.

He was the only one out of the four kings that stayed awake at night pondering the unknown, the "what if" of the dawn of an unwanted day or haunting of a lethal night. The first time he had returned from the unknown territories beyond the kingdoms, the Wolf King Feyedor scoffed at Palimus when he told him he believed there were other clans beyond their realm that may be a threat to their kingdoms. The Gorilla King Brock laughed when the bird king asked him to go with him to explore the mountains beyond the jungle the next time around to share with him all that he had seen. It was not until he had gone to see the lion king Luther, that Palimus knew he was completely on his own as he sought to look at the bigger picture in life, rather than just the present moment on any given day.

"Palimus, whether there are kings and queens beyond our realm, matters nothing to me. Should they try to take what is not theirs to claim, they will die. Should they attempt to start a war with we four kings, they will be slaughtered. Should they try to bring their people to occupy our land, their clans will be destroyed before they even set foot near our borders. This idea bores me, for the only concern I have is for that sea. And Cassius thinks he can battle it out with us kings to rule this realm and bring down our houses. Mark my words: any king or queen who threatens the den will be burnt out before they even know what hit them. So go. Go on another one of your quests to subdue your curiosity or conquer your fear, but be ready for when the time comes to strike the lesser clans down. I will need your armies in the sky."

My armies in the sky.

His birds. There were no other creatures like those in his own clan. They could see what no man could; they could hunt like no other lioness. They lived in the ground, stood watch in the trees, hunted in the waters and in the sky. No other king could claim as such.

But then again, no other king honored the Sun like Palimus had. No other king stood before the fire and asked which way he should go. And no other king had the vision he had one night as he stood before the fire in honor of the Sun.

"Show me what I need to do to protect my clan. Take me where I am supposed to go to strengthen my house from within."

The flames burned hot that night, giving the ravens and the crows pause, for no other king before this one dared to move in the direction of the flame. And whatever Palimus had seen when he looked into the fire, fueled him and set him on a path that no man could drive him from.

He saw what the kings wanted. He understood what they needed. And he knew what they would be after — *his land.*

One needed something to offer, something to defend. And when Palimus looked out at the lush gardens filled with blooms and massive fields filled with crop, he knew what that something was: food. No one could live without it. And because of that basic fact, everyone would want it. His lands were plentiful enough to supply it to the entire realm forever. That was what part of the vision revealed as the flames spoke to him when he stood before the fire. And so he knew his army would need to be fierce enough to defend it.

So Palimus had called a meeting with the bird chiefs within his kingdom. He explained to the ostrich chief that the clan borders to the northeast side of the kingdom needed to be solidified, for it left them vulnerable to the lion's den side.

"Use the caves. Dig the pits and the ditches," he commanded.

And the ostrich chief obeyed.

Palimus described to the crow chief that there was more land beyond their borders that they could expand and grow more crops.

"Take it. Cultivate it. Make it grow. Fill it with your warriors to watch and guard from invasion from the outside — to those unknown."

And the crow chief fulfilled his king's wish.

To the eagle chief, the bird king commanded, "Build me an army of thunder and lightning, that watches as fiercely in the day as the ravens do at night."

And the eagle captain bowed and gave rise to the Thunderbird Guard.

The fire burned twice as hot as the bird king looked at the chiefs of his clan, knowing that the vision he had for his kingdom's future would one day come to pass. There was only one task left, the one that drove Palimus into an era of continuous sleepless nights as he thought to remedy the one thought that plagued his heart. It was the one piece of knowledge he had yet to decipher as he fought to fit its truth into his skewed perspective of his and his clan's destiny. The vision he had seen in the fire had one more piece of information.

"It'sss the lionsss…"

Palimus stared into the coal-colored eyes of his raven chief, the master assassin in all the land. The bird king nodded, feeling the tightening in his chest as he thought of the lion king.

"Luther is our ally against the lesser clans. If I am to believe all that I have seen, then I must distance myself from the den."

"What isss it that you have ssseen, my king?"

Palimus' olive skin suddenly paled as he looked at the raven chief. "The lions are not to be trusted, Damon. I have seen it in my vision. It was what I saw in the fire. They do not honor the Sun."

The feathers on the young raven chief's crown rose up all at once. *"The Sun…how can they not honor the heart that warmsss thisss realm!"*

To which the bird king replied, "They do not believe in the Old Ones, the Creators of this world. They believe they are illusions of an uneducated mind. They believe, Damon, that all the masters of this world are the ones who choose to be."

"The king or hisss beastsss?"

"In the den, there are no beasts. Only masters. I have seen the future.

And within the den will come a man, one who will be king, who will wish to rule over all. He will attempt to abolish the belief in the Creators; he will seek to wipe us out — an heir to our clan. I saw neither when nor how, but this can never be. For the time revealed to me..." He did not say the last part. It sickened him to do so as he thought of the last part the fire had revealed.

The raven's eyes darkened even more. *"Fire will not allow it either, my king. For our clan hasss alwaysss honored the burning Sun. Fire will show usss when. Fire will show usss how. Until then, we build for that moment. We grow for that time. We become...for what we need to be. In thisss, the ravensss will alwaysss defend."*

The mighty raven knelt down and lowered his large ebony head, exposing his neck to his king. Palimus laid his strong hand on top of his raven assassin's neck, breathing a little bit easier as they stood alone in the dark — the raven and his king.

"Our clan will never go down, Damon, this I promise you. I only wish I knew when the time would be so I would know when to act."

The raven chief lifted his ebony head, and in the moonlight, his coal-colored eyes seemed to glow. *"We will know the moment, my king. Fire will show usss. The sssign will come...from the Sun..."*

VI

Nathan was standing amongst his lion warriors, still surrounded by a flock of ostriches, when he saw a swarm of birds approaching from the sky. The ostriches craned their long necks around and screeched in excitement the moment they came into view. Nathan watched their faces as their reaction went from one of joy to one of absolute fear.

"RAAAAEEEKKK!!!"

The ostrich warriors rose up, crying out with the most shrill shriek Nathan had ever heard. Like a stampede, the warriors raced forward, leaving the lion king and his squadron all alone as they raced toward the swarm of oncoming birds.

Chester shouted, "Where are they going?"

Nathan's eyes slit to a cat the moment he realized what was happening. "DANIEL!!!"

The birds were falling from the sky.

The king and the guard took off directly behind the ostrich stampede. Nathan watched in horror as his grandson slipped from the eagle's grasp and began free falling toward the ground at rapid speed.

The ostrich warriors continued to race toward their falling brethren. As the eagles rocketed toward the ground, the ostriches gathered into a cluster as one, lowering their necks to the ground, linking arm to wing, creating a net of feathers to catch the bodies of their falling kinsmen. Daniel hit the net first and bounced off of it, rolling over the ostrich warriors, colliding onto the ground.

Cheetah immediately hit the feather net next and steamrolled Daniel, knocking the wind out of him. He looked up just in time to see the Thunderbirds fall onto the ostrich warriors; they bounced off of the makeshift net and rolled onto the ground. Daniel's eyes grew wide the moment he saw an eagle rolling his way.

Daniel immediately dove for cover under the ostrich barrier and barely avoided getting crushed by the large eagle warrior. While under the feathers, he looked up and saw that he was eye to eye with one of the ostriches. The soldier's almond shaped eye was right next to his face.

"Lion…"

Daniel crawled back from under their wings just as Nathan and the rest of the lion's den warriors raced up beside them. Nathan roared upon seeing his grandson. *"OUT OF THE WAY!"*

Nathan grabbed Daniel by the shoulders, lifting him up and inspecting him for any sign of injury. "ARE YOU HURT?!?"

He shook his head. "I'm all right."

Nathan breathed deeply, still clutching onto his grandson's shoulders. "You're all right." He rested his hand against Daniel's face.

Daniel nodded his reassurance. Nathan hugged him tight. "You're all right."

Daniel exhaled deeply, trying to catch his breath as he said, "I awakened the queen, grandfather."

Nathan released him from his embrace. "You were not supposed to leave the den, Daniel. Not ever."

Daniel lowered his head, unable to meet his grandfather's stare. "I know, but something deep inside me told me I had to go. I'm sorry."

The ostrich warriors suddenly lowered down as one. The tigers growled as Nathan and Daniel looked all around them. The eagle warriors were sound asleep; the ostriches had fallen into a deep sleep as well. Nathan looked out at the Bird Kingdom past the Great White Mountains with a pained look on his face.

"What's wrong with them?"

"I don't know…" Nathan looked down at the eagle warriors. He could feel the weight of his arms and legs as the adrenaline pumping through his veins began to slow. "It has to do with the queen." He looked up at Daniel with a fearful look in his eyes. "What did she say?"

Daniel could hear the pain in his grandfather's voice. "She's angry. And sad. I could see it behind her eyes. All her pain." Tears formed in Nathan's eyes as Daniel spoke. "I was hiding in the shadows after I had awakened her. I watched as all her birds came to life." He paused. "They are strong. Stronger than we are."

The lion, tiger and panther warriors were standing on edge, listening in silence as their young prince spoke.

"She loves them…like a mother…she loves her clan."

"Yes, she does."

Daniel continued on, " I…I saw something else behind her eyes. It was strange. They seemed to change colors with her mood." Nathan listened in silence, remembering Rebekah's eyes as Daniel now described them. "Cheetah protected me and wanted us to go but I didn't listen. I wanted to stay and hear what she had to say to her birds."

Nathan noticed the shift in Daniel's tone. "And what did she say?"

Daniel looked at his grandfather and his king with a look of dread. "That she would never let anything happen to them again. They were all that mattered now. Only them. I got scared. So I ran. Like a coward, an utter fool. I ran…"

Nathan placed his hand on his grandson's shoulder, "You are not a coward. Any one of us would have run when alone in a room with warrior beasts and no den beside them."

"Well, I didn't get far. Her raven found me and carried me back to the queen's chambers."

Nathan suddenly noticed his grandson's bloody wounds on both sides of his shoulders. "Poe…"

The hair on the lion warriors' fur stood on end as they growled lowly, gripping their weapons tight. Daniel could not help but notice that the raven's name was one everyone seemed to know — all except him.

"What happened then?"

"I spoke to the queen. I told her that I awakened her because of what Reginald told me. I could tell that that meant something to her. Her eyes suddenly turned gray. I told her that we needed her help. That the five kingdoms were in dire need of it." Daniel shook his head, reliving that moment. "Then her eyes turned dark — like the color of her raven."

Nathan turned and looked at Chester. A knowing look passed between them. A look of dread.

"She was angry and thought I had misspoke." He looked at Nathan with pleading eyes, "I begged for her to help us but she did not answer me. I shouted! I even said your name…"

Nathan tried to calm Daniel down as he listened to him speak. His own emotions had risen to the surface as he imagined the scene his grandson described. "It's all right, Daniel…"

"No! It's not! I failed!" He turned to the lion's den warriors. "I failed all of you. She will not help us! I don't understand…why was I the one worthy to awaken her if she won't help us…"

Nathan touched his grandson's shoulder. "No…you did not fail us, Daniel. You alone were noble of heart. You alone were worthy — *a lion*. And that hasn't meant anything in a long time. You have lifted the pride of the den this day and the lands quake and hope resounds because of you."

Daniel looked at his grandfather with gratitude but still felt hopeless all the same. Nathan smiled faintly, "There is a history here that goes far deeper than what you know. And I take full responsibility for not keeping you better informed. That will never happen again, Daniel, so long as I live. I will rectify it. I can only imagine the courage it took to stand before the queen to beseech her. Not even I could have done it. You threw a gauntlet down at the queen's feet and she has much to think about before she answers."

"But she already has!"

"No, she hasn't. She didn't say no."

"No! She ordered her birds to attack anyone who came to their gates!"

"Yet she returned you to us. Even we are unharmed." He turned his gaze to the sleeping birds on the ground. "Look at the birds. They are sleeping — exhausted. They mirror the state of their queen." He turned to his warriors. "The birds did not attack us. They returned our prince to us — and his warrior." He looked back at Daniel. "You have brought honor back to the den by this single act." The lion king roared to the guard, "Lions! Tonight we celebrate! My grandson...your prince...is the Noble Heart!"

The lions roared in reply.

Nathan placed his arm around his grandson. "A lot can change in a day, Daniel. You have reminded me of that one simple thing."

Daniel looked at his grandfather, "I'm sorry I left the den without telling you. I didn't mean to make you gather a squadron to start a battle over it."

"I'd fight to the death to protect you. You're the only hope left for our den." He looked proudly at Daniel. "What a king you will be one day...better than those of us who came before you."

Daniel shook his head. "No, my king. I can only be the king you think I can be because of the kind of king you have been to me."

The lion king and the prince walked back to the den with a new strength in their step. The steps of the warriors walking beside them, however, were not filled with the roar of excitement or pride they might be mistaken for; instead, they were filled with dread.

VII

Rebekah opened her eyes and found herself lying in her bed inside her chambers. Night had fallen, filling her room with a midnight glow as the moonlight trickled in. She spoke to the shadow crouched in the corner, feeling the angry, pent-up energy emanating from the darkness. "I'm surprised you aren't flying over the realm to see if what the lion prince said was true."

"All that mattersss isss you, my queen. Your sssafety for the sssurvival of our clan…"

"We are not what we once were, are we, Poe?"

From the shadow of the room, the raven assassin stood. *"We are better…"* His raspy voice answered his queen, *"Even though our enemiesss are all ssstill here…"*

She paused, letting his words sink in. He was right. They were still out there — but which ones? She closed her eyes and inhaled with a heavy sigh. "You wanted them all to die. You still do. I can feel it in your heart. I can see it in your eyes."

He paused, *"Yesss, my queen, they deserve to perish. Even you sssaid ssso not ssso long ago. When you fed them their liesss…I cannot hear the criesss of those in the other clansss…it meansss nothing to me even if I could…yet, I..ssstill hear the criesss of my kind that are no more — especially my ssson."*

"I hear nothing."

Poe craned his large head toward his queen. He lowered it down, leveling his eyes at her. *"Liesss…you hear him…I know you hear him…I hear the voicesss inside your head. Our king…Palimusss speaksss to you…"*

Rebekah shifted her gaze to the darkened corner where her raven stood. Poe emerged from the shadows and walked toward his queen; his footsteps were slow and lethal. *"Tok...tok...tok...you brought him with you from the grave. I could not hear him before. Now isss not the sssame asss then..."*

He knelt down beside her bed and tilted his head sideways to study the look on his queen's face. The feathers on his head rose slowly and fell gently back into a sleek crown around his head. *"Yesss....he livess behind your eyesss. I can ssseee it. I am glad, queen. No more sadness when you think of our king."* He could see the cool brown settling behind her eyes as he spoke the words. *"Why have you not called the eagle?"*

"Reginald, Poe. Your captain."

"Why, queen?"

She studied Poe's face before answering, "Because what he has to say matters. And I'm not quite ready to feel that it does."

Poe continued to stare at her. *"It should not matter what he hasss to sssay. Only what you think about what you know. That isss all the truth we need."*

"It's so dark...but I can still see...like the owls and the ravens. I can see far and wide — like the eagles and the hawks. The dark, I feel, is helping me see the light. But I need the light just as much as the dark. I will call him when it's time."

"He is a traitor in the ranksss! The lion prince knew about you! He knew your private thoughtsss!"

She slowly sat up, "I asked Reginald to stay behind, Poe, on behalf of the entire clan — to be my eyes when I could not see and my ears when I could not hear. Whatever Reginald chose to do with his time and whom he chose to do it with is an intention that I trust. I've never had any reason to distrust him. Nor have you."

Poe immediately rose from his position and began pacing back and forth. *"Not when it comesss to the lionsss! What secretsss hasss he revealed? What strengthsss will be turned against usss asss our weaknesss?!? He doesss not know what we know! He hasss never ssseen what Palimusss saw! In our slumber, my queen, we saw hisss vision in the fire! Our king'sss!!!"*

"Did we? I saw his vision from long ago. I heard his voice but there was no meaning behind it. Look me in the eye and tell me you heard what Palimus was saying while we slumbered. Tell me you know what he is saying now."

Poe remained silent.

"I didn't think so."

"He isss speaking to usss for a reason..."

"I am your queen! And I do not rule under the guise of a dead king! Even if it is Palimuss!"

"We do not know if thisss new lion prince isss the one Palimusss foresaw!"

"You don't believe then that it was Gunthar that Palimus' vision foretold? And I, the heir?"

Poe stopped pacing. *"You are the only heir. And you are ssstill a target until another remnant isss born."*

Rebekah knew he was right. But the more he challenged her, the more defensive she became. She leaned forward and worded her next sentence carefully, "And what king would you be satisfied with to help bring that about?"

"Tok...tok...tok..." His chest rose rapidly and fell as if his breaths were a heartbeat and a pulse all their own.

"Therein lies another problem, Poe." She sat back. "I agree with you on many counts but not all. We need to understand the state of the realm and how we fit it into it now. Besides, the young lion was deemed noble of heart to awaken us, chosen by the Creators to be the one. He is not a threat, nor is he to be harmed in any way. Is that understood?"

Poe stood in silence and slowly nodded his head.

"I know this prince does not represent the rest of the beings in the realm. If that were true, we would have awakened long ago. So, I must know..." She tapped her finger against her leg. "What kind of kings am I dealing with?" Rebekah suddenly stopped tapping her leg. "There's only one way to find out..."

Poe narrowed his eyes as he watched the idea forming in his queen's mind. He loved to watch the wheels spinning, for he knew her cleverness was from his side of the clan. He cocked his head to the side and slowly moved forward until he was kneeling beside her. *"I trust you, my queen. I feel the fire burning through your veinsss asss it doesss in mine."*

Rebekah extended her hand and gently touched the side of his large ebony head. Her eyes began to droop in exhaustion until she fell fast asleep. Poe remained where he was, listening to her breathing until it fell into steady breaths. As she rested, sitting straight up against her pillow in her large canopy bed, Poe continued to study her face, memorizing it as he peered down at her sleeping in the moonlight. The wind blew gently across the balcony and into her chambers. Poe craned his head around, absorbing the feel of the wind as it blew through his feathers. He looked back at his queen and lifted his black, taloned hand, gently moving a strand of hair from his queen's forehead. He listened to her breathing; and with each breath, his body relaxed until all the tension drained from his muscular form, filling him with peace.

He looked at his queen one last time, feeling a curiosity about her that he had never felt before. He loved his queen. He felt more connected to her now than he ever had before — as if they were now one. For what he had seen when he had awakened was a portrait of the image he had hoped for all these years — a painting of power, cunning and fearlessness on the face of his queen. And now she had it. The painting he had always imagined finally lived — and it was all because of pain. She had stepped out of the painting behind his mind's eye and rose from the ashes of betrayal, pain and heartache — a little less trusting, a little bit wiser, and a bit of something else. What was it? He could not put his talon on the word.

Whatever it was, Poe understood it. Knowing his queen had it, brought him a kind of peace, a sense of confidence and calm ambition, for what happened fifty years ago was not over yet. There were scars that had yet to toughen. There were tears that had yet to be dried. There was damage yet to be repaid. There were deaths yet to be avenged. And he knew that he was not alone in his thinking. He knew his fellow brothers in the scavenger clans felt the same — the crows, the vultures. He saw it in their eyes the moment they laid eyes on the lion prince. The tension, the detached feeling of emotion as they looked to kill. And he knew his queen felt the same. He had seen it. He had seen it behind her eyes. He had felt it shooting down his body — her anger and her rage. And for all the loose ends that still remained, Poe had felt the need to wait and not jump into action — not yet. For this new queen that had awakened was not the same as the one he remembered from before. And as he looked out at the moon, he felt truly at peace as he knelt beside his queen's bed. He knew that something had shifted that could not be swayed — the pendulum had swung in the opposite direction. He smiled at the moonlight knowing what it was.

Just like Palimusss…

VIII

It was dawn. Marcus stood on the balcony just outside the Great Library doors of his personal sanctuary. It was the sun that had drawn him toward the ledge, for it was ordinary. And like the monotony of days and nights that seemed to repeat themselves into the dullness and comfort of no further change, he thought of the sunrise from the day before. That was the moment when he stirred from his routine and took notice, for it was different. It was unlike any other sunrise he had ever seen before. Its red burning fire was a sign shouting to the entire realm that it was a dawn of no ordinary day. The scarlet tint was the banner he had come to recognize and associate with one person alone. He knew exactly what he was seeing as he stared at the flames of the sun: the color of the roses that branded itself across her gates, the color of her raven assassin's eyes as it zeroed in on those he deemed enemy, the color of blood that he had seen spilt over and over again throughout the years, and it was the color of anger as he stared out at that sun.

But the crimson fire from yesterday had vanished into the golden hue of today and was now as it always was. Yet he wondered...what would she do? Was she coming for her vengeance or would she give aid? He did not know which queen had awakened, but it did not matter. He had dared to stop hoping her awakening would be anything good years ago, after all the bodies continued to pile up and the cries of the starving and the fearful and the hunted echoed across the realm. Thinking upon all that had happened to his kin, his enemies, and his own clan, Marcus' dread continued to grow the more he stared at the sun.

"*Remember...remember...*" The old toad chief's voice echoed in his ears. "*Angry she will be...wrath of the raven cannot be...good queen, good queen, peace...*"

34

"Rebekah…" He had not spoken her name in years — not until Daniel had mentioned it. And now it seemed to be the only name he was thinking of. He remembered how, when he was a boy, her name used to make him wonder, it used to make him dream. But now, as an old man who had pondered much over starless nights, her name brought an emptiness that could easily shift between the pendulum of anger or fear. For her action so long ago, her choice, had destroyed any wonderment or hope of dreams for all the pain and suffering Marcus had seen on all the other sunrises and sunsets he had seen before this one.

Neither Daniel nor Nathan had returned, yet the sun had reverted back to what it always was. He had been praying the entire night, a silent prayer that he hoped would be carried on the wind if what he believed to be true…was.

"I beg of you, have mercy on us all…do not harm Daniel. Do not harm the prince." As he spoke his whispered prayer, it was almost as if the wind itself spun all around the old lion prince and carried his plea from the balcony and out onto the grounds below and out toward the Bird Kingdom. It was strange for Marcus to remain inside pondering the unknown instead of racing across the fields alongside Nathan and the rest of the den to rescue his nephew. He had stripped himself of fear and inaction long ago and had not looked back since. But something about yesterday and today made him stand still, as if he were the boy and the young man who had pondered and philosophized about the world, as he used to, but only inside his own head. He had not done that in ages. And yet, here he was, standing alone behind a sheet of glass pondering and philosophizing about the way the world would be now that Rebekah had arisen.

Marcus turned and looked back at all the scrolls that covered his desk and filled every corner of the room. They never made any sense. He never could figure it out. But there was one thing he knew to be true: there were others beyond the realm that could shift the wrong into the right — and he sought to find them. That is what he understood years later when he remembered what the old toad chief had said when he had taken the stone from his headpiece the night Rebekah had been poisoned. *"A gift, a gift, a gift for me…it is what the earth gave to me. Remember, young lion, you will see…"*

What had Marcus seen?

Nothing.

No one.

Not a single footprint.

Not even a stone.

And yet he still wondered. And like all the silent introverts who ponder about the world and its meaning, Marcus wrote all of his thoughts down. Thoughts that he drew from the realm's history, ideas he thought would lead him down a path to answers, but none of which he shared with anyone.

What had it mattered? Nothing he had done changed a single thing except for filling the passing of time. And now time had brought him back to a moment to where it had all changed, reminding him that he was insignificant in changing it. The doorway to an unbreakable door had been opened and the queen from time forgotten would soon be walking into it as a remembrance of what the world he had once known could have been. All that mattered now was her footsteps. The scrolls behind him meant nothing. The adventures he had taken outside the realm to find a means to save it were wasted travels that led to nothing and nowhere.

And as the old lion prince gathered up his maps and collected his scrolls, he wondered at his life and what purpose it had served. He suddenly felt old. Strange how the changing color of the sun could bring about thoughts of examining one's own life by simply turning red one morning. But as Marcus knew from past experience, it was often the little reminders from the past that triggered the idea of who you were, who you are, and who you want to be to keep you on a path of doing something different — to make something better than when you had it long after you gave it away.

And what had Marcus wanted to do?

Be as strong and brave as Nathan — and wasn't.

Open the bird queen's doors — and couldn't.

Stop the violence in the realm — and didn't.

Find a means to bring the rain to the dying kingdoms — and failed.

The more he pondered at his life, the more depressed Marcus became as he looked down at the maps and scrolls collected in his arms. He decided to throw them into the fire. He marched swiftly over to the large hearth in the library and hurled them inside. He grabbed for the candle burning over the mantle and crouched down to light all his life's work afire. The moment the flame was about to come into contact with the paper, the wind blew and the flame went out. Marcus grabbed for the other candle on the other side of the mantle and tried again. The same thing happened — the fire went out. Exasperated that not even this action would go his way, he turned to go and get the candelabra off of his desk.

The moment he rose to cross the room, he heard something fall with a soft THUD behind him. He turned and saw an emerald green book on the floor. He recognized it immediately and slowly looked around the room, wondering how it had fallen from the bookshelf at that exact moment. Marcus walked toward the book and knelt down to pick it up. He opened the first page, recognizing his own writing as he read the words. Tears filled his eyes as the flood of emotion filled his heart at the words he had written so long ago. They were words filled with a purpose, of intent, and they were his. The tears continued to stream down his face in the reminder that his intent behind his actions meant something — even if it only meant something to him. Reading his own words from long ago was the reminder he needed right at that moment of what his purpose was, commanding him that he should keep going. He buried his face in the crook of his arm and wept — silently and alone — feeling that someone, somewhere out there was reminding him of one small thing: what you do with your time in this life...*matters*.

IX

Rebekah stood at the bank of Wolf Lake watching the sunrise as she did so long ago. How many times had she stood by its waters, listening to the waves lightly crash along the shore? Now, nothing moved and the silence amongst the trees was all she heard, for not even the waters could be heard, remaining silent, as still as a sheet of glass.

Fifty years had passed, and for Rebekah, it was not long enough. At least, that was how she felt as she looked out at the darkened lake: that there was nothing…until she came face to face with the lion prince.

"I came here…I believed him…"

Her chest tightened as she battled out her emotions against her conscience. And still, she had not called for Reginald. Instead, she had flown with Poe to Wolf Lake wanting to linger alone in the dark for a little while longer.

And as the sun rose and the sun's rays cascaded down over the lake, Rebekah could not help but look up at the sun. She lifted her hand to grab hold of her medallion around her neck, when she realized it was not there. It was then that she remembered…Reginald had it.

She knew the moment she called out to him, he would undoubtedly come. The fact he had not flown to the kingdom of his own accord reminded her that he understood her heart all too well. He had been waiting for her to call to him. She had felt his heartbeat of rage, loneliness and sorrow the entire time she was asleep, yet awake. Her connection to him now, however, was dulled now that she had awakened. Strange that it would be so. She could only sense Poe — which was not altogether good. She needed them both to feel at peace, but right now, she was all right without the connection to the two. She was not quite ready to hear what Reginald had to say but knew it must be heard. For the world does not wait for your grief, it does not sit by as you try to heal. And whether or not you recover, it moves on without you and your pain. And for Rebekah, that was fine by her. She wanted to be a bystander for a while, not wanting to engage, unwilling to participate in the theater of this world. The real reason she did not want to speak with Reginald yet was because she knew he would feel the need to tell her the right thing to do at the moment. Like all moral compasses, one tends to avoid them the moment one knows they should do something better. Why it was her who had to be that person now, made her chest squeeze even tighter. She had asked for it to be so. She had desired for the moment to drive it home. And now, she begrudged the idea she ever felt her purpose in life should be so important. Who was she but a queen to a clan without an heir to carry on? Wasn't that the most important thing now? Wasn't that the cycle of life that everyone seemed to agree to?

"My grandfather…he loves you still!"

Rebekah cringed at that moment, feeling a sharp pain drive its pointed edge directly into her heart.

And then she saw it.

Whatever pain she felt was immediately squelched by the stunning horror of what her eyes beheld the moment the sun's rays shone down upon Wolf Lake. The water was still and dark even as the sun shone down upon it — there was no life in it. An ominous feeling pulsed through the bird queen's veins. Her eyes roamed the trees; they were dying. There was no sound, no echo. It was then that Rebekah realized that the entire time she had stood on the banks, there was not a single wolf that howled.

There were only five.

Rebekah suddenly whistled sharply to the sky, its shrill sharper and more urgent than it had ever been before. She searched the sky for him, looking north toward the Great White Mountains, but she saw nothing. She heard only silence.

She screamed his name *"REGINALD!!!"*

She whistled again.

Moments passed and seemed like hours as she stood there alone.

"It can't be the wolves…not the wolves…"

She refused to allow the panic to take hold of her rapidly beating heart. Even now, there was no sound off of her shout or her call to Reginald. He heart continued to sink. And then it came: the high, powerful shrill. Rebekah exhaled in relief, her heart pounding as the great warrior descended through the clouds. As he soared over what was left of Wolf Lake, she took off in an all-out run, her heart racing in relief as he approached. The moment they were feet from one another, she jumped.

Reginald swooped down underneath her and caught her on his back. Feeling her warm body on top of his own, he closed his eyes and sighed, "My queen…"

Poe emerged from behind the trees and ascended quietly as he trailed them from behind.

"What took you so long?"

He looked down sheepishly. "I was hoping you would call for me like you did so long ago. I've been waiting for it. It was the only way I imagined seeing you again." He lifted his head sharply, his eyes dilating to the size of a pin. "What took *you* so long?"

She smiled, realizing she had been caught. Her smile slowly faded as she looked into his eyes. She shook her head, refusing to answer. He nodded, understanding her thoughts.

"Who was the One?"

The bird queen looked out at the sun. "Your friend, Prince Daniel."

Reginald smiled to himself, feeling the pride of knowing it was the young lion prince.

Rebekah looked out at the nearly dried up lake. "Are the wolves still alive?"

"Yes, my queen. They are."

Rebekah closed her eyes and let out a slow breath. For all her anger toward the Lair the last time she had seen them, they were her kin, her only family. She opened her eyes and patted her hand against Reginald's back but said nothing more about it.

"Show me the realm, Reginald." He craned his neck around and looked at his queen. Without looking at him, she said it again, "Show me."

The great eagle captain, spread his wings wide, proud to carry his queen as they flew across the five kingdoms of the once-mighty realm.

X

Is it you, my son, that is to be betrayed?
Palimus stared into the gray-tinted eyes of his infant son. A heaviness weighed on his heart as he memorized the tiny hands that clasped around his larger, stronger ones. He lifted the tiny hand to his face and rested his cheek gently against it.

"I promise you, it will not come to pass. The lions will bear down to the will of the ravens. In this, you will have nothing to fear. You never need worry about what evil lurks around the corner and if its goal is to take you out. I will end the fear in my lifetime for the next. I have asked the Sun for this one thing, I have stood before the fire, and in this, he will answer me."

The cock crowed three times.

Palimus turned his head just as the gorilla king Brock stepped through the archway into his chambers. The moment Brock saw Palimus, a large grin spread across his face.

"King." He stormed inside the large room and moved toward a table filled with a pitcher of nectar and empty goblets. He immediately strode toward it and poured himself a large portion.

"You don't look well, bird."

"I haven't been sleeping."

Brock eyed him. "I heard that you found more land and evidence of other creatures outside the realm." Brock grabbed a fistful of grapes on the plate beside the tray of goblets and swallowed them whole. Turning his perfectly sculpted athletic body in Palimus' direction, his bone scepter at his side, the two kings could be mistaken for brothers. They resembled each other with their jet-black hair, chiseled faces, muscular bodies and olive skin. Where they differed was in height. Whereas Brock was fit and stocky with large biceps and shoulders, Palimus was tall and lean. For all their similarities and differences combined, one thing was clear: these two kings liked and respected one another.

"I love these things." The gorilla king tossed another handful of grapes into his mouth. "So, tell me, what did their tracks look like?" He leveled his eyes at the bird king, his jovial tone turning serious. "Were they smooth?"

"They were paw prints."

Brock slowed his chewing as he digested the news.

"And they were larger than the wolves'."

"Larger than the lions?"

Palimus nodded.

Brock pondered this news while taking another sip of nectar. "Luther will want to know."

At the sound of Luther's name, Palimus stood. "I doubt he will. From what I recall, neither of you cared much for what lay beyond the realm."

He chewed another handful of grapes. "The rumor of an uprising of the lesser clans is no longer just that. Knowing if we have more enemies or allies outside the realm has changed our perspective."

Palimus' eyes darkened.

"We may need more allies in the mix." He turned and looked at the bird king. "You never saw any of these creatures, only their tracks?"

Palimus nodded in reply.

Brock sat deep in thought. "So long as Cassius does not know. The last thing we need is clans from the outside borders attacking us while the lesser clans battle us within."

Palimus tapped his hand against his leg as he thought about what Brock had just said. "I doubt Cassius or any of the kings of the lesser clans would find their way to other allies."

"Why is that?"

"The land…seemed to change. Every day the path behind me was different than what it was the day before when I crossed it. I can't explain it, but it seemed as if some force far greater than what I have ever born witness to protected the path to other kings and clans. We are not meant to find who or what is out there. At least, not yet."

A smile slowly broke out across the gorilla king's face. He understood the force Palimus was making reference to. "She is beautiful indeed…and if she is protecting what is on the outside, then we are protected from within. Cassius is a fool. Always has been. Entitlement is the banner he breeds. False ego and undeserved pride will bring about his fall."

"How long?"

"Hmm?"

"How long before the lesser clans start their war?"

Brock took another drink from his goblet. "Two moons from now." He popped a few more grapes into his mouth. "The mariner men keep no secrets when they visit my jungle." He smiled knowingly and rose from his chair. "I am sending my scribe to you."

"What for?"

"I want him to write down everything you saw on your travels. Leave nothing out. Until then, king, I suggest your gather your armies and tell Feyedor to do the same."

The gorilla king walked over to the bird prince and patted his hand on the young heir's head before exiting the bird king's bedchambers, his bone scepter swinging against his side. Palimus watched him go just as Damon emerged from the shadowed corner in the room. *"The gorilla king enjoysss your company and our kingdom."*

"He always has. As much as the wolves are kin to our clan, I could easily claim the gorillas as the same."

"Shall I summon the eagle captain to relay to him the gorilla king'sss recent newsss?"

"No. I only need the ravens."

The raven assassin said nothing more as he bowed to his king.

XI

Reginald and Rebekah flew in silence across the desolate realm. The queen was abnormally quiet as she rode atop his back. She had wanted to see the kingdoms — and she wanted to start with Critter Country. As they flew over their side of the realm, she quietly took in the decrepit state of the land. It was so unlike the last time she had flown over the territories on her way to the Lion's Den for the gathering of the clans. A peace treaty was the talk then — a treaty to unite the realm for fear of a great famine and drought that would destroy the clans…and it had.

The fields were now yellowed and dried out, weeds covered the ground everywhere she looked. The waters surrounding Mariner Sea had retracted. They had lost their royal blue color and were now black with a tint of red. All was still. The tower itself was burnt out and abandoned. The swamps and ponds were practically dried up. No amphibians of any kind could be seen.

"What are you going to do?"

"I'm going to feed them their lies."

A sharp pain pierced Rebekah's heart causing her to cry out. Reginald faltered as well, filling the night sky with a loud screech of agony. Somewhere off in the distance, the eagle captain could hear another cry that echoed his own. He knew it was Poe. He could sense his fellow brethren nearby and longed to see his old friend face to face.

Rebekah tried to catch her breath to squelch the pain. "Take us down, Reginald."

Reginald craned his neck around and looked at his queen with weary eyes. Without another word, he descended toward what was left of Critter Country. Rebekah immediately jumped off of Reginald's back the

44

moment they were close enough to land. She walked with hurried steps toward an enormous headstone. She fell to her knees and let out a cry of anguish as she read the writing of the great chief's name etched in stone.

"Rayford..."

Rebekah looked all across the field and saw miles and miles of endless headstones.

"I buried them all after Rayford fell." Reginald walked up beside her.

"How did it happen?"

"Brutus' clan."

A flashing memory of Brutus' face as he bowed before her at the Lion King's Ball. *"Queen..."*

Rebekah could barely speak. "Did the lair suffer many losses?"

Reginald's voice was barely a whisper, "King Alexander did not engage."

Rebekah's body froze. "Why not?"

"His argument was that they were not his to protect."

Rebekah's pulse thundered in her ears.

"King Nathan came to their aid and drove the gorillas out. He killed Brutus in the process."

The bird queen was reeling, "But not in time."

She reached out to touch Rayford's headstone, seeing the vines and roses adorning his grave. They were in full bloom. Rebekah gently touched the petals. "The Sister..."

Reginald lowered his head in respect. "She protected him as best she could. The battle was over before it really began."

Rebekah whispered solemnly, "She guards the remnants with such fervor."

"As do the brothers, my queen..."

As if in reply, the sun shone brightly down upon the eagle captain and his queen. Both of them looked to the sky as the rays continued to shower down all around them.

That was when he heard it — the voice of a man. Reginald's feathers spiked straight up. The man was speaking to Rebekah in gentle tones and whispers. It was so faint, he could not make out what he was saying, only that Rebekah seemed to ignore the sound of his voice as she stared at the sun. She turned her head and looked at Reginald with a sad smile. "You hear him too."

"Who is it, my queen?"

She paused before answering. "It's Palimus."

The pupils in his eyes constricted to tiny pins.

"It makes me sad that you can hear him now." She turned and looked back at the sun. "He has been speaking to me since the night I was poisoned at the lion king's ball. Sometimes I listen, sometimes I don't. But ever since that darkest night, we *all* hear him — especially Poe."

Reginald's heart was pounding ferociously inside his chest. "What is he saying, my queen?"

Her chin started to tremble as she tried to hold back her emotion. "Nothing."

"Why do *I* hear him?"

She slowly looked up at him and gently touched his face, but she did not answer. She was suddenly filled with a deep sadness.

"Don't listen to him, Reginald. He doesn't have anything good to say."

"Then why is Poe listening?"

"Because the ravens have always admired Palimus so."

Her eyes drifted down toward the golden orb hanging around his neck. Her fingers moved to touch the sun-blazed emblem. They moved gently over the head of the eagle and over to the raven. Reginald watched the changing expression on his queen's face. Upon her touch, the medallion began to glow.

It was then that the eagle captain looked at his queen with a new set of eyes. She was different yet the same. What he remembered in her was not fully there. For that, he could understand, for she was still locked in a day and time when all was about to be lost, only to be awakened into an era where she had everything to gain. Reginald's heart was filled with a sudden heaviness, weighted down by the look of his queen. For what was lost behind her eyes was the remnant she had left him with all these years — and he could not see it, he could not feel it. His heart sank as the look he had longed to see behind her eyes could not be found.

"Take me home, Reginald. I want to read the history of all that was lost."

She climbed onto his back, pondering the news about Alexander and Nathan as she stared at the grave of the forgotten critter chief, wondering what more she was going to learn as they headed toward the Great White Mountains.

Nathan walked through the banquet hall, relishing in the laughter and joy that filled the den. It had been a long time since there had been anything to celebrate. Even now he had mixed emotions as to whether or not they should be celebrating at all. But looking at his grandson glowing with pride as he told his cousins and warriors the story of the vines and how he had awakened the queen, he relished in the legacy of a truly great story. And he enjoyed this one, simply because it was the first one his grandson had to tell. It was a life moment, a small victory to existing, and in this…Nathan was resolved that it was a celebration worth having.

He walked on, feeling a little distant from the group, as if he were suddenly the outsider. And he was all right with that. He had been king for a long time. Seeing his grandson be heralded, he felt the oncoming of the passing of the torch. He walked down the hallway, hearing the faint echo of laugher as he headed toward the Great Library. Nathan knocked on the large doors.

"Come in."

Nathan stepped inside his brother's sanctuary, taking in the warm glow of the candles lit all around the room. It suddenly looked different. He could not place his finger on it, but the room had somehow changed. What had not changed, however, was finding Marcus pouring over a book while sitting at his large desk that overlooked the lion's den courtyard.

"You didn't come to the banquet."

"I wasn't in the mood. I'll speak to Daniel later."

Marcus continued to read and write inside an emerald-colored book as Nathan moved further inside the room. He looked up at all the portraits of all the ancestors before him hanging on the walls. "All these kings…what have they meant to you?"

Marcus suddenly stopped writing. "What?"

"What have they meant to you?"

Marcus suddenly looked up at all the painted portraits. His eyes settled on the portrait of his father's. "Nothing."

Nathan turned toward his brother. "How can that be? Why have them fill your walls if they matter not?"

Marcus went back to writing his last thought. "What is a portrait but a false image of a man born out of rocks and oils? These kings mean nothing to me."

"Then why leave them hanging?"

Marcus put his quill down and leaned back against his large chair. "For all the rest of you to admire…or mourn. The library is not completely mine."

Nathan stepped even closer. "Not even father?"

"What are you asking me, Nathan? If I loved him? Respected him?"

Nathan chuckled, "I've just been thinking about what it means to be king."

Marcus let out a deep breath. "You're thinking about that *now*?"

"Because of Daniel."

His answer seemed to soften Marcus' tone just a bit.

"Have I equipped him enough? Are these kings hanging in this room and down our halls ones that should influence or inspire him to be the kind of king he can be in this age and time?"

Marcus crossed his arms over his chest. "And what kind of king is that?"

"One that's better than me." Nathan continued to study the portraits, settling his eyes on his father's. "You know, for all of our father's faults, he loved us. He loved the den. I didn't always agree with his reasons or his actions, but his intent was always clear — regardless of how it turned out. And I wonder at times if he did it better than me. Would he have let things get to be the way they are if he had lived as king? What would he have done differently?"

Marcus stared at his brother for a long while. "You have done the best job you could, Nathan, given the circumstances upon which you became king. You've been a good one."

Nathan turned and looked at his younger brother.

"If ever I were to hang a portrait of a king in this library that mattered anything to me, it would be yours."

Nathan was taken aback by his brother's admission.

"You have always been what you claimed to be. You have never lied to me. You have never cheated anyone with cunning or any other hidden agenda. You have always strived to keep honor in this den. You have fought to keep your heart guarded yet still found a way to love. And you realized that to be king in the kind of realm we have been cursed into living in, means that sometimes you have to guard what is yours rather than guard what others are meant to protect...and haven't — and you've been able to do it without any other war coming about while you fought that battle. Not an easy task to accomplish, my brother, but you have done it. Which is why both your brother and your grandson admire you so."

Nathan stared at Marcus completely speechless. "What's gotten into you?"

Marcus laughed. "You're not the only one pondering the life lived and the lives that will be long after yours is over." He picked up his book in his hands and closed it. He walked over to the bookshelf and placed it back in its designated spot.

"So when are you going to see her?"

Nathan immediately changed expressions. "I'm not." Marcus leaned against the bookshelf and stared at his brother. "All these years of standing on the hilltop overlooking her kingdom, waiting for her to awaken, and now you grow afraid. Which tells me one thing…"

Nathan looked up at him.

"You didn't really believe she ever would."

"Sometimes, brother, you believe in miracles hoping there could be some for you as well — but not really believing it."

"But the miracle happened. So what's stopping you?"

Nathan sighed deeply. "Time. I'm an old man now. Nothing like the young prince I was before. Not the young man on the verge of becoming king when I gave her my heart filled with all the promises I dreamed about; I *am* king. But this life has not turned out anywhere near what I had hoped or imagined. The dream I had dreamed for myself has never come to pass."

Marcus absorbed his brother's words, being completely reminded of how he was feeling, reminded that you are never as alone in feeling how you feel; there are others who feel the same. And just like him — rarely share it.

"When I was young, the years ahead had so many possibilities, ones that consumed my desires, ambitions and every form of imagination. But life has had a means of keeping my dreams in check, making sure that what I want and what the world demands are opposing needs. I feel as if I ended up being its sacrifice in evening the plain."

"Whose?"

"The world's. I have often felt as if my life were being used for some other purpose I never signed up for on a contract I never agreed to sign. And yet I found myself pushing through this life past all I had been dealt to stand up on that damned hill every morning of every day, as if life had never aimed its arrow of woe at my heart. I wanted the promise I made to Rebekah to remain true — to show that the world and all its pain had never broken me from keeping the one promise to myself and her that I always wanted."

"What was your promise?"

"To never give my heart to any other woman so long as I lived." He looked at Marcus. "And I kept it. And now I am trying to find every excuse in the book not to go see her. I did not think I would be this old when she awakened."

Marcus looked down at the floor. "You think that dreams are on a timeline upon which they can come to pass?"

Nathan nodded. "In this, I do. There are certain dreams I have had attached to loving this woman that are meant for the young. I'd be a fool to think…" He stopped himself and shook his head, standing tall once again as he looked at the portrait of his father. "Ah, never mind. I'll leave you alone now. All this talk has made me depressed. And I'm not a fan of self-pity…" He smiled softly at Marcus and turned toward the library doors.

"Nathan…"

Nathan turned.

"The awakening of a dream placed deep in your heart is meant for a certain time. That time was not then. It is meant for now. Even if it doesn't make any sense. You are still among the living now that she is alive. She is still a remnant and needs an heir." He smiled encouragingly.

"That has not escaped my thoughts, brother. But there are other kings in this realm that have grown to match her stride that could suit her needs far greater than I could."

"Nonsense! You are the greatest king amongst them. And if Rebekah is as she always was, you are the only king for her."

"And still, the rain has yet to fall." Nathan smiled and walked through the library doors.

Marcus pondered the conversation he just had with Nathan, feeling a sense of connection to his family — one he had not truly felt between he and his brother in a long time. He looked up at his father's portrait filled with a myriad of thoughts and emotions as he stared at his painted face. "You brought your fear to fruition, father. Let us hope that fear has no more fruit to bear."

XII

Rebekah walked inside Reginald's home on the highest peak inside a nestled cave. She took in her surroundings, surveying the cozy nook Reginald had made for himself over the years. He had a wooden table and chair placed close to the edge of the cliff that overlooked the entire realm. There was a small candle resting atop the table, halfway melted down. Rebekah pictured Reginald sitting there at night as he read or wrote while looking out at the starlight and out toward the sea. She turned her attention to the direction of Mariner Sea.

"The king or queen who controls the sea, rules the realm."

"What was that, my queen?"

"That was what they all believed — the clans — from the beginning. I never understood it. I always thought it was the birds that brought the rain and filled the sea. Something about the sea though, that I have seemed to have forgotten." She sighed. "Like all philosophies and bits of wisdom that are meant to be remembered for a specific time and purpose, I'm wondering why I'm remembering this one."

He followed her gaze. "Perhaps you are thinking of Mar — the mastermind behind all that transpired so long ago."

"And yet, for me, it's not so long ago."

The sun was slowly rising. She looked out over the mountaintops and into the distance. She tapped her finger against her leg and turned to Reginald. "I can't see Mariner Sea, Reginald. What happened to it?"

Reginald picked up a large book from his desk and handed it to her. "I have written the history of the last fifty years in this book, my queen. The answers to all of your questions are written here. May its memories and tragedies be your eyes as you look upon the history that still has yet to be written."

Rebekah took the book from his taloned hand. "You have served the clan well, Reginald."

His feathers puffed at her remark. "My home is yours, my queen." He pulled the chair out for her to sit. She sat down and reluctantly opened the book to the first page. "I shall leave you in solitude. I wish to see my brethren."

She nodded. "Yes, of course. They will be overjoyed to see you, Reginald — especially Kenuen."

Reginald beamed. He extended his long arms and wings and dove outside toward Bird Kingdom. The moment he left, Rebekah flipped through the large book, looking at the dates on each of Reginald's entries. She closed the book and looked out at the land below. She closed her eyes and inhaled deeply, knowing that she needed to read the words inside but not truly wanting to. It was a cowardice move on her part, knowing she had asked Reginald to remain behind for this reason alone — and that he had. The hour had come…but she was not quite ready for the brutal wind of time to sweep over her with all of its forced memories. Like a babe comfortable in the womb, she was not yet willing to travel through the comfort of that tiny space of peace and back into the world where the book resting on the desk in front of her now was going to take her.

She looked out at the realm beyond, "Whomever controls the sea…"

She knew the wielder in the sky, the soldier in the deep; she felt the warrior in the wind, and felt the growing comfort of the earth as the trees consoled and comforted her.

But she did not control the sea.

Yet, she honored the Sun…and he answered her.

She bent to Fire and it kept her spirit comforted.

She reached for the light and could heal others, but she had yet to be healed.

But the sea…it continued to summon her attention…what was it? It was as if it were calling to her like the ticking of time to an hour that would answer all her questions and doubts and fears of the world she was now living in, daring her to dive into its waters and see who truly commanded its tide.

What did it mean?

Rebekah shifted her attention to her current surroundings. There was a bed in the far corner at the back of the cave; in the other corner were Reginald's armor and weapons. Her body stilled the moment she saw them. They were tarnished and stained with old blood. Seeing the worn armor in the corner, she could only imagine what he must have battled over — even when did not have to. He owed nothing to anyone, yet he had chosen to engage. How much, Rebekah was about to find out. She was about to read it all: everything that had happened in the last fifty years.

And as the bird queen opened her eyes to read the large volume between her hands, she suddenly noticed the rosebud carvings etched into the wood of Reginald's desk. She narrowed her eyes knowing they were not there moments before. She lifted her hand and gently ran her fingers over the detailed carvings. Upon touch, the carvings began to bloom.

Reginald's heart raced with excitement as he soared through Bird Kingdom. He had not seen any of his kinsmen in our fifty years. Fifty years of solitude, being the only bird warrior in the realm, was a loneliness all its own. He felt alive again, young, as he descended from the clouds and into the fields that stretched out across Bird Kingdom…his home.

He could see Poe and members of the Thunderbird Guard clustered together around a small patch of land down below; the looks on their faces were grave. Reginald landed softly on the lush green grass behind them. Feeling the sprouts beneath his taloned feet, it took everything within him from humming as he felt the cool grass against his skin — so different from the burnt-out weeds and dust he had come to know. Poe lifted his head and stood the moment he saw Reginald.

"*Tok…tok…tok…*"

Kenuen and the other Thunderbird warriors spun around, gripping their weapons tight as they turned and stood face to face with their beloved captain. Kenuen's pupils dilated rapidly as he deciphered the being that now stood before him. "Reginald!" The feathers on Kenuen's crown stood on end and slowly relaxed as he moved toward his captain. "Old friend!" They immediately rubbed foreheads together in welcome as the other eagles reacted in excitement. They gathered around the old captain, cawing and speaking salutations through shouts of joy, followed by a flurry of questions.

"Quiet down!" Kenyan commanded. "I'm sure we will be catching up with our friend for quite some time to learn about the state of the realm!"

He turned back to Reginald. "As I have many questions."

Poe stared at Reginald with his crimson eyes. *"Asss do I…"*

Crouching down again, Poe extended his black taloned hand to the ground directly on the spot where the eagles had gathered.

"You all look so serious. What's going on?"

Kenuen answered, "We found a creature's footprint on our lands. It's unlike any we have ever seen before."

Reginald moved past Kenuen and crouched down on the opposite side of Poe. Both the eagle and the raven looked down at a footprint framed in the soil. Reginald's eyes dilated to the size of tiny pins. He recognized its resemblance to a clan of old, but it was larger than what he remembered. He looked north and wondered. A chill suddenly filled the air as the idea of what this could mean began to sink in. He turned to Poe. "It looks like the mark of a bear but not."

Kenuen's eyes dilated rapidly to the size of pins. "The bear clan…" His voice was barely a whisper. "They haven't been seen in centuries. Not since the civil war between the bears and the bulls."

"Thisss isss not one of theirsss…it isss larger in size. The bearsss do not live in the north."

"No, they don't. But one of their kind does."

Poe slowly lifted his head and stared coldly at Reginald; his eyes scorched a fierce shade of red. Reginald was taken aback by the look of hatred emanating from behind Poe's eyes. *"Enemy…"*

Reginald's body froze as Poe spat out the word. He could not tell if it was meant for him or the unknown creature.

Kenuen touched the dirt around the footprint. "This was freshly made."

Reginald finally tore his eyes away from Poe. "No one has been able to set foot on our side of the realm."

The entire group looked north.

"Until now." Poe suddenly stood and hissed at Reginald, *"Protect my queen!"* He immediately cried out in a loud shrill and rocketed into the sky. The eagles watched as the raven assassin headed north out past the lands of Bird Kingdom that lay behind, completely taken aback by the aggressive speed upon which he flew.

"Where is he going?"

Reginald watched Poe in flight until he disappeared from view. "A better question to ask would be, Where has he gone?"

Kenuen interrupted his train of thought with, "We did not find any other prints but this one. We were lucky to find it." He lowered his voice to a whisper, "As a matter of fact, we've all been on edge since we awoke.

The haunted memory of the lesser clans marching toward our gates is still as fresh in our minds as that unknown creature's footprint."

Reginald turned and placed his taloned hand on Kenuen's shoulder. "I understand." They stared at one another for some time before Kenuen finally spoke. "What happened while we slept?"

Reginald breathed in deeply and exhaled slowly before he spoke. "Let us gather our brethren and head to the Great White Mountains. I shall rouse Chief Ume and his warriors, and I will tell you all."

They walked back through the fields as the wind softly blew through the crop, but not before Reginald looked one last time at the strange footprint etched in the soil and found that it had disappeared.

XIII

Poe flew as fast as his wings could carry him as he soared over the unknown territory that lay beyond Bird Kingdom. He was angry and he was scared. No creature would have ever dared step foot in his queen's land before — not without the fear and apprehension of coming face to face with the fortitude of the eagles and the wrath of the ravens. *The ravens...*

His diaphragm constricted as the realization hit home. *There are no more ravens.* And yet, others had dared before.

He faltered in the sky. Soaring across the clouds, he was reminded of that last flight as he flew from Mariner Dam back toward Bird Kingdom. He felt it then — the poison pumping through his veins. He couldn't think. He couldn't feel. But he knew. He knew he needed to warn his queen. But it was too late. He fell from the sky as the poison worked faster than anticipated. He would never make it the kingdom. Instead, he crawled his way home. And what he saw when he got there was unlike any nightmare Poe had ever experienced before.

The forest in Raven Territory was on fire as his brethren were dragged from their homes by bull and amphibian warriors. They were crying out for mercy, shouting to be spared.

And not one of them was.

Poe watched in horror as the ravens were thrown into the fire, one by one, burning alive, helpless to save themselves — too weak from the poison. Poe crawled his way to his nest, searching for his wife and son. But he was too late. His wife had been slaughtered; her body was lying just outside the door. Poe dragged himself inside the doorway and found his son crouched in a corner, barely breathing as the blood oozed from his multiple wounds. Outside, the shrieks and cries of his brethren kept coming.

Poe grabbed hold of his son's body. His son, Damian, looked at him with terrified eyes. "I...could not...protect her...I'm sorry, father..." Damian closed his eyes and breathed his last breath while Poe held him tight.

"No..." Poe rocked his son back and forth while the fires blazed all around him until all went dark.

Skoll had found him. The Wolf Pack had discovered what was left of Raven Territory. It was a miracle, they said, that he had survived. He was the only one.

They took him to his queen. He had to tell her. She had to know. *It was the lions.* As she held him in her arms, Poe saw a look in his queen's eye that he had never seen before. She was calm yet her eyes were as black as his feathers. That was the last thing he remembered until he had awoken to find a lion prince and cheetah warrior running across the plains of his beloved kingdom.

He wanted nothing more at that moment than to kill them both, but something had stopped him. It was the wind. It would not allow him to descend, not until he decided to bring the prince back to his queen and lay him at her feet. It was as if the wind knew what he was thinking, for its force suddenly relinquished, allowing him to dive down.

And what had his queen done? She let him go. She always lets them go — the ones who deserve to die. The threat to his queen was allowed to live on, and now there was another threat beyond that teased at a greater reveal. Another creature had crossed into their land without any obstruction. Without permission. Just like fifty years ago...

He felt trapped, helpless. Between the memories of the past and the events of the present, Poe felt as if he were in a cyclone of the insane without a center to anchor him down to that of the sane. And for the first time since he had awakened, Poe erupted. He cried out in the loudest caw the realm had ever heard. Even the trees surrounding him seemed to tremble off of his cry of torment and pain. Exhausted, he collapsed onto the ground, unable to move and too exhausted to think.

"*Poe...*"

Poe's heart stopped the moment he heard the whispered voice, unsure if he really heard it.

"*Poe...*"

He listened closely, trying to locate where the sound was coming from. He slowly rose from the ground. He looked all around him, his crimson eyes searching for the source.

"*Remnant...*"

His heart began to pound rapidly inside his chest. He did not recognize the voice as it continued to speak and sound all around him.

"Protect the clan…"

And then the voice was gone.

He looked up at the sky and waited for any sign of further communication, any sign of movement around him. He honed in on the sun — but he could not see it. It was hidden behind the clouds.

The wind suddenly swirled all around him, blowing past him as if urging him to move ahead. Poe looked off in the distance. It was then that he saw the peak of an oversized mountain eclipsing the clouds above. He ascended into the sky and flew toward the massive mountain. It was the first time he had ever left his kingdom. It was the first time he had ever ventured outside the realm. And it was the first time since he had awakened that he heard the silence amongst the cries.

By the time Reginald had returned, Rebekah had barely finished half the book. It was an hour or so before dawn, and she was mentally and emotionally exhausted. She was lying in Reginald's bed, staring up at the rock ceiling with one arm draped across her forehead, and the other hand resting atop her medallion. Reginald remained silent as he slowly approached his queen.

"The reptile clan is no more, hunted to extinction as food. Mar reaped what he sowed. Without my vultures to dispose of the carcass…plague. Tatiana and Ivan are dead and now only my enemies remain…and they need my help or they will die."

Reginald remained silent.

She looked down at the medallion hanging around her neck. "My mother once told me that the eagle represented wisdom to rule, and the raven cunningness to protect. Maintaining the balance of the two was the duty of the clan's king or queen, for the way the pendulum swung was the basis upon which the kingdom would rise or fall."

He saw the darkness behind her eyes; he could feel the weight of her thoughts against his chest as she spoke.

"How should the pendulum swing…I've been laying here, Reginald, thinking about a lot of things. I remember thinking that I wanted to do something good in my life, but I didn't know what exactly. I knew I wanted our clan to be trusted and loved, but I really didn't focus on how. And what I'm thinking about now is why that even mattered. The world will forget all the good you ever did in your life — if you did any; and you have no control over what others think or feel about you no matter how hard you try or what your intent is. So why does it matter? Why try? We were loved on our side. We did well for our kind. So why did I try to do anything different?"

"Where are you going with these thoughts, my queen?"

"You don't want to know." She turned her head, "You would be disappointed in me."

He thought for a moment before answering, "I disagree with you. It has mattered, my queen, that you sought to go outside your comfort zone and do the impossible."

"I have yet to see how."

"The end of the book is not yet written."

"But what has been written gives me pause."

He looked at her tired eyes, feeling the heaviness in her heart. He understood his queen all too well, but he also knew that being a part of this clan, being loyal to this queen, was the greatest honor of his life. If it mattered to anyone in the realm what his queen had tried to do, it mattered to him.

"Don't stop, my queen. Keep going. Continue on the path you once started. Plant your seeds in the field anyway — and eventually the right one will grow."

The queen did not reply.

"It is easy to give in to the shadows of the heart, my queen. And it is common. Only a rare few fight against the tide to turn it toward something good so all may ride. You are not common, that is why you are queen."

She stared up at the rock ceiling, sighing deeply. "I don't always want to do what is right and what is good. I am tired of doing the right thing and getting nothing for it in return while I watch others get everything they want. Cheat a little, lie a little, do what needs to be done to even the plain. And what do I get? Nothing but pain. The one thing I wanted, Reginald, the one thing I ever desired — that I felt I deserved — was something I never got a chance to have." She looked at him. "For once I want to turn to the dark and be the reason justice is served — not just sitting back, letting it go and hoping one day it happens. So why not do what everyone else has done. They always seem to get they want."

Reginald replied, "If that were true, your enemies would not be kneeling at your feet pleading for mercy. What they have done is easy.

The path you are walking upon is a much harder road to travel and very few can do it. You *can*. What weighs on your heart is hard. The greater the struggle, the grander the victory."

"And what have I really won, Reginald?"

"A chance to change the world in the moment it was meant to be changed. You have been given a gift to rise just now. The Elements, the Creators, are on your side. The Sun…has given it to you. Not by your will that it should be done, but by the Sun's. Who chose the noble heart? Who claimed there was to be one? You are not so alone on this quest to bring about a great change as you think. You have help — and they are leaving it up to a rare few worthy enough to do it. And if you don't, you are accountable. It matters, my queen, to wonder at life, to seek a great purpose, to accomplish a dream. For if it did not, none of our lives would matter anyway. And I know mine does." He knelt down beside her and looked at her with pleading eyes, "How do you want to be remembered?"

His question hit its mark. Her silent prayer came rushing back to her from so long ago.

Better than this day.
Wiser than the others.
Kinder than the rest.
An eagle that soars rather than the scavenger who settles.
To do something great.
To be someone unexpected.

The last line, she kept to herself. Clenching her teeth, she draped her arm over her eyes. She knew he was right. She knew what she was supposed to do. And whether or not she was ready to or felt the overriding impulse to do it, she knew she needed to do it. She let out a heavy sigh and issued the command, "Send the birds to the fields, Reginald. Feed the clans."

His heart hammered with pride, relief and excitement. "*All* of them, my queen?"

She breathed in deeply and nodded without another word. Reginald dove down toward the fields faster than he had flown in decades; it was the moment he had been waiting for, and she knew that not all the birds would feel the same sense of joy. Rebekah opened her eyes and looked at the shadow in the corner of the room. Even though Poe was not there, she could feel his scarlet eyes on her anyway as the clouds rolled in and the thunder and lightning followed.

XIV

The doors to the Great Library burst open and Prince Daniel peered inside. "Uncle Marcus!"

The library was completely dark. The only light illuminating the room was from the candelabra Daniel held in his hand. He was completely drenched, having stood outside as water fell from the sky. The rain continued to pour nonstop, as if the sky itself were making up for lost time. Daniel looked out as the droplets cascaded down the large windows on the other side of the room. He was mesmerized by rainfall, never having seen it before. He had been listening to the sound it was making as it pitter-pattered against the rooftops in the lion's den. It made him want to light a fire in the large hearth in the library just to sit beside it and listen to its constant rhythms and melody as it danced upon the lion's den rooftops.

Daniel walked further inside the large room clearly noticing that all the maps had been put away. Not a single scroll could be seen anywhere — none piled up on the floor, none draped over the furniture, and definitely none on Marcus' large desk. As he set the candelabra down on top of it, Daniel realized it was the first time he had actually seen the desk in its entirety, and it was a masterpiece of craftsmanship.

He gently laid his hand out across the wood, feeling the many carvings etched into its surface. There were various lion faces carved into its edges. Each head depicted a generation or sovereignty that had reigned before now. Between the lions, however, Daniel saw the intertwining of vines and roses. He narrowed his eyes, recognizing that this particular flower did not grow in the den.

"I told you to knock."

Daniel jumped at the sound of Marcus' voice. "Uncle! What are you doing sitting alone in the dark?"

"Watching the rain. Watching you stand in it." Marcus was seated in the corner, facing one of the windows. "It's been a long time since I've heard that sound."

Daniel leaned up against the edge of the desk and looked out at the rain. "Strange, to feel comfort in the shades of gray clouds and rolling sound of thunder. It's peaceful."

Marcus turned his head and looked at his nephew through his monocle. "And was she…peaceful?"

Daniel looked at his uncle, knowing exactly whom he meant. "Only when I mentioned Reginald."

"Hmmm…" Marcus looked back at the rain. "I envy you this moment."

"Why?"

"It was you who was worthy. We've been waiting for the noble one for decades." He smiled softly. "To know it was a member of our clan is ironic, indeed." He removed the monocle from his eye and tucked it carefully inside his breast pocket. "I had hoped to be the one, many moons ago, to open her gates and awaken her. I used to sneak out of the den at night just to try and see if tonight was the night. I was a foolish child then, wanting to matter. Wanting something to fight for and win. Feeling the need to do something important, something that defined me as a person who added something to this world before I left it." He paused before finishing his last thought, "I suppose it didn't matter. It's funny what does."

Daniel took in his uncle's words, baffled by such an omission. "What do you mean?"

Marcus looked at the lion prince, a sad smile forming on his tired and weathered face. "When I was a young boy, the Den was one of the most powerful kingdoms in the realm. Every lord, master and chief within each of the clans was filled with men — warriors — beings that desired nothing more than for something to fight for. There weren't any wars, mind you, which is why we ended up fighting and challenging each other over pride and conquests of women mostly. But each of us knew that inside the den, you had to prove yourself worthy of the house you belonged to — almost as if it were a right of passage that said you had something to offer that made you and turned you into a man. That's how Nathan got those tattoos on his neck. It was a sign of manhood given by the panther chief when a quest had been accomplished. I never got mine. The moment the shockwave rolled across the kingdom, everything changed: order, justice, even tradition. And yet, even with all the loss, all the chaos, I was fearless. I still did what I wanted, when I wanted, how I wanted, without realizing the consequence — intended or otherwise. All I understood was that I was a prince in a den of prideful masters used to getting their own way. And I wanted mine." Marcus continued to stare out at the rain. "Her eyes turned black."

Daniel stood straight up. "What?"

"When she was angry. Queen Rebekah's eyes turned as black as coal." He peered at Daniel. "You've seen the same look. I can tell." He looked back at the rain. "That's what I have been afraid of…"

Daniel turned closer toward his uncle. "The queen was angry when she was awakened, yes, but there were moments where they suddenly changed to gray. She was angry when I told her there were only five kingdoms that remained, when I told her my people needed help…" He thought of that last moment when Queen Rebekah's eyes swirled to dead pools, "And when I mentioned grandfather…"

Marcus breathed in long and deep. "No doubt those were daggers to her heart, Daniel, for they touched on the three things she loved the most: the realm, her desire to help the people, and Nathan. All of which betrayed her."

"When did you see her angry?"

Marcus looked at Daniel for a long while before answering, tears welled behind his old, tired eyes. "I made the mistake of killing a warrior from another clan — the Critter Clan. He was a squirrel running for his life across the plains, trying to get back home, and I thought he was nothing more than a bit of prey. I hunted him down and killed him, like his existence made no difference in the universe. He was a leaf that had fallen from a tree that I longed to step on and crumble just to hear the sound — that's how detached I was from what I had done. When I realized my mistake; that was when the fear in my life took root and began to grow." He paused before continuing, "Life is a very precious gift, Daniel. And those of the living will fight to survive regardless of how insignificant we find their existence to be. It was Queen Rebekah who taught me that lesson…and I've never forgotten it. It haunted me for years."

Marcus took a small compass from his breast pocket, touching it with respect. "Fear cripples you, Daniel. It strips you of all your strengths and magnifies your weaknesses. It is a chain that makes you second-guess your every action, your very gesture, for fear of the consequence you alone imagine or feel you know. So you live, analyzing your own behavior as being witness to life or slave to watching the lives of others." He looked out at the rain. "You do not dare to engage — not with the world, not with the people around you, and most certainly not with your own mind and destiny. You have none at that point. You squelch the you, you could have been or always wanted to be because of the fear, the fear of making a mistake. Of being found out and reminded of all the ones you made before. Live in it too long and it's like a disease — no one wants to be near it and you are your only physician — a physician without the means to self-medicate in anything but helplessness, anxiety and hopelessness. That disease crept up on me slowly and all at once. I'm surprised I wasn't driven to complete despair."

He looked back at the compass. "I could not engage with this world. How I hated everyone and everything in it. Because I knew...I was not worthy enough to be the one to open the doors to the one who could."

Daniel watched his uncle as the scars of adventure etched all around his face moved with each word he spoke. He had never known this side to Marcus. He had only ever seen the one who lived without fear. The one who could not be held inside the den for long. The one who dared to push the boundaries to funnel hope others had lost long ago.

"And yet, you changed it."

Marcus looked up at Daniel in reply, "Changed what?"

"Your life."

"I wasn't talking about changing my life. I was talking about being the one to change others'."

"But that's the start, uncle...changing your own life before you can for others. And you did. What made you strip yourself of fear and engage?"

Marcus breathed in long and deep. "There comes a point when you have to ask yourself, what is it all for? This time that I was born into, the circumstance that I was grown, these thoughts no one knows, and these dreams I share with none? What is it all for if you are not meant *to do?* And it was time for something to be done — and I knew it was time for me the moment I realized...my existence did not matter. My thoughts, no one heard. My dreams would be snuffed out with the last beat of my heart if I did not engage. I lost my fear the moment I realized I had nothing to lose, for I had already lost it. Everyone had given up on me and written me off as not really mattering. The only thing left to do was rise and become." He looked at the rain once more. "Or what is it all about if you don't? I didn't want to simply be wasted space."

It was then that Daniel understood: the maps being packed away, his uncle dressed in lounging clothes instead of wearing his travel gear.

"You matter, uncle."

"I don't know that I do. I don't know that I ever have. All the things

I've done and tried to do all these years…but it's all right."

It was then that Marcus turned and looked at Daniel; almost as if he were seeing his nephew for the first time. Looking into the prince's blue eyes, he saw Princess Lara's kindness behind Nathan's face. He could see Matthew's strength in Daniel's frame; it carried power and athleticism. And he could see Tara's mischievousness twinkling behind his eyes. And there was a bit of something else — a humility in all the power he bore that balanced out the strength. This young man was a quiet man who listened, who understood, who loved deeply, and would fight to the death for honor, integrity, and the good. He bore the mark of a man who stood for…nobility. And it was then that Marcus understood why it was Daniel who alone was worthy. A sudden sense of peace and pride welled up inside Marcus' heart as he let that understanding settle inside, for he finally had the answer to his question. What was it all for? It was for this one; the one who stood before him now.

He grabbed a small envelope that had been resting on his lap, and suddenly stood up, patting the chair no one was allowed to sit in but him. "Here. Sit. Listen to the rain." He looked all around the walls of the library, the only piece of space he felt was his and could claim as his own.

Daniel was shocked. "Really?"

"This room is yours. Come and go as you please." He smiled softly. "No need to knock anymore." As Marcus headed toward the doors, the thunder rolled across the sky.

"Uncle Marcus…"

Marcus stopped in his tracks, his hand resting on one of the scrolls in the corner of the room.

"Even if no one told you, you need to know…you gave the den years of hope that there might be something beyond the realm to go after and hold onto."

The rain continued to beat down hard against the windowpanes. Marcuse looked to it. "I don't know about that, Daniel." He turned and looked his nephew with an appreciative smile on his face. "You may have been the only one who ever noticed or cared."

"Isn't one enough?"

Marcus pondered the question. He nodded his head in reply, "Only if it's you." He smiled to himself and walked out of the Great Library leaving Daniel alone in a room filled with a multitude of mismatched scrolls secretly packed away. He reached down to grab the candelabra. That was when he noticed it — the markings on the desk. They had moved. He angled the light down over the room and peered a little bit closer.

65

BOOM!

Daniel looked up and saw a handful of scrolls spill out onto the floor. He moved across the room to pick them up. As he set them upright, his eye caught sight of a bright, emerald green book with gold embossment on the outside. Curious, he pulled the book from the shelf. There was no title on the front, but the moment he opened it up to the first page, he recognized the handwriting — it was Marcus'.

He read the first sentence aloud, "Long ago, before the realm became what we know it to be now, man and beast lived side by side. The intellect and ability to reason was a commonality between the two, but unlike the other, the will and desire to rule their own territory outweighed the combined effort to keep the peace between the two kingdoms. So a blood truce came to be, a balance and a bond between man and beast.

"Man and beast continued to evolve, living side by side as the clans had formed — each with the lethal and the good, each with intelligence, each with skill, each with a loyalty to his or her king and queen, and the king and queen to the beast clan leader, for now they were bound — their blood interwoven with a pact and an oath. One could not live without the other, for with life comes death, with love comes hate, and with dominance comes submission. The Master cannot be slave to the servant, but without a people gathering in, a Man cannot be king. And while the remnant — the sole heir to the throne — lived, the clan would survive. Should the remnant die, all would fall. That was how the balance of the dominant and dominated could remain and has.

"But there are some who say that it is the elements in this world that watched and maintained the balance."

Daniel paused, "The elements?" He had never heard this tale before; he began reading once more. "Fire, Wind, Ice and the Earth were said to be the protectors of the kings and queens of the realm, claiming a king or a queen for a time and purpose." Fascinated, he sat down in his uncle's large chair and continued to read. He neither noticed that it had suddenly stopped raining; nor did he notice the outline of his uncle walking outside Lion Den Courtyard in his travel gear, heading straight out from its gates and toward the haunted forest that once terrified Marcus as a child — the one that led straight toward the Wolf Lair.

XV

Rebekah stared at the moon from the balcony just outside her bedroom chambers. It had not changed, yet the world she had known was altogether different. The people now in it, she did not know. The kingdoms were no longer the powerhouses they once were — Reginald's historical account had made that quite clear. They were simply quartered bits of landscape that bore the branded name of their former empires.

Strange to feel a sense of strength in the pulverized landscape of the starving and the weak. It was a feeling of unrelenting confidence that she had never really had before. It was almost as if she had always been waiting for a chance to run free, and now the path to do so had suddenly been cleared. Rebekah did not know if she was grateful or simply begrudged the idea of it altogether, for her dreams had suddenly changed. Her desires to lift her clan up were no longer there. And after all that had happened, the one thing that was new to her was the sudden feeling of being utterly alone in the world, for she had no one anymore upon whom she could share her thoughts or emotions. And even if there were such a person, Rebekah did not believe her desire to share herself with anyone anymore would take hold of her heart ever again. For what had it gained her? It had only cost her — a little too much.

The wind suddenly blew all across her gardens as the sound of a wolf howled outside her gates.

The cock crowed twice just outside her chamber doors.

Her entire body froze.

It was him.

Her crows only heralded his arrival in such a way.

"Rebekah..."

She could barely breathe the moment she heard Alexander's voice. She exhaled slowly, sensing anxiety and earnestness in his tone as his tall, lean frame stood in the doorway behind her. Rebekah noticed that his voice was a little bit deeper, the sound of someone a little bit older, yet she could not answer him. Rebekah could not bring herself to turn and look at him just yet. She was not entirely herself, ready to face this world, for she still felt as if she had one footstep in it and one in the world beyond. Although relieved to hear the sound of his voice, she cringed the moment he spoke her name. Rebekah could feel the heat in her body rising as she listened to his footsteps move across her marble floor as he slowly approached. She listened even closer, noticing his gait sounded quite different. They were not swift with the sound of strength and youth anymore. They had slowed, moving with the sound of tiredness and age. He moved inside and out toward her balcony.

"Bird, look at me..."

She could not bear to turn as his final words to her echoed in her ears, *"Don't you cry, Rebekah, not in front of me and not over this..."*

Tears of anger trickled down her face as that last moment resurrected itself all over again. "I don't want you here, Alexander."

"You...*are a disgrace to your clan!*"

The pain drove straight into her heart.

"Nathan didn't love you at all."

She could barely breathe as her chest continued to seize.

"I know."

How she wished he would go back to his lair. The anger and sadness she felt the last time she saw him was constricting in her heart, twisting and turning as her head pounded as she thought of all the things he had said to her. Even now, as alone as she felt, as much as she needed a friend, the last person she wanted to see was him. "Wolf, if you have any decency in you..."

Alexander suddenly grabbed her shoulders from behind and spun her around to face him. He pulled her into his arms and held her tight. She tried to break free from his embrace. "Let go!" But he held her even tighter. He rested his cheek against hers and whispered the words, "I'm sorry."

She continued struggling against his hold.

"Do you hear me, bird? I'm sorry."

She stopped and exhaled harshly as she tried to squelch her rage. Alexander could feel the tension in her body lessen. "I know you are angry with me. I wouldn't blame you if you decided to hate me forever, but know that this is but a fraction of how I felt the last day I saw you…so long ago."

He held her tight. "If it pleases you to hear that I have suffered, know that I was level to the ground and groveled there for quite some time. If I could take back all the things I ever said to you, know that I have wished for that moment a thousand times over ten thousand days. For all the rage you feel toward me now, know that I have hated myself far more than any rage you could fuel toward me." He rested his head against hers. "But I had to come here. I had to see you and feel you in my arms today to know you were real, and to say, I'm sorry."

Alexander could feel her exhale deeply; her body's tension loosened until she went limp. It was then that the bird queen began to weep. Her body racked for what seemed like an eternity as all the pent-up emotion she held deep within her heart suddenly broke free.

"Ah, woman…I hate it when you cry."

Rebekah could barely breathe as she tried to control her cries. Alexander slowly lessened his hold on her. She turned away from him and grabbed hold of the balcony railing. She leaned over it, closing her eyes, trying to calm her emotions and simply…breathe. It was not until she looked up at the moon, focusing all her attention on the pale orb, that she finally began to calm down, clinging to a moment of peace.

The wolf king stepped up beside her, joining her as he leaned over the balcony alongside her, staring up at the moon. "I can only imagine what you must be going through. When I think back to all the events that led up to that day, and all the tragedy that followed that darkest night, I understand the rage caged within your heart; it has nowhere to go. I understand the grief and loss you are experiencing right now as the world around you has continued to shift and refuses to wait for your moment to mourn. And I understand the desire to want to be alone in a moment like this, unwilling to talk to anyone, desiring nothing more than to go back to simpler things, easier steps, and the burden of lesser responsibility and duty than what the day commands. I have lived where you are living, Rebekah. I was still in this world with nowhere to go and no one to share it with…because you were not in it."

He turned and looked at her, suddenly realizing she had been looking at him the entire time he spoke. He stopped and caught his breath as he looked at her. She was as she had always been. Time had not touched that last moment as her raven-colored hair glistened in the moonlight. Her gray, eagle eyes twinkled slightly from the moonlight catching just behind them, illuminated by her tears. His heart ached for a moment, thrown back into the past when he was a young man, and she the only one he ever wanted.

"It was you that I loved most in this world. Only. Ever. You. I lost you on the same day I lost my mother. It was the day I lost myself, only to drown in a day that was never a better tomorrow. But I learned to live on. And what a life it has been. The realm is in shambles waiting to be put back together. And I believe it is you who are meant to do it."

He extended his wrinkled hand, still bearing strength beneath his touch, and moved a strand of hair away from her forehead. He watched as her eyes roamed the features of his face. He could not tell what she was thinking as she did so. All he knew was that she was no longer crying.

"Alex…"

"What is it?"

"You're old."

She began to cry even harder.

His eyes flashed silver. "Mourn me not, Rebekah, I'm not dead yet. Of all the things…*that* is what you have to say to me after everything that's happened?"

"Well, you are. It had to be said. It's a bit of a shock, you know. Yesterday you were dashing and young. And today, well…"

"You thought I was dashing?" A boyish grin spread across his face.

They stared at each other for a long time.

"Rebekah, you are exactly the same."

"Am I?"

She stared into his eyes but said nothing more. He was used to knowing exactly what was on her mind. And what he could not decipher, he was ultimately able to gauge by merely interpreting the look on her face. But this look she was giving him now was a new one; one that no matter how deeply he looked into her eyes, he simply could not read.

"I mourned you for so long. You were my life, and life has been quite different without you in it. Yet, you seemed to be everywhere without really being here anyway, impacting all our lives."

Rebekah's body stiffened. He knew he should not say what he was about to say next, but he could not help it. Just like he had always done before, he needed to push her, test the waters, in order to understand what it was she was feeling.

"Even Nathan has been shaped by the loss of you."

That had done it. She immediately turned away from him and walked to the opposite end of the balcony. She stared into the darkness, tapping her finger rapidly on the stone ledge.

Relief flooded Alexander's veins as he watched her trying to calm herself down — it meant that she still felt, that she still contemplated, that she was not entirely numb to the world around her. And even with that bit of knowledge, the wolf king pushed her even harder.

"Not quite ready to hear his name, hmm? I never took you for a coward, bird."

She slowly turned around; her eyes had swirled to dark, black pools. "Didn't you? Isn't that what you called me when you last stood at my gates?"

Alexander's entire body went cold. "You heard that?"

Her face twisted into a cruel snarl — he had pushed her too far. "You come here throwing your darts of pain at me, seeing which one will hit its mark. Why? To show me that whatever pain or heartache I feel is nothing compared to yours! Or Nathan's! That somehow mine doesn't matter!"

Alexander did not dare reply.

"You all had years to work out your grief and your rage and your suffering! Fifty years may have passed for all of you, but for me it was *yesterday! Yesterday*...my enemies stormed my gates to slaughter my people! It was *yesterday* that Nathan married the Mariner! *Yesterday* that all the ravens were murdered in their homes! It was yesterday...when you threw it all in my face! And *today* the realm demands that I forgive them for all of it! That today, I should remember and embrace the idea that they are right."

The rage behind her eyes almost seemed to make her dark eyes ignite in flame. "I didn't ask you to come here, Alexander. I didn't ask for that lion prince to awaken me."

His eyes narrowed. "That's who it was? That boy?"

"That *man*! He is near my age...whatever age I appear to be." She shook her head as she looked out over her balcony.

"What did he want?"

"What they all want. What they wanted from the beginning...food. I'm left with these same clans and these same people who keep coming to my door — not with weapons this time but with pleas. I can't wrap my head around it." She turned her head without looking at him, "And you're not helping me."

Alexander sighed deeply. "I..."

"Don't you understand? I may look the same to you but I am not as I always was. My heart..." Her voice caught as she tried to finish her sentence. Whatever she was going to say next was what Alexander had been waiting for. It was the pathway to what he had seen behind her eyes.

"Say it."

Rebekah did not reply.

"Say it, Rebekah. Your heart..."

She looked down at her medallion hanging around her neck, letting her eyes roam over the eagle and the raven. "I have no love in my heart for those living in this realm."

Alexander paused before asking, "And what else?"

Rebekah finally turned around and looked at him. For all the years he had aged, the moment she looked into his eyes, she saw the same man who knew her best staring back at her. The look on his face at this moment, however, was one that tried to shield a look of dread as he waited for her answer, one he already knew.

Her eyes were locked onto his as she said, "Palimus was right."

A cold wind blew across her balcony, chilling Alexander to the bone.

"I should have stayed on my own side. Then none of this would have ever happened. I have cursed myself, Alex."

Alexander looked her up and down, studying her. "What happened to you while you slept? You said you heard me. How can that be?"

The bird queen looked out at the moon in an attempt to avoid his eyes. "I heard you all. All your voices. All your cries. A melody of pain played over and over again the entire time I was in my own self-proclaimed limbo." Her face slowly changed as the thought planted itself deep within her heart, but she did not speak it aloud.

"Rebekah."

She looked at him.

"What else? What else did you hear?"

Rebekah's eyes lightened to gray; her face softened until it fell into one of deep sorrow. Watching its sudden transformation, Alexander could not help but be moved by the grief written all over her face. "Tell me."

"I still hear him. He never leaves me."

The wolf king's eyes narrowed, "Who?"

Her voice was barely a whisper, "Palimus."

She looked down at the floor, trying to focus her mind and body. Alexander slowly moved toward her. He took her hand in his, stroking it gently as he ran his thumb over her soft skin. It was all he could think to do to comfort her. "What is he saying?"

She looked up at him and simply replied, "The stories are always the same, except for the last one. I can never quite hear what he is trying to say. Perhaps, it is to let them all die." Tears streamed down her face. "And part of me wants to."

Alexander lifted his hand to her face and wiped away her tears. "And yet you sent food to the clans anyway. And the rain."

She gritted her teeth as she looked into the shadows of her room. "Poe will be furious with me. He told me I should never give my gifts away; there is a time and a season for all things under the sun, and I yet I still cannot help but want to give freely all that I have at the same time wishing I had never done it."

He wiped away a tear. "I'm proud of you."

She shifted her gaze, "No, you're not. Every choice I ever made, you disagreed with. You are a lot like Palimus. You think a lot alike. Stay on your own side. Love only your own. It was probably the better way to go in the end." She looked back at him. "If it pleases you to know it, I think you were also right. I should've listened to you."

"Bird, it's not in your nature to agree with me. You have a mind and purpose all your own. And why you would listen to the voice of a dead king when you never listened to me..."

"What?"

"You know, Rebekah, the one thing I have learned after all these years, is that no matter how dark the night, the sun always rises." He moved a strand of hair from her face. "And it is in the sun that you shine best. If it were otherwise, you would have awakened in the moonlight." He looked lovingly at her then. "And it does please me to hear that you thought I could actually have a good idea."

"I didn't say it was a *good* idea, just *an* idea."

He shook his head at her and could not help but smile. Rebekah tilted her head to the side and let her eyes roam all across his face.

"You've had your share of pain, haven't you, Alex?" The smile on his face slowly faded. "But you have also had joy. I can see it in your eyes. You have a twinkle I've never seen before."

The crow guard cocked twice. Rebekah did a double take. That announcement had only ever been for Alexander.

"Father..." It was a female voice.

Rebekah looked wide-eyed at Alexander. A slow smile planted itself on his old face.

"Alex, you have a daughter."

He nodded. A glow resonated behind his eyes. She could see the pride and the love exuding from his face as he acknowledged his heir. Reginald had mentioned nothing of the wolf princess in his account. What else had he left out?

"And your wife?"

His smile softened as he replied, "Marriage was not meant for me, Rebekah."

Rebekah studied his face as he looked toward the doorway. Time had been good to Alexander — as time seemed to be for many men. Although his hair was completely silver, and his face was etched with the lines of time, he was still devastatingly handsome. And as she saw his eyes brighten the moment the wolf princess stepped through the archway and into view, Rebekah's anger toward him melted just a little, for she knew he had found what he was ultimately looking for. The queen turned her head just as a young woman stepped into her bedchambers.

Rebekah whispered, "Your cornerstone."

Alexandra stopped dead in her tracks the moment she saw Rebekah standing side by side with her father.

Alexander spoke first, "Queen Rebekah, this is my daughter, Princess Alexandra."

Alexandra looked helplessly at her father, unsure of what to do next. He nodded at her encouragingly. Nervously, she curtsied to the queen. Rebekah, recognizing her shy, timid nature, stepped forward. "It is an honor to meet you, Princess Alexandra." She curtsied back as they rose, staring at one other — a queen and a princess.

Alexandra was tall and athletic. She had Rebekah's same long, black hair, but that is where their resemblance ended. Rebekah could see the princess had Alexander's blue eyes and his lean frame, but her cheekbones were higher than any wolf female she had ever seen. Her lips were full, and her shoulders were wide, her hands strong.

Alexander stepped up behind her and whispered in her ear, "Don't say it."

"I wasn't going to." Rebekah tried to hold back her knowing smile. "Alexander, your daughter is beautiful."

The wolf princess looked gratefully at the bird queen, "Thank you, Queen Rebekah."

"We are kin, Alexandra. Call me Rebekah."

Alexander stood staring at the two women he loved most in the world and felt his heart ache. He was grateful for this day, knowing he had lived long enough to see it. He knew he had been holding out for it — just like Nathan. And now that this day had come, he knew he needed time to do a few things more.

"Not only is Alexandra beautiful on the outside, but her intellect brings out the beauty within." Rebekah raised her eyebrow in curiosity. "She can play a mean game of chess."

Rebekah's eyes narrowed at the challenge. "We shall see. Set the board."

XVI

Poe landed atop a gigantic tree, clutching onto the thick branches as he surveyed his surroundings down below. He had yet to see any movement other than the wind as he followed its path toward the enormous mountain before him. He had never seen anything like it; it was monstrous. Poe's scarlet-colored eyes scaled the base of the mountain all the way to its peak, unable to see the top from where he stood. The mountain was so colossal, Poe was overwhelmed by the supernatural power exuding from it.

What kind of fortress isss thisss?

As if hearing the question inside his head, the mountain rumbled and groaned in reply. Every feather on Poe's body stood on end. He reached for one of his daggers, clutching it tight. His heart was pounding so fast, he thought his heart was going to explode. As he stood there, his breath began fogging on the air. The temperature continued to drop until it was absolutely freezing. It was then that Poe watched as snow and ice sprouted on one side of the mammoth rock. He silently dropped from the tree, weaving through the shadows as he moved toward a cliff. He looked from left to right, searching for any sign of life as he made his way toward the snow. He extended his arms, still gripping the dagger in his blackened talons. He landed atop a small overhang and knelt down. He found what he had been looking for. Imprinted in the snow was the same footprint he had seen in the fields of Bird Kingdom.

Poe's body stilled as he memorized the markings of this new enemy. It had travelled far and wide to come to his kingdom. Why? What was this mountain fortress? And what creature or creatures resided here? It could not be a bear, for the bear clan disappeared centuries ago on the eastern side of the realm. But if it were the one species from that clan that the footprint belonged to, it meant that the clan it joined forces with was the one clan he had hoped did not exist, for they were a myth — a legend — to those who lived on Poe's side of the realm.

There was only one way to find out.

Poe laid his black talon down upon the rock. His heart pounded violently as he tried to siphon the sounds from the elements surrounding him on the outside in order to feel the sounds from within. His head slowly tilted to the side as the vibrations and rumblings beneath his talons pulsated. He shifted his scarlet eyes to the mountaintop, feeling the sense of power contained beneath the thick rock.

He didn't even realize that every feather on his body was standing straight up as the wind gently blew all around him.

"Your king was right..."

Poe immediately whirled around, spinning around so rapidly at the sound of the whisper, no other creature would have seen him do it. But the voice on the mountain did.

"The ravens are no more..."

Poe's eyes rapidly moved across all angles and positions surrounding him as he tried to locate the source of the voice.

"Finish what he started...start over."

That was when he saw it: snow and ice were blooming all across the mountain as if growing like mold. Each time the voice spoke, more snow emerged.

"Kill them all."

And right in front of where Poe stood, a small mound of snow rose up from the rock ledge and the same footprint he saw in the bird clan fields formed on the white crystals.

"Or others will come to your realm and do it instead — with or without your kind."

The wind slowly blew the creature's print away the longer Poe stared at it. And as the snow blew off the mountaintop, Poe jumped off the ledge and flew with it. It was then that the clouds had separated and a land beyond his realm was revealed. It was a land the color of ivory, built on snow and ice.

And for all the curiosity that Poe had felt as he flew to the unknown fortress, it soon dwindled when he saw the massive kingdom that lay beyond. It was then that he heard a low growl echoing up the mountaintop.

Poe shifted his red eyes from the land beyond to the fortress below. Although he could see no other creature, he knew they were there. His

76

mind was on overdrive as to what he should do next.

He remembered the oath of the ravens that had been born and bred into his veins from the beginning. *"Fire will not allow it either, my king. For our clan hasss alwaysss honored the burning Sun. Fire will show usss when. Fire will show usss how. Until then, we build for that moment. We grow for that time. We become...for what we need to be. In thisss, the ravensss will alwaysss defend."*

But this was not the voice of Fire. It was that of Ice — and Wind seemed to be on his side. No raven before had been summoned by any other Element. What did this mean? Start over...

Enemies were outside and within. Old enemies and new.

They would not survive if they were not prepared.

And there would be no time like the last time.

A new wall would need to be built, and whether or not his queen agreed to it or not, he would make sure that no other clan members marched onto their grounds ever again. The next battle they faced would be the one the birds would be bringing...to the realm and beyond. He looked up at the mountaintop and saw the clouds up above. His scarlet eyes searched the vapor. But no matter how hard he looked, the raven could no longer see the sun.

XVII

Daniel had fallen asleep at the large wooden desk while reading the green emerald book Marcus had written. He looked around the room, confused and out of sorts as to where he was and what day it must have been. He suddenly remembered it was morning and that he had been up all night reading the book his uncle had written. Sunlight trickled in through the large glass windows behind him burning away any remaining raincloud.

There was a loud commotion coming from the courtyard. Daniel jumped up from Marcus' chair and opened the windows to see what all the ruckus was about.

"Cheetah!"

From down below, Cheetah looked up at his prince and smiled widely, exposing his sharp fangs and blackened lips. "My prince! The eagles! They brought food!" Daniel looked all across the courtyard grounds and saw fruits, herbs, spices and vegetables of every type imaginable. The lion prince could not help but feel the sense of excitement as he saw the joy on the clan's faces and the roar of laughter as they devoured the feast before them. *She did not say no.* "Where is the king?"

But Daniel knew.

"Never mind!" Daniel ran out of the library and through the castle gates when he plowed straight into SinJin. He bounced right off of the old lynx warrior and landed flat on his back. "Ow."

SinJin extended his large hand and pulled his prince up to standing. "Are you all right, my prince?"

Daniel rubbed the back of his head but brushed it off. "I'm fine. Where's my uncle?"

The cat warrior's face changed and a deep look of worry filled his old cat eyes. "He's gone. He went on another one of his missions but…without me." He handed Daniel a small envelope. "He left this for you."

Daniel took the envelope and placed his strong hand on the old warrior's shoulder. "Don't worry, SinJin. Uncle Marcus can take care of himself."

"It's not that, my prince. It's that he's never gone without me before. We have always stayed together." Before Daniel could say another word, SinJin turned and walked back into the courtyard, his broad shoulders drooping a deep disappointment. Daniel looked down at the small envelope in his hand and placed it on the mantle over the large hearth. He ran through the courtyard doors. The moment he was about to hit the open field, Cheetah dropped the morsel of food he was consuming, growled loudly and charged after his prince. They ran side by side to the hilltop in Bull Valley that overlooked Bird Kingdom. They were going to see their king.

Marcus had finally reached it: Wolf Lake. He had not dared venture through these woods since he was a young boy when he first met the Bird Queen.

"I, Prince Marcus of the Lion's Den, am forever indebted to you. This night, you are no longer my enemy. I shall call you…friend."

Even now, the leg she had healed was strong. Thinking back on his life and how terrified he was then when he last ran through these woods, he could not help but feel a little uneasy at his present surroundings. Whereas before, it was the sounds of the night that had made him fearful — owls hooting, the wind blowing, the trees creaking and the wolves howling — the woods in the Wolf Lair — now were eerily silent. In addition, there was a large wall built along the entire border of the lair. Marcus had to climb over it to enter it.

Everywhere he looked, he could only see death and decay. The trees were barren and diseased. The ground was cracked and dried out. Even the lake's shoreline had receded to a point that shocked even Marcus the moment he realized that not even Alexander's lair had been spared.

Marcus had come this way feeling the need to retrace his steps as a young boy, yet knowing the path he wanted to take meant he had to travel through Wolf Lair to get there. What he wanted seemed to be north — the only place he had never ventured forth. He deciphered that in all his travels, all the years of searching and finding nothing meant that this was the only way left. This had to be the path that would lead to all his unanswered questions. It was the emerald book he had written long ago that had reminded him of this and propelled him to be where he was now.

Marcus had made up his mind to keep trying, to keep going — even though Rebekah had brought the rain. The realm had to survive with or without her help, for what if she withdrew it again? He knew he had to try to find the key to the door he was looking for. No king or queen should be relied upon for everyone's survival — no one should be allowed to wield that kind of power over anyone — even if it was Rebekah.

The thought of her swaying between the dark and the light was what had been keeping him up at night; especially after what Daniel said he had seen behind her eyes the day he awakened her. Marcus had been reminded of what the toad chief had said to him so long ago.

"Remember, remember..."

Those words were what was driving him into the woods in order to go beyond it.

Seek and ye shall find.

Knock and the door shall be opened unto you.

He knew he needed to go on this last venture alone, for he had decided this would be his final attempt to see if there was any other sign of hope that lay beyond the realm. He knew SinJin would be upset with him, but Marcus felt that the journey of life — even when surrounded by others — is a lonesome one. You are born, you dream, you fight, you love, and you die — *alone*. And Marcus, who always felt alone, had never really been alone. Not since that night he ventured into the woods all by himself when he was a young boy. And as Marcus hiked past Wolf Lake with the sunshine on his back and the wind blowing in his face, he knew that to be alone at a moment like this meant he was free and right where he needed to be.

XVIII

Alexander stirred awake, shifting in his seat, having heard the faint stirring in his lair — there was someone from the outside who had found their way in. He looked around the room and saw Rebekah and Alexandra playing a game of chess. Seeing them concentrating on the board, unmoved by what he thought he heard, he turned his head and peered out toward the balcony to listen.

He closed his tired eyes, concentrating harder on the sounds of the night. He had heard the same stirrings the moment Rebekah stood before his lake days before. But who would venture into his woods now? He would find out soon enough when he returned to the lair. Besides, if it were an enemy, his wolves would soon take him out.

Both the wolf princess and bird queen studied the board with rapt attention; it was Rebekah's turn. Alexandra snuck a look at her, trying not to stare.

Rebekah tapped her finger in frustration against the board; she was impressed, "That was a good move." She glanced up and caught Alexandra staring at her. Embarrassed, the wolf princess' cheeks turned bright pink as she looked down at her own pieces. She quickly shot a glance in Alexander's direction. Seeing him sleeping, she sheepishly looked at the board and looked as if she were about to speak.

Rebekah spoke softly, "You have something you wish to ask me. What do you want to know?"

Alexandra bit her lower lip in hesitation.

"We are kin, Alexandra. What is it?"

"Were you and my father lovers?"

Rebekah looked up from the board; not exactly the question she thought she was about to be asked. She smiled wryly, "He wished."

Alexander let out a loud snore.

Alexandra's face fell into one of disappointment at Rebekah's answer, but she did not pick up on her father's reaction. "You know, when I was a little girl, I truly believed you were my mother. He talked about you…all the time. Whatever story he told, you were in every one. So I thought it had to be you. I wanted it to be you. I used to talk to the clouds, thinking that you could hear me." She smiled sadly.

Rebekah shifted her eyes to Alexander; his body had stilled.

"He raised me to be like you…at least, that's what it seemed like. But sitting here in front of you…I realize we're nothing alike. And yet, I wanted to be. I stared at the portrait he painted of you for hours. We had the same hair…"

"Alexander paints?"

She nodded; Alexander let out another loud snore. The princess continued, "I never knew my mother. And now that you're here, I want you to know you're the first queen I've ever met. I've pondered a lot over the years about the past as both Reginald and my father told it to me. I've also worried about the state my clan is in, and I've fantasized about the kind of queen I want to be. All these years, I've wondered, how did you know…to make the kind of choices you did? Because you seemed to make all the right ones."

The room was absolutely silent.

Alexandra shook her head apologetically. "I'm sorry. I've put you on the spot. I just feel as if I know you. As if you've been a part of my life all along." She laughed nervously. "Even Reginald talked about you all the time. They both told me so many stories. About the treaty from long ago, the ball you asked for from the lion king, how you were poisoned. I just…I just have so many questions that I have wondered about and always wanted to ask."

Rebekah's chest began to constrict. She reached across the chessboard and grabbed Alexandra's hand and squeezed it with a gentle reassurance. "Alexandra, don't apologize. I am glad you are asking me these questions." She smiled. "When I was a princess, my parents taught me that the most powerful act a king or queen could bestow…is mercy. It is the greatest weapon against the harshest of crimes — especially on the most undeserving kind. The irony of that philosophy is that my clan was not known for being merciful. My clan committed a crime against a king of old."

"You mean Palimus and Luther. Hood, our wolf captain, told me about the Old War."

"Hood? Skoll was the last captain I remember."

"He died when I was very young. Hood is his son."

Rebekah nodded and stared at the board for a moment, digesting the news, realizing that most of her conversations would be like this one the more she encountered those that now lived in the realm.

"Hmm." She shifted her gaze to the fire. "The Old War..." She let go of Alexandra's hand and sat back against her large velvet cushion. Rebekah felt as if she had just come full circle, remembering the night that Reginald told her about the Old War. It was the night when she pondered whether or not to answer the lion king's request for a truce amongst the clans, only to find herself sitting across the chessboard reasoning out her answer and her legacy with the wolf prince.

Now it was his daughter asking questions that reminded Rebekah about who she was and what she wanted to be; something that she herself had forgotten and was trying to forget.

"Well, my clan was hated. Despised. And I didn't want to be. There was something deep within me that made me think I could change the image branded in the hearts and minds of those in the realm who thought so poorly of my clan."

Alexandra remained silent.

"It would have been wonderful to simply reign as queen side by side with my clan on my side of the realm, the way I was. Live, die and be succeeded by any offspring I had to bear. Not to care about what others thought." She gently laid her hand over her heart. "But I knew I couldn't be the one to have it be so simple." She looked at the pieces on the chessboard: the pawns, the knights, and the queens. "I knew it was time to be and do something different. And if no mercy was going to be shown to me and my kind, then I would be the one to bestow it on others...because I wanted to."

"Why did you want to?"

"Because of time. My father died when I was very young. And my mother soon followed. Life changed for me then. Whatever fantasy I envisioned for my life took a different turn because the people I thought were going to be in it, suddenly weren't. Life can change so very quickly, Alexandra. Time in this world can be shortened. And so I asked myself, what does my time in this world mean? Is there something I have yet to do to leave this place better than when I came into it? Is there something that I am meant to do? And if I don't do it, why didn't I? If there was nothing in my way, why shouldn't I?"

"Do you still feel that way now? That you want to do something better?"

Her eyes fell on the king piece on Alexandra's side of the board. "No, I don't. I don't have that stirring now. And I don't know if in this place and time, whether I'm meant to. I've been feeling as if all my choices were actually the wrong ones. Even now, I don't know that I have truly done what is best for me or my clan."

Alexandra stared at the bird queen, seeing the faintest glimmer of tears behind her gray eyes.

"Many of the choices I have made have been based off the mistakes of others. But most have been based on the idea that if anyone said anything against me or my clan, we would live and I would rule so no one would believe it. Not all my choices have been good, nor have they been right. I've just hoped that they would be in the end because of the intention behind them. I haven't succeeded. My dream has not come to pass. That's what I've been thinking about since I've awakened…whether the dream should have ever been."

Alexandra narrowed her eyes at the queen. "But that's what I'm in awe over. You had one. And the one you have *will* come to pass. You have no idea what you have meant to my father…and to me. You don't see…everything that stood in your way before is now gone! Failure is not an option! It *can* be or why else would you have been held and protected for a time when it could actually be done!" Rebekah stared at the young princess. "I see it so differently than you, and it's clear what you are and what you are meant to do. You aren't just meant to bring honor to your clan. You are meant to bring life back to the realm. And in that, you have your honor."

Rebekah stared at the young princess, struck by her words.

Alexandra looked out over the balcony. "But the pack in the lair…I don't know any of them. My father is king, and it's his voice they listen to — not mine. He is the alpha. All the stories I have are his stories to tell. Whatever dream I am supposed to have, I have not had it." She looked at her father sleeping in his chair. "He wants me to be something I don't know how to be. And I'm terrified of the day I have to be…queen." She looked back at Rebekah. "I would not have known to do what you did in order to save them if they were in danger. I wouldn't know anything…" Tears suddenly streamed down the young woman's face. "I don't know what kind of queen I want to be. I just know the kind I'm supposed to be…and that I'm not."

Rebekah stared at Alexandra, contemplating the wolf princess's words. "Have you ever been outside the lair?"

"Just with Reginald when we go flying."

"You go flying with Reginald?"

Alexandra smiled brightly and nodded. "I love it! That's the only thing that Father allows me to do. He says it's still not safe to actually land."

"I see."

"Actually, outside the portraits hanging in our halls, you're the first female I have ever really known." She smiled. "It's nice. I don't feel so alone." She laughed nervously. "I've never known anyone like you. I can see why my father loves you above all others."

Rebekah tapped her long finger on the board. "Correction. It is you he loves above all. You know, you don't need to be just like your father, Alexandra. Your grandmother was loved and respected by the pack — even with the king at her side. She had a voice all her own, and the pack listened. Tatiana was a lot like you — gentle, loving — and she knew when to be fierce. I can tell you have that within you too."

Alexandra's spirits seemed to brighten.

"Besides, being a woman should never be linked to be more like a man. That is not what makes her strong or a force to be reckoned with in this world. That's the mistake people often make. It is in being a woman that better defines you against any man." Rebekah picked up her queen from the board. "You have nothing to fear, Alexandra. When the time comes for you to be queen, you become the alpha to your pack. And they will listen to you. They will help you. Poe and Reginald have helped me find answers to questions I needed. They have challenged me on my thoughts and opinions. Hood and others in your pack will do the same. As they should, for their livelihood rests in you."

Alexandra seemed to breathe a little bit easier.

"But if I have any bit of wisdom to give you, there's one thing you must remember…it's something I've come to know in ruling in a kingdom of men." Alexandra leaned in to listen even closer. "It is that the queen is the most powerful player in the game. As a woman, you have a great power that no man has. That is why your enemy will always try to eliminate you first. Take out the queen, the king and the men who fight for her crumble — for love has left them. The king's decisions shift from the head to the heart and he is left unprotected because his heart is either laid bare or solidified by pain. Depending on the king, either he hangs on and wins or he succumbs to the enemy."

Alexandra listened intently.

"Know that it is you who your enemies will try to take out first. It is you who holds the power to shift the odds and win the game. It is you who can make the king crumble…because you are love. And love is the most powerful weapon in the entire universe. Even if you don't have all the answers on how to rule your kingdom — and you never will, you know — it is how you love, Alexandra that defines the kind of queen you will become."

Alexandra looked at all the pieces on the board.

"So use your power and wield it over your king and your kingdom — use it for something good. And if the day ever comes when your enemies stand before you and you don't know what to do, remember your power and wield it over them to win. Your love can bring the world to its knees, for it is the queen, Alexandra..." She put her queen piece down. "Who rules all." Checkmate.

XIX

Marcus had finally reached it: the border that led from the Wolf Lair and into the land of the North beyond. He had taken with him only one map. It was one of the first ones he had ever drawn, and it always seemed to perplex him, for he remembered seeing a mountain fortress one morning only to find it gone the next. It was the fortress he was hoping to find, for he had never seen it again. Almost as if it did not want to be found.

Marcus moved forward, winding through the trees when he felt someone watching him — *from above*. He stopped and stared at the trees, knowing someone was there. But everywhere he turned, all he could see were branches, leaves and shadows.

He gripped the hilt of his sword, listening intently for any movement among the leaves. He moved forward, cautiously, until he heard the sound he hoped he would never hear again.

"Tok...tok...tok..."

Marcus whirled around, whipping his sword out, ready for any oncoming attack from the one enemy he never wanted to encounter again. But he could see nothing. It was then he decided to focus on the shadows of the trees, remembering the first moment he saw Poe rising up from amongst them so long ago.

"Why do you hide, bird?" Marcus continued searching. "It's been a long time since I've seen your face, Poe."

"Lionsss cannot be trusted..."

A large being dove down and wound around the trees.

"Nor can birds!" He continued to watch for Poe's movement.

"Lionsss....my queen isss the best of you all. Like our king..."

"Palimus? You dare compare your beloved queen to that traitor!"

A loud shrill screeched throughout the forest.

Marcus honed in on the direction the voice was coming from. "I'm not in the Lair. These lands are not yours to claim, raven. Show yourself!"

Whatever Marcus expected, he did not anticipate that the raven would emerge slowly from the shadows of the trees — unarmed. Poe's scarlet eyes glowed in the darkness. Marcus was unnerved as his red eyes moved up and down Marcus' body, sizing him up.

"You've ssseen much, lion. You ssseem to know your way. Why are you here and where are you going?"

Marcus remained silent.

"Tell me...what creaturesss lay beyond our realm?"

Marcus was taken aback. "There are no creatures beyond our realm. Only land." He shook his head, still gripping his sword tight, as Poe walked slowly across the ground circling him.

Poe stopped walking and hissed. *"Liesss!!! I've seen their footstepsss in our fieldsss and on the mountaintop of the great fortressss..."* His eyes blazed like fire.

Marcus' heart stopped the moment Poe spoke. He had seen it — the fortress. He had to get out of here. He had to keep Poe talking. "There aren't any! I've searched beyond this realm for decades and have never seen any other being!"

Poe cocked his head to one side. *"And yet, you are still sssearching."* His eyes roamed the trees in the lair. *"Why do you go this way? What are you looking for?"*

Marcus swallowed hard, inadvertently giving himself away. Poe slowly turned his head and looked north. Marcus could see the wheels spinning behind the raven's sinister eyes.

"Are you looking for help? Trying to recruit another clan to wipe usss out once and for all?"

Marcus remained silent. He had no idea what Poe was talking about — or who.

"There is no one out there, raven."

Poe turned his large ebony head in Marcus' direction. *"Yesss, there isss. I have seen their land beyond the great mountain. I have seen their path leading back to oursss! You go to seek them out to destroy usss!"*

It was then that Marcus knew that there would be no bargaining with Poe. Whatever Poe thought he saw, Marcus knew the raven would never see again. The land they had ventured into would soon change. Marcus knew he had little time to get to that fortress before the land changed once again.

He watched as Poe extended his right hand, examining his talons. *"Tell me, lion...isss that it?"*

Marcus watched in horror as Poe knelt down to pick up a rock, sharpening his talons one by one against it. He wasn't going to wait around to see what Poe was going to do next. He had to take his chances. There was only one thing left to do...*run*. Marcus turned and raced into the woods feeling nothing but the cold wind behind him.

XX

"My king, it is of utmost importance that you remain absolutely still."

Palimus exhaled with impatience as he posed before the critter artist Jocke; he was the most talented raccoon in all the realm. The bird king had no patience for such frivolity but he knew his clan would be pleased.

The crow cocked twice, and the wolf king Feyedor strolled inside the room.

"Don't say it."

"I wasn't going to say a word, king." The wolf king stood leaning against one of the tables with his lean arms crossed over his chest. His silver eyes almost danced as he contained himself from all the things he wanted to say as Palimus posed for his portrait.

Palimus had had enough. "We're done for the day."

The raccoon artist threw his hands up in exasperation while Feyedor replied, "Please, don't stop on my account. I wanted to see you if he could capture the warm glow behind your soulful eyes."

Jocke ignored the wolf king and muttered to himself as he exited the room. "No appreciation for art…"

Feyedor laughed as he watched the raccoon artist scuffle out of the room. He walked over to the portrait and began examining it in detail. "He's being very generous. Your biceps aren't nearly that large."

"Shut up." Palimus smiled in annoyance at his long-time friend and kinsmen.

"I have to do it. My wife says it's time."

"Well, she's right, you know. Time isn't good to everyone, and you may be one of the unlucky ones. Have him paint you at your best rather than what once was your better moment. But I must say, the ruffles are a bit much. I would have suggested battle armor."

"I borrowed the ruffle idea from your attire. Besides, it wasn't my idea."

"Idea or not, you still have a say."

"Why are you here?"

Feyedor's face grew serious. "Brock told me about your latest venture outside the realm. Tell me what I need to know."

"Tell you what?"

"What you saw in the fire." The room suddenly stilled as Palimus and Feyedor stared at one another.

"How do you…"

"You were in my lair. Don't think for one moment that my pack doesn't have eyes and ears everywhere you turn. And what they don't see, I hear."

Palimus studied Feyedor. "And what did you hear?"

"You had a vision that rose from the flame." Feyedor stared at Palimus for what seemed like minutes. "Tell me."

Palimus sat down in a nearby chair and looked off in the distance. "Do you trust Luther?"

"With my queen or my life?"

The bird king looked at his long-time friend. "For me, it's one and the same."

Feyedor pulled up a chair opposite Palimus. "That's because you're a hopeless romantic — both for your woman and your clan. You love them all as if they were all your sons and daughters."

"They *are*."

"No, my friend, they are not." Feyedor's eyes glowed silver as he spoke, "They are creatures with a will all their own. One in which you have no control over — whether or not you are their king."

Palimus did not like Feyedor's answer. "They're more than that, Feyedor."

"No, they're not. Don't make that mistake, Palimus. If it weren't for the simple fact that they are bound to us, to serve, to ensure that they survive so long as there's an heir, they would not bow down to your will."

Palimus shifted uncomfortably in his seat.

"Haven't you ever thought about what your clan could do to you if you were the last remaining one? They could throw you in a dungeon and feed you scraps to eat so long as they could breed you so that they could live on."

"My birds would never do that."

"Wouldn't they? Not even your ravens?" Feyedor continued to hold Palimus' stare. "You think they care about your portrait hanging in your halls more than their own survival?" The wolf king shook his head. "You asked me if I trusted Luther. I trust no one — not even my own clan." Feyedor leaned forward in his chair and looked Palimus dead in the eye. "Tell me what you saw when you looked in the fire."

Palimus tapped his finger against the armrest, weighing what he was about to say next. "I saw death."

"And who brought it?"

Palimus looked the Wolf King dead in the eye, "The lions."

Feyedor paused before he asked his next question. "And who died?"

Palimus could see the images he saw that night rising up from the flames as he looked into the fire. He leaned in toward Feyedor so that they were eye to eye. "We all did."

Feyedor sat back against the large chair and stared at Palimus for a long while. "No wonder you aren't sleeping." The two kings sat in silence for some time before the wolf king spoke once more, "What do you intend to do?"

"A war is coming, my friend. There will be many losses."

"I see." Feyedor stared at Palimus for a long time. He could see the dark circles under the bird king's eyes, the tension in his body. "Are you sure that what you saw in the fire was for this time? In our era?"

Palimus shifted his eyes to the wolf king. "Why should it be for any other time if I were meant to see it in this one?"

"Then you would argue that all prophecies are meant for the here and now?"

Palimus shook his head in frustration. "I know what I saw."

Feyedor was losing patience. "You saw your son die? You saw me die? You saw the jungle go down?"

"I saw…"

Feyedor stood up and leaned over the table, "WHAT!?! What did you see, Palimus?!?"

Palimus slammed both fists into the table and shouted, "IT ALL BURNED TO THE GROUND! ALL OF IT! THE REALM! THE SEA FILLED WITH BLOOD! THE LAND BARREN! THE BIRDS WERE GONE! BONES LINED THE VALLEYS! ONLY REMNANTS SURVIVED! KINGDOMS DESTROYED! CLANS PERISHED! AND IT WAS THE *LIONS* WHO IGNITED THE FLAME!"

Feyedor stood straight up and walked over to the portrait. He stared at it for a long time. "But you did not see your son. You did not see me. You could not see when."

Palimus was still reeling from his outburst.

Feyedor continued, "I have seen many visions in the flame. Some have come to pass, while others never came into existence. I often wonder why. Is it that our decisions have shifted the path, or is it our choices that drive it home?" He turned back toward Palimus. "I don't know the answer. All I know is that you may be right about the lions, but you may be wrong. You don't have the entire vision. And that is a dangerous thing, my friend. Especially when it involves all of us. You may be the key to this hidden door that brings the vision to pass because you believe that it inevitably will — without all the facts."

"What would you do, Feyedor, if it were you who saw this in the flames?"

He exhaled deeply. "I don't know. I might keep my eyes on my friends as closely as I do my enemies." The wolf king looked out at the sun. "I might look for the signs...just to be ready." He turned back at Palimus. "A war is coming, my friend. Let us agree to focus on winning that one first before we bring another that will split this realm in two."

Palimus nodded his head in agreement. "Perhaps you are right, Feyedor. Maybe it is not for our time."

Feyedor nodded in reply. "Or just a later day. Know that if I ever chose to trust anyone, it would be you, bird. Yes, you. If no one else. And if one day you see the signs and act on what you know, believing today is that day, where you lead, I will follow."

The two kings looked at one another with respect.

"Get some rest, Palimus. You're beginning to look as dark as your raven."

Palimus half-smiled as the wolf king walked out, leaving the bird king alone with his thoughts. He stood and walked over to the portrait hanging in the room. He studied it for a long time, memorizing the expression the raccoon artist captured in his face. Feyedor was right. He had not seen his son in the vision he had when he looked into the flames. He had not seen any of the faces of the generation that surrounded him. And because of that, the bird king decided he would wait to annihilate the lion king. He would do as his friend suggested and wait for the signs.

XXI

Rebekah was pouring Alexander a glass of wine when he noticed a large book on the table beside the chessboard. "What's this?"

"A book Reginald wrote."

He picked it up and looked at it in disapproval. "On what? How to fly?"

She handed him his glass. "No...on the last fifty years. I asked him to be my eyes for me. He wrote a history of everything he saw. Strange to read about your life through someone else's eyes."

"He wrote about me?"

Rebekah sat down on the floor beside his chair, snacking on a large bowl of grapes. "Yes."

He flipped through the book in disgust. "And what did the eagle have to say?"

"You'll have to read it."

Alexander scoffed, "I despise reading...and why couldn't the bird draw a few pictures. He had enough time."

He stopped flipping and placed the book next to his cane; it was leaning against his chair.

"Not everyone seems to have your talent. When did you start painting?"

He narrowed his eyes at her. "I've always painted. Just because you didn't know about it, doesn't mean my talent didn't exist."

She smiled at him coyly, "Alexandra said you painted a portrait of me."

He eyed her. "It was the best damn painting I ever did."

"Hmm...I wouldn't be naked in this painting, would I, wolf?"

Alexander's eyes flashed silver. "You wish."

"What's it of?"

His face softened as he looked at her. "A moment when you looked the most beautiful in my eyes. You dancing in my woods before the fire."

Rebekah's eyes grew wide, "You did not!"

He smiled with a devilish grin. "It's true."

She shook her head in disbelief. "Alexander…"

"And you were naked in it, but then Alexandra got older and I had to paint clothes on you. It's hanging across my bed."

She threw a grape at his head. "You're terrible. I never danced naked."

"In my mind you did."

Rebekah put the bowl down beside her and grabbed hold of his hand. "I love seeing you with your daughter."

He held her hand tightly in his. "You didn't think I had it in me, did you?"

"What?"

"A selfless love."

Rebekah studied his expression for a long time, seeing the love he had behind his tired, blue eyes. She lowered her head and rested it against his knee.

"I feel very protective of her…like she was my own."

Alexander gently placed his hand on the top of her head. He began playing with her hair. "You will make a wonderful mother one day, Rebekah."

She looked up at him with hopeful eyes. "Do you think so?"

"Do you see my face, bird? I know so. I raised Alexandra to be what I remembered best in you." He touched her hair. "I listened when you didn't think I was. I watched when you thought I wasn't paying attention." He grabbed hold of her hand and held it tight. "I want Alexandra to shine. I want her to be happy. Promise me that when I'm gone, bird, you will protect her. Watch over her and help her. Teach her what I could not."

She closed her eyes and shook her head. "Alex…"

"I'll haunt you if you don't. Maybe conjure a means to speak from the grave through those toads. If Palimus can figure it out, so can I."

Rebekah opened her eyes and rested her chin atop his knee. Her heart was heavy as she thought about the loss she had felt so long ago, and the loss that she would no doubt face as those that were still alive would one day be gone. Tears streamed down her face as she thought about how much she loved Alexander — he was her best friend, her only family.

"It's overwhelming, you know. So much has happened. So much has changed."

"That would be the understatement of the century."

"Who would have thought that this is how it was going to all turn out when we ventured to the den that day."

He stroked her hair as they reminisced about the past. "Yes. I was about to be engaged, you were about to save the realm from a made-up famine, and Mar was plotting to take all of us down. Now, here we are, recovering from a real famine where no one is engaged, and there are none of us left around to take anybody down."

"Correction. There are other kings I have still yet to know. Have you ever met them?"

"Once…a long time ago."

"What were they like?"

"Desperate, scared. But they were a trio — bound together by brutality and violence. Who knows how they turned out. Nathan would be the one to ask. He is the king on that side of the realm."

"Stop bringing up Nathan."

He pulled her hair.

"Ow!" She sat and looked at him. "What?"

"If ever there was going to be a happy ending to a tragic story, it would be that you and Nathan finally marry."

"He was already married."

"That's not quite fair, Rebekah."

"Well, he was." She turned and looked out onto her balcony. "Until I met Nathan, I never thought I'd be married, yet I knew I had to have children if the clan were to survive. And now, I still have to have children for the clan to survive…"

"*A* child, bird. Just one."

She tapped her finger against her leg. "And what if it isn't supposed to be with Nathan?"

"What do you mean?"

"What if there's just too much pain to get past?"

"Yours or his?" Alexander looked at Rebekah and suddenly felt sorry for her. "I haven't read this foolish book your eagle wrote, but there could be volumes written on Nathan's pain alone. Not to mention the pain he continues to put himself through every morning."

"What are you talking about?"

Alexander was annoyed. "Of all the…where is that bird of yours?" He grabbed the book and flipped through it. "How could he not put it in here?"

"Put what?"

"*Bird*, don't you know…every morning since you went away, Nathan has stood on the hilltop in Bull Valley waiting for you to awaken. Even when he was married. Even when she died. Even after his son was slaughtered and his daughter-in-law perished. He stood there…waiting for you. He stands there still."

Rebekah was stunned. Tears streamed down her face as Alexander continued to speak. "If the love you had with Nathan was true, then time can never change it. If what you are after is an heir, there are plenty of imbeciles left in the realm who could pull off the act. But if what you are seeking is love, a child who will rule your clan long after you die with the same honor and strength as you have brought to it, then there is only one choice in the matter of whom that person is. And he is still here. Loving you even when you aren't there. So, no, I will not stop bringing up Nathan. You've put that man through enough torture by not even going to see him now that you've awakened. That's downright cruel, Rebekah, and I will have none of it anymore! Go see him! Marry the bastard and be done with it!" He closed his eyes, exasperated and tired.

"Alexander…"

"What!"

She was trying not to smile. "Thank you."

"For what?" He opened his eyes and looked at her.

"For what you just said. And for not painting yourself out of my life now that I'm here."

"Don't you know, woman…side by side in all our adventures is where I have always been. And where I will always be." He shifted his eyes to the book. "The filler in your book."

She looked up at him, resting her chin on top of his knee once again. "Alex, you are no filler. You are a tale all your own. Read chapters thirty through sixty."

"Stupid bird. Toss that book into the fire."

He closed his eyes and breathed in deep. She took in his tired face. She whispered, "I love you, Alex."

He did not respond.

"Did you hear me, wolf?"

With a peaceful smile on his face, he answered, "I heard you, Rebekah."

XXII

Daniel walked in to the Great Library and found Nathan seated behind the large, wooden desk. The moment he saw his grandson, he stopped writing, looking a little sheepish, as if he had just been caught doing something he shouldn't have.

"Who are you writing?"

Nathan quickly finished with one last scribble before sealing the piece of paper in an envelope. He shouted toward the doorway, *"CHESTER!"*

A lion roar followed and Chester moved through the doorway. "King."

Nathan stood and moved swiftly over to the doorway, handing the great lion his letter. "I need you to go to the Great White Mountains and deliver this letter to Chief Ume. Tell him it is to be delivered to his queen."

Chester stared at Nathan. Daniel could not quite read the look on the lion warrior's face, but knew the captain of the den was not happy. Regardless, Chester nodded his consent and took the letter from his king and exited the library.

"What did it say?"

Nathan finally turned and looked at his grandson. "It said, 'yes'."

Daniel narrowed his eyes, "To what?"

Nathan walked back toward the desk and peered out the large glass windows to watch Chester race out the courtyard. "Queen Rebekah wanted to know if you would come for a visit."

Daniel could immediately feel his shoulders throb, still healing from Poe's talons. "Just me?"

"That's correct." Nathan looked down. "She's not quite ready to see me, and that's all right...for now."

Daniel shifted uncomfortably. "What if I don't want to?"

Nathan turned, "What are you afraid of?"

Daniel was rubbing one of his muscles around his shoulder. "Nothing. Maybe I'm just not in the mood."

Nathan, amused by his grandson's response, moved toward him. "You have something better to do than represent the entire den on an invitation from a queen who has give our people food, brought the rain..."

"Well, not when you put it like that."

"Good. As you said, you are to go alone..."

"No way! When I asked if it was just me, I didn't mean me alone! Cheetah would have my head if I went without him."

Nathan looked at his grandson curiously, "As if you didn't go to Bird Kingdom without him before."

Daniel stopped rubbing his shoulder. "That was different. I didn't wait for him to follow me."

"Why not?"

"In case he tried to stop me."

Nathan moved toward Daniel. "Trust me, Daniel. Cheetah will try to stop you."

"I don't understand."

"Cheetah will try to stop you from doing what Queen Rebekah is asking of you upon your arrival. Therefore, he must not know. You are to go alone."

Daniel exhaled deeply, "Fine. What is it she wants me to do?"

"When you get there, you'll find out."

Daniel stared at his grandfather, clearly seeing the twinkle behind his eyes. He was enjoying this moment. And just seeing the joyful look on his grandfather's face alone, Daniel consented. "When do I leave?"

"Now. And more important: it's *how* you're going to get there." And for the first time in almost a decade, the lion king smiled.

XXIII

The crow cocked once. Reginald immediately turned and saw Prince Daniel walking through the archway into his queen's chambers. Reginald looked at her, bewildered, unsure as to what his queen was up to. Rebekah smiled upon Daniel's approach. "The noble heart."

He bowed to her. "Queen Rebekah, on behalf of the den...thank you...for the rain and the food."

"To hear the cry of one's people and desire to find a way to answer it is noble indeed, young lion."

"Thank you. My grandfather sends his well wishes. I've never seen him look so happy. Especially when he told me how to get out of the den unnoticed. He said that was how he came to see you."

He watched for her reaction but she gave nothing away. He looked all around her room and out past her balcony. Rebekah nodded her head, signaling her permission for him to explore further. He took it all in, looking out over the parapet. The large bird warriors tending to her garden and fields below overwhelmed him. "There's so much color here. So different from the den."

Rebekah smiled with pride. "Yes, but not as green as Gorilla Jungle." She caught herself. "Or at least, as green as it used to be."

"Was Mariner Sea as beautiful and blue as I've read about?"

She nodded. "It was stunning. The blue looked just like the turquoise color of your eyes."

He blushed.

"You have your grandmother's eyes."

Daniel's face changed to one of excitement. "You knew her?"

"Just a little. Princess Lara had a kind nature about her that I always liked and respected."

Daniel absorbed her words. "My Uncle Marcus said the same thing."

Rebekah's face changed upon hearing Marcus' name. "Marcus! Young lion…"

Daniel laughed. "Well, he's not that young anymore. He's gone off on one of his trips again outside the realm."

A look passed between Rebekah and Reginald. "Outside the realm…what for?"

"To find a means to make it rain and fill the lands and sea with water again. He still believes there's a way to do it — with or without the birds." Daniel realized what he had just said. His eyes grew wide in hopes that he had not stuck his foot too far inside his mouth.

"Not to worry, young lion. You have not offended me. It's a good thing, what Marcus is doing." She smiled. "But…I do have a favor to ask of you."

He nodded.

"Reginald kept an account of the last fifty years of all the happenings in the realm. I've read about it through his eyes, but I'd like to see it through yours."

"Why?"

"Because you are the future of the realm. You are the generation that will rule it, so I need to understand how you see it — without Reginald's perspective of how he once knew it to be and without my prejudices of how I think it should be. I want to see it through your eyes, lion."

Daniel took a deep breath. "I'm honored that you asked me, Queen Rebekah, but I'm afraid that I cannot help you."

"Why is that?"

"I've never seen the realm outside of your lands or mine."

"Well, now…" She looked at Reginald with a mischievous twinkle in her eye. "Let's change that."

Two falcon soldiers landed on the balcony beside the queen just as the crow cocked twice.

Daniel took in the height of the seven-foot-tall soldiers; his look was that of a wide-eyed young boy who suddenly saw a ghost. A female laughed softly behind him. He quickly turned to find the most beautiful young woman he had ever seen standing opposite him. She had the most striking blue eyes, dark black hair and high cheekbones set against olive skin. She was exotic in appearance with long, lean limbs that made her appear taller than she was.

"Alexandra, this is Prince Daniel of the Lion's Den. Prince Daniel, this is the Wolf Princess Alexandra."

Daniel could not find his voice. He could do nothing but stare at her full set of lips.

"Just like a lion...a mute."

Alexandra smiled at Daniel.

"Prince Daniel, Princess Alexandra has agreed to scour the kingdoms along with you. Be back by sunrise. We'll have an early breakfast together so I can hear your report of the realm."

Alexandra mounted the falcon. "Knack won't bite, I promise." The falcon narrowed his eyes and scoffed. Daniel moved toward the large falcon warrior. He attempted to jump onto his back, but only made it halfway up the bird's spine. Instead of letting go and trying again, he held on and tried to pull himself up the falcon's feathers.

The falcon soldier swiveled his head in Daniel's direction. "You are pulling on my feathers, prince."

"Sorry."

Daniel finally jumped down and tried again; this time he made it. The bird warriors immediately took off. Rebekah watched them go as Reginald approached her from behind. "Playing matchmaker, my queen?"

Rebekah continued to watch her work take flight. "Did you see how that lion looked at her?"

"It's the same way your lion looked at you."

"I have great hope for those two; the manner in which they view the realm will shape its course."

"Does the wolf king know of your plans for his daughter?"

She shifted her attention back to the task at hand. "Did you see the way she looked at him? Alexander will know soon enough." She turned back toward her castle. "Any sign of Poe?"

"No, my queen. The Thunderbird Guard has been keeping an eye out for him as well. Interesting that the lion prince has gone outside the realm as well."

"Hmmm...I hope they don't run into each other. Reginald, come get me before dawn. I need a ride to Bull Valley."

Reginald nodded proudly, understanding her meaning. "Yes, my queen."

XXIV

Marcus hid behind a waterfall that poured powerfully down the rock above from a river he had never seen before. He was inside a cave just beneath the falls, watching for the raven assassin. He knew he would see him from this position, for Poe's giveaway was his scarlet-colored eyes; they magnified against the light.

It did not escape Marcus' attention that he had found something he had been searching decades for: the waterfall. Years ago he had discovered it on the eastern side outside the realm. But the following morning, it was no longer there. And now, he had found it again. He had found water. Lots of it. And it was flowing from an unknown source that Marcus had yet to discover. Ironic, indeed, that he had now discovered a resource the realm could build upon to live while he was hiding in hopes that he would not die at this moment before sharing the news.

He had raced into the forest running as fast as he had ever run in his life. Marcus thought for sure Poe's talons were going to dig into his shoulders from behind him to rip his body up from the ground. He did not dare hope he would be carried back to Bird Kingdom for questioning the way Daniel had. Marcus had the feeling the queen did not know what Poe was up to.

How had Poe come to the land outside the realm? And why?

Marcus was bewildered by Poe's questions about another creature and another kingdom. And where had it come from if he had decided to step inside the realm and onto the Bird Queen's lands? It sounded as if the kingdom were far north, but one could never know for sure the way the lands continued to change. Marcus ran through the memories in his mind, searching for any inkling or proof he had ever found that gave rise to the idea of another being or creature living beyond the realm.

There was nothing.

Not even the summer when Marcus had reread the histories of the clans collected in the library. He had read them all with meticulous care, remembering all the details; and there was never any mention of any other clan for at least a thousand years.

What kingdom could it be? And what did it mean for the realm if what Poe had said were true?

As if on cue, Marcus heard a low growl coming from deep inside the cave. It was unlike any kind of growl he had heard before. Whatever was behind him sounded *big*. He slowly turned to see two eyes mirroring in the darkness — and they were not Poe's. Marcus slowly backed up toward the waterfall just as the pair of eyes blinked. The growl became more menacing the more he moved, and Marcus braced himself for what was coming next.

He dove toward the waterfall just as the creature lunged forth from the darkness; Marcus plunged to the bottom of the river. His body buoyed back up to the surface as the tide carried him rapidly downstream. Marcus looked back at the cave and saw a large snout sticking out of the water. Its eyes were watching him as he was carried helplessly down the river.

And just when Marcus did not think it could get any worse, two black talons dug into his shoulders and ripped him out of the water and into the sky.

The lion king stood on the hilltop overlooking Bull Valley just as he had so many times before. He loved this spot — seeing the sun rise up over the Great White Mountains, shining its rays down upon her kingdom. It reminded him of an oasis in the desert: so close, yet so out of reach — just like all the things he ever wanted. And although he had the constant yearning to believe that he would one day have what he had always dreamed about, he still had that seed of fear pitted in the bottom of his stomach that said, *You will never get it. You don't deserve it. Peace is for the gentle and the kind. Love is for the worthy not the proud.*

And yet, he still dared to hope that Rebekah's heart would melt to him one day so that he could tell her all the things he had been holding onto all these years. That he tried to do what was right even in all the wrong.

"*Nathan...*"

He froze, barely able to breathe as he heard her voice call his name. For a moment, he did not even believe he had heard it, that it was a trick of his mind.

"*King...*"

Nathan closed his eyes, and breathed in the sound of her voice, feeling his entire body go limp. She was here.

It was then that he slowly turned around to face her. The moment he saw her, his breath caught in his throat. She was exactly the same, untouched by time as she stood there opposite him. The same black hair of her raven. The same ruby red lips. The same gray eyes of her eagle.

And for all the sunrises he stood on this hilltop, this was his favorite one. He could feel his heart calm, as if her very presence healed something deep within his soul. He could not move.

So she moved instead. Rebekah walked slowly towards him. There was no anger in her eyes. They were shining their brilliant gray as she closed the distance between them. It was then that he reached out to her to touch her. She closed her eyes the moment his hand rested against her cheek; she laid her hand on top of his.

He exhaled the words, "You are real."

He pulled her toward him and held her tight. Nathan buried his face in her shoulder. He breathed in long and deep, smelling the faint aroma of roses in her hair.

"Lion..."

Rebekah could hear the slightest rumble of content vibrating in his chest as he held her. She clung to him in complete surrender, listening to his heartbeat as her head lay against his chest. How long they had both waited for this moment — her in tormented state of limbo; he trapped in the world of the living. She could hear a low purr revealing his satisfaction as he held her close.

As she approached the hilltop that morning, she had been watching him standing there before she spoke his name. His profile was still one that exuded strength and power. Even with his back to her, Nathan still had an athletic frame accentuated by his strong, broad shoulders. And as he turned to face her, there was not much change. His face was still as lean and rugged-looking as she remembered. There were a few lines of age around his eyes and there were gray streaks running all throughout his hair. And to Rebekah, he was to her as he always — devastatingly handsome.

Nathan softly spoke her name, "Rebekah..."

She held him even tighter; it brought her a complete sense of peace being in his arms. She could suddenly breathe easier. As he held her, Rebekah could feel Nathan's body relax into hers. She slowly lifted her head from his chest and looked into his amber-colored eyes. She felt her heart skip a beat the moment their eyes connected.

"Lion..."

That was when she saw the change. His gaze suddenly shifted from looking at her to looking past her. His entire body suddenly stiffened; Rebekah heard a vicious growl rumbling from inside his chest. And before she knew what was happening, Nathan's eyes slit to a cat. He grabbed her and shoved her behind him in a protective stance. She was at the top of the hill, however, and Nathan's shove was so forceful, she lost her balance and fell backward, careening down the hill. She hit the bottom and looked up to see what was going on. A huge Black Angus warrior charged straight toward Nathan. They collided into one another and a brutal fight between them began. That was when she spotted a second warrior at the top of the hill. It was a silverback soldier — and it was looking directly at her. Rebekah scrambled to get up; she searched the sky and whistled sharply.

Nothing.

The warrior was charging down the hill straight for her. She shouted as loud as she could, *"REGINALD!!!"*

He was nowhere to be seen. The silverback was almost on her when she reached inside her cloak and pulled out her small, silver boomerang. She was running backwards as the gorilla rushed forward. She hurled her boomerang at the soldier, but she could not run fast enough. The boomerang sliced through the air and clipped the warrior's head, but the warrior kept coming.

She cried out, *"Nathan!!!"*

Nathan whirled around and saw the gorilla charging the queen down below. *"Rebekah!!!"*

The bull rammed Nathan from behind and wrestled him to the ground. Rebekah's boomerang circled back around and sliced off another chunk of flesh from the gorilla's head, but nothing seemed to phase the beast from charging. She reached up and caught her weapon just as the silverback soldier tackled her to the ground and all went black.

Poe's entire body constricted the moment his queen was hit. He could feel it. His body flinched so violently, Marcus felt as if Poe's talons were going to go straight through his entire body. He shouted in pain. As he looked up at Poe, he could see the conflicting look in the raven's eyes. It was one of terror and anger. Without even knowing it, on instinct, Poe was racing back toward Bird Kingdom with Marcus clenched helplessly in his grasp. Marcus knew something must have happened. It must be the queen.

"I saw it!"

Poe looked down at Marcus, almost as if he had forgotten he was even there.

"In the waterfall! Your creature!"

Poe did not say a word. He merely swiveled his head back in the direction they had just flown. His eyes did not glow crimson like

Marcus thought they would. For a split second, they almost looked sad. Then it was gone. Poe's eyes seemed to glow brighter and brighter as the anger seemed to build. He suddenly lowered his ebony head back down and looked at Marcus. Marcus' heart stopped the moment the raven assassin looked at him. It was as if Poe were looking right through him; as if he were a thing rather than a person. That was when he knew…his time was up. He tried to plead with Poe anyway. "I would never harm your queen! I did not summon this creature! Listen to me, Poe! I want what you want! A means to survive! Without a war! Without more death!"

"That isss where you are wrong, lion. My clan will survive…but death isss eminent to the guilty onesss still living in the realm. The lionsss will bear down to the will of the ravensss. They will all die. Starting with you…"

And as Poe began his vicious attack on Marcus, the lion prince's shouts vibrated across the land. The only ones to hear him were the raven in the sky and the creature still watching down below.

XXV

The four kings, along with the Critter Chief, had gathered in the Lion's Den. Luther sat at the head of the large table where a map of the seven kingdoms was laid out between them.

"Cassius' only chance is to spread his army across the four rivers that lead out from Mariner Sea. His warriors can't last that long on dry ground. He'll try to attack as swiftly and violently as he can to do as much damage as possible in a short period of time."

Luther turned to Brock, "I'll need you and your warriors to attack them close to the canals on the Bulls' and Reptiles' sides before they get a chance to surface. I'll join you on the bulls' side while Feyedor, you attack closer to Reptile Desert and Amphibian Swamps." He turned back toward the map and stared at the icon for Mariner Tower. "Cassius is a fool to think the sea is his shield. He has forgotten about the land that it feeds. That is where your warriors come in hand, Garmon." He turned to the critter chief. "Destroy the lesser kings' strongholds from underground."

Garmon nodded.

Luther shifted his eyes to Palimus. "Cassius has also forgotten about the sky. Your vultures and scavengers will tear their warriors in two."

Palimus answered, "They will. My eagles have been ordered to take out the chiefs in the lesser clans."

"Yes, I understand your eagle has formed a Thunderbird Guard."

"He has."

"And your ravens…"

"My ravens…I'm saving them for the Buffalo Soldiers."

Luther nodded with satisfaction. "These kings will wish they had never risen up to claim what they could never own, and rule over what was never theirs to begin with. They'd destroy it and bring it down to their level of mediocrity, base desire, and mob mentality of entitlement without the sacrifice." Luther sat back in his chair utterly disgusted.

Feyedor asked, "And what are we going to do with these kings when the war is over?"

Luther's eyes slit to a cat as he answered, "Kill the kings. They have their remnants. We strip the heirs of all their weapons, power, and privileges to sit at the realm's table. Their authority will be whittled down to nothing but a title and land to watch over without really watching. We will be the kings over their castles." He shifted his eyes to the map once more. "We will be the ones they pray to instead of the relics and ideology they claim for their religion. That's what started this war to begin with. Cassius with his soothsayer prophesying that he would rule the realm. Fool!"

Feyedor looked over at Palimus. Whatever the bird king was thinking at that moment, the wolf king could not tell.

Brock shifted uncomfortably. "Strip them of their weapons, rule over their lands, but leave their beliefs in the spiritual realm alone."

Luther scoffed. "What for?"

"Because a people cannot be enslaved into thinking one way at all times. They are not designed that way. Wonderment in the miraculous cannot be siphoned, Luther, nor should it be."

"You mean to tell me that you believe in all that hodge-podge of beings beyond this world who are calling each of us to a greater purpose than the ones we ourselves create? That somehow, our fate and our destiny can be influenced by elements — *signs* — that we cannot see, hear or touch, yet tell us which way to go?" He shook his head. "I never took you as a champion of the feeble-minded."

Brock clutched the top of his bone scepter. "I don't believe the same things the lesser clans do, but I have a belief in the Creators of this world. Just as your jaguars and panthers do."

"No, they don't. They believe what the lions, tigers and cheetahs believe: life is in their own hands. Whatever our will is, is the will that is done. No hocus pocus bonfires in the Lair or toads mixing magic potions." Luther rubbed the temples of his forehead. "Once you all learn that it is your own logic and reason that shifts the way of the world into higher thought and greater action, we will have no more wars." He looked up, "For everyone will see what should and shouldn't be done and by whom."

Feyedor jumped in, "Survival of the fittest."

"Yes!"

"And everyone agrees."

"Yes! Because it makes sense."

Feyedor leaned in. "We don't need to agree on our beliefs, Luther, to maintain the peace. All we need to agree on today, is how we're going to win this war. And if my pack believes they have the wind on their back carrying them swiftly to victory, they can go on believing it."

Brock added, "And if my gorillas believe the earth will wield a perfect day for battle, *they* can believe it."

Luther exhaled deeply and looked at Palimus. "And you, Palimus? No doubt your ravens will be lighting bonfires all over your lands to summon the confidence and rage they already have inside them but feel the need to ignite by staring at flames." He shook his head without waiting for an answer. "Fine. Whatever it takes to bring the lesser clans down and bloody the sea." He looked a the kings and critter chief. "But when this war is over, you do what you want with your clans, but the lions will banish these fables and beliefs within the clans we rule — just as we did with the jaguars and the panthers." The lion king stood. "We march at dawn."

With that, the kings exited the den. Palimus and Feyedor walked down the corridor in silence until the wolf king spoke, "What are you thinking?"

"I'm thinking we allow Luther too much reign in bossing us around as if he were king of the entire realm."

"He's always thought that. That's how the lions are."

"Yes, but we don't have to let him think that. He needs us."

"As much as we need him. That is the difference between us and Cassius." He studied the look on Palimus' face. "I noticed your expression when Luther mentioned the Elements."

"And the bloody sea."

"This whole war is going to be bloody."

Palimus stopped walking and turned to Feyedor. His eyes were dark pools; it took the wolf king off guard. "Yes, Feyedor, it will." Damon suddenly landed beside his king. Palimus mounted his raven and vaulted into the night sky.

A large grey wolf stepped up beside Feyedor. "My king, the pack has gathered in the den."

"It begins when the sun rises."

"Yes, my king."

Feyedor continued to stare up at the night sky. He saw the moon shining down over him. But the moment he saw what appeared to be a red halo encircling the moon, his insides churned. "Fire, light the way. Wind, keep us strong. Ice, steel my men. And Earth…" He looked down at the ground, "Forgive me for the carnage that will soon follow."

XXVI

Rebekah opened her eyes and found herself lying in a large bamboo bed in an unknown bedchamber. She looked all around the room, taking in her surroundings. The last thing she remembered was the gorilla soldier colliding into her, but she had no idea how she got to where she now was. And from the looks of it, she was no longer in Bull Valley. Amidst the bamboo, there were larger green leaves she had seen only once before. She slowly sat up, wincing in pain when she tried to move too fast. She reached up and felt a large bump on the side of her head. The room was warm and dark except for the glow of a fire burning in the hearth across the room. There was a window on the other side of the room where she could see out. And although the clouds had gathered in, no rain was falling; it had completely stopped, leaving the room slightly humid.

"I like seeing you in my bed."

She turned toward the direction of the man's deep, sultry voice; it was coming from the fire.

Rebekah looked across the dark room and saw a handsome man just beside the hearth; his chair was facing her. As her eyes adjusted to the room, she looked closely at his features and recognized the olive skin, dark hair, muscular build and dark sable eyes.

"And here lies the great, legendary queen. You know, they say you ate your own clan to stay alive all these years throughout the famine. Eating your own kind — no wonder you remain so beautiful."

"The gorilla king..."

He slowly rose and moved from his chair and over to the edge of the bed to sit beside her. "You're thinking of my father, Brutus. He died long ago. I am his son...Byron."

Rebekah was adjusting her position in bed to move away from him when she realized she was not wearing any clothes; only the sheet covered her; that, and her medallion. "Where are my clothes?!?"

"My servants are cleaning and stitching them for you. I brought you this instead."

He reached across the bed and laid a beautiful strapless burgundy dress in front of her. The gorilla king was young. The same age as Brutus when Rebekah knew him. He had Brutus' strong, masculine features and deeply intense eyes. She could feel them penetrating into her very soul as he stared at her; it was a bit unsettling. He lifted his hand to touch the bruise on her head. "I didn't mean for my gorilla to do this."

"Where is the lion king?"

Byron removed his hand from her head; his face hardened. "Back in his den. He has the bull warrior still. No doubt what will become of him."

"Why am I here?"

He reached for her hand and slowly brought it to his lips. He looked at her with his deep, dark eyes and kissed it. "I wanted to thank you...for feeding my clan. I shall leave you so you can dress. There is much I wish to say to you, Queen Rebekah."

The moment he left the room, Rebekah continued to sit there contemplating her strategy for when he returned. Her heart was racing — less from the introduction to the new gorilla king and more from being captured and taken away from her clan. What would her birds do if she wasn't returned soon? And more importantly, what was Nathan going to do? She had to get out of the jungle...but how? A cold breeze suddenly blew inside the room from the open window. She shifted her gaze to the corner of the room and stared directly into the shadows. She reached for the dress and put it on, readying herself for what was coming next as she heard the gorilla king's footsteps coming back down the hall.

XXVII

Alexandra and Daniel soared over the lands of Gorilla Jungle and on toward Mariner Sea. They could see its dried up rivers and shrunken, dead waters even from the height from which they flew.

"I didn't realize it looked like that."

"Now that the rains have come, I wonder if the sea will rise up once again."

"Another dam will have to be built."

Alexandra nodded, "Yes, but there are neither beavers left nor a Critter Clan to help."

"The bulls will have to do it." Daniel looked at her, "How is it that you know how to fly?"

"Reginald visits my father often. I've grown up flying with him in the moonlight. It's my favorite time of day."

"The night?"

She nodded in agreement. "It's when I feel most alive. We wolves stay up *all* night in the lair."

"You know, Reginald visited me in the den too."

"He did? Did he ever mention me?"

Daniel shook his head. "He never really mentioned anyone on your side of the realm. Did he ever mention me?"

She shook her head. "He must have felt the need to remain

neutral by not speaking about either side. He mostly spoke of Queen Rebekah."

"The same with me. He gave me one of the journals he wrote. It was filled with all sorts of stories he could remember about her."

Alexandra's eyes grew wide. "What! He never even told me he had one! I can't believe he gave it to you!"

Daniel laughed. "I'm sure he had his reasons."

Alexandra was still trying to decipher this news when she asked, "What is it like in your den?"

"Dry. Dusty but beautiful. Our den is built out of marble and brick. The clan homes within our walls are thatched huts — and they are not small. They're more like mini-castles all along the plateau. My grandfather told me that there used to be large trees, flowers, grass and streams that wove their way all throughout our land. There's none of that now."

"Where did the streams come from?"

"Mariner Sea."

Moments passed in silence between the two before Alexandra spoke. "I wonder what it looked like. I often think about what the realm was like before the famine. Seven kingdoms..."

"And what's it like inside your lair?"

Alexandra brightened and a large smile spread across her face. "You have to come and see it! No one's ever been inside my lair! Ever!"

Daniel smiled. "I would love to."

"Then you can meet my father."

Daniel's smile faded. "King Alexander?"

Alexandra nodded. "He's wonderful!"

Daniel looked pale. "I was never allowed outside the walls of the den. The first time I ever escaped, I went straight for Bird Kingdom."

"How did you know where to go?"

"I looked at the direction of the sun."

Alexandra smiled at him. "How did you do it then?"

"Look at the sun?"

"No, awaken the queen. How did you know you would be the one?"

"I didn't. I just...decided to find out."

Alexandra laughed and shook her head. "You must have given your family a heart attack when they discovered you had left. My father would have killed me. I've never been outside the lair either. Just when I'm flying with Reginald." She looked at him curiously. "Your story amazes me. It sounds so easy to do what you did."

"Well, it wasn't entirely easy. I thought the queen's raven was going to rip me in two when he spotted me and my cheetah warrior racing across Bird Kingdom. I didn't even see him coming. He just swooped in out of nowhere and scooped me up and brought me back to the queen. I'd never flown before."

"That isn't exactly flying, Daniel." Alexandra narrowed her eyes. She turned her attention to the bird warriors they were riding, suddenly realizing they were utterly silent as Daniel told his tale.

"Are there any other men and women on your side of the realm?"

Alexandra's attention shifted back to Daniel. "A few. What about yours?"

"Just my cousins from the Cheetah clan. Our panther clan only has a few members left, but no lords or barons anymore. Same with the lynx and jaguar clans. I know that there are other kings still on our side of the realm though."

"Do you know them?"

Daniel shook his head. "Not a one. I don't know anything about them. I just know that there are three left: the Gorilla king, and the Amphibian and Bull kings."

"I've heard about them too. My father told me about them — but only a little bit. They're young from what I know. I wonder about them from time to time. Thinking about what their kingdoms look like and what type of men they are. I wondered about you too."

Daniel blushed a little. "Really? About what?"

"What you looked like, what you did all day. I knew you were the only other prince and I was the only princess." She paused. "Did you...ever wonder about me?"

Daniel stared at her. "I didn't even know you existed. I only knew of your father. I thought he was the remnant."

Alexandra's face fell in disappointment. Daniel jumped in to try to rectify what he had just said. "But...now that I know you exist..." She looked up. "I hope I won't have to wonder. I hope I can escape the den more often now."

Alexandra beamed at him. The look of joy on her face made Daniel's breath quicken. "Yep, definitely more often."

Reginald searched high and low for his queen. He had heard her whistle followed by her shout, but he had not made it to her in time. He chastised himself over and over for keeping so far a distance from his queen. He had only wanted to give her some privacy with the lion king, not thinking that there would be any true danger in the moment, other than if she chose to attack Nathan herself. He could not fly as fast as he once did, so he felt with his heart instead. He could feel his queen, her rapid pulse as it spiked and settled. He knew it was her adrenalin. He had felt a sharp pain in his head sometime after that. The fact that it was still throbbing now, he knew she had been hurt.

When Reginald found Rebekah's boomerang at the bottom of the hill in Bull Valley, his body went into overdrive. Seeing the tracks of both gorilla and bull warriors on the ground, he surmised that something had gone terribly wrong. Reginald had flown to the lion's den but could not find the king anywhere. Chester, the lion guard captain, had informed him there was no sign of the king. And for one so territorial, he did not seem to be too concerned, which meant that the lion warrior was lying. He knew exactly where the king was. It was at that moment that Reginald knew, whatever bond he had formed with these warriors over the years, was gone. When he looked into the lion's eyes, he saw what he had seen before: loathing. It was the same look the old lion warrior Apollo had given him long ago when he had first ventured inside the den. Whatever happened, Reginald knew he would not be getting any help from the den anymore.

Reginald, however, did not sense his queen's presence in their kingdom, so he listened to his heart and flew on determined to find his queen. Along the way, he had looked for Poe but again, could not sense him anywhere. As a matter of fact, as he soared over the sky, he could not hear any other birds. Strange, especially since they were so protective of their queen now that she had awakened. He had sensed the tension they felt when any other clan was mentioned outside their own. His brethren had been changed during the time they slept. They had awakened with a deeper sense of possessiveness over their territory...and their queen — especially the scavenger clan.

So where were they?

Reginald soared over the den and headed toward the Amphibian Swamps and on toward Gorilla Jungle, searching. Still searching...

XXVIII

Rebekah was tying a gold belt around her waist when she heard the gorilla king's deep, velvety voice, "You are beautiful."
She looked up in surprise. He was standing in another doorway, leaning against it.

"Do you always sneak up on queens when they're dressing in your room?"

"I would if they all looked like you. But there are no queens, dear lady. Only us kings."

Her medallion was lying on the bed. Byron moved toward it and picked it up. He stepped behind Rebekah to clasp it around her neck.

"Are you your father's only son?"

Byron smiled, "Good old Brutus...he tried for a long time to make an heir with any one of his fifteen wives. I had two sisters, but they died from the plague. I came along twenty-some years after you disappeared."

He moved in front of her and moved a piece of hair away from her face.

"You are young." He moved in closer. She slowly backed away before hitting a wall as he continued to advance. "Young enough to have sons and daughters of your own to rule your clan long after you're gone." Byron touched her necklace, running his fingers gently over its metal. His face was inches from hers. "I want many sons."

"With your many wives, I'm sure you'll have them, king."

"You mistake me for my father, queen. I have no wives. Unlike him, I only desire one." He leaned in towards her and opened the door beside her. He backed away from her.

"Then you're a remnant."

"Yes. And I'm not the only one."

Byron took her hand and led her down his halls and into a library, closing the door behind them. She took in the massive shelves filled to the ceiling with all the gorilla king's books.

"You're surprised to find I enjoy reading here in Gorilla Jungle. We have scribes who have been recording the histories of the clans for centuries."

"I did not mean to offend you, king."

"Byron."

She nodded. Rebekah saw two other men standing opposite her in the room. She froze the moment she saw them.

Archer. Rom.

Her attempted murderers. The two men looked at one another unsure of her reaction and what she was thinking as she stared at them. Byron caught Rebekah's look and spoke to her calmly, "Queen Rebekah, I'd like to introduce you to the bull and amphibian kings: Minotauro and Sebastian."

For a moment, Rebekah could not move. It was completely uncanny how similar these two kings looked like their fathers. Sebastian had Archer's long, lean frame; his eyes, however, were not solid green like his father's but a strange hue of green mixed with speckles of violet. Minotauro had Rom's build: wide, sturdy and strong. Whereas Rom had a steely, cruel look resting behind his eyes, this new bull king had a haunted one.

Minotauro knelt down in front of her. "On behalf of my clan, I thank you for the rain."

Sebastian knelt beside him. "And the food, good queen. My people..."

His voice suddenly caught as he tried to contain his emotions. He looked down at the ground but said nothing more. Byron placed a hand on the king's shoulder.

Rebekah swallowed hard before replying, "You are welcome, kings."

They stood up in unison, looking like they had a heavy weight on both their shoulders. Byron motioned for her to sit opposite them. He pulled a chair out for her. The three kings sat down together; Byron sat in the middle of the other two. Rebekah could tell that the other kings were waiting for Byron to speak as he reached for a handful of grapes in a bowl on the table in front of them. She was reminded of what Alexander had said about them — a trio.

"I've never tasted anything so delicious."

Byron motioned for Rebekah to drink from a goblet at her side. It had already been filled with some kind of drink prior to her entering the room. Her face paled and her insides constricted as she stared at it. Byron grabbed her goblet and drank from it himself. "I am not a frog waiter, queen."

He offered it to her again. This time, she took the goblet from him and drank from it. She was trying to relax but struggled to do so — even as the kings tried to make her feel at ease. One could feel the tension in the room as Byron cleared his throat and began, "We kings are the remnants of our clans. We are fully aware of the names our fathers have handed down to us. Names that we wish to change, for our clans continue to be punished brutally for the choices our fathers have wrought. Your gift of mercy has given us great hope that we can change the course of our peoples' futures. You have given us the confidence that there will actually be one."

Rebekah listened on in silence. She was studying them, searching their eyes for their character. She was impressed and a little taken aback by the gorilla king's choice of words. They were words that mirrored her own. She looked at them closely. What was it she saw?

"I know the manner in which we brought you here was not a wise one, but we didn't think you'd come on any invitation we had to offer."

"Yet, you didn't even try. No, it was not wise. My clan will not be pleased with you for what you've done, and the lion king and his den will not take this lightly as your warriors attacked him as well."

Sebastian and Minotauro shifted uncomfortably in their seats.

Byron answered, "We had to risk it anyway." The men remained silent knowing her words rang true. "We've kept silent on our side of the realm for too long. And we fully realize that our three clans were the ones that marched on your kingdom so long ago."

Rebekah shifted in her seat, seeing the armies in her mind's eye, remembering the night she sent the shockwave. She looked down at her hands, suddenly realizing how tightly she was gripping onto the arms of the chair.

"Our jungle was flooded the night of the Mariner wedding."

Rebekah looked up, surprised by this piece of news. Reginald had not written about the shockwave's damage to the other kingdoms; he only wrote about the slaughter of the Mariners.

Byron continued, "Thousands of people died, and many more were left homeless. Even Bull Valley and Amphibian Swamps suffered many losses that night." Byron looked at the other two kings. They did not say a word and seemed to be lost in their own memories as he spoke. "Our kingdoms have been in shambles ever since." He looked at Rebekah. "We need your help. We're sorry for what happened today, the way everything transpired. Please believe me when I say there was no other way."

Rebekah stared at the gorilla king for a long time. He was honest; she could hear it in his voice. The kings were humble; she could see it in their demeanor. She relaxed a bit, feeling a sudden connection to these kings — unlike she had ever had with any other kings before. She knew she had a decision to make, and this was easier than most of the ones she had ever had to make before. If only they could all be this way.

She tapped her finger against the armrest of her chair. "Kings, you do not have to worry about food or the rains any longer. I will not wield that kind of power over your clans. My birds will continue to feed your people." She looked at their gaunt faces and desperate eyes, remembering their fathers before them. "We will always feed your people — so long as you keep the peace. You have my word."

What was it she saw?

Hope.

Byron rested his hand on Minotauro's shoulder and squeezed it. The bull king was looking down at his clenched hands. The queen could see them relax, deeply relieved — as if part of the weight he had been carrying were suddenly lifted; it was the king's only emotion. Sebastian's eyes filled with tears as he stared at Rebekah; his jaw was tight. His teeth remained clenched as he tried to smile while holding back his heartfelt emotion.

"Thank you, queen..."

Byron was clearly the rock in this trio as he continued to speak for the kings. "It does my heart good to hear you say that."

Rebekah added, "But there is more..."

"We have drawn up a treaty between our clans. We wish to make an alliance with you."

"There is no need..."

"Yes, queen. There is."

"King, in signing this contract with your clans, who am I signing against?"

"The wolf and lion kings."

"The Wolf Lair is kin to my kingdom. I have no alliance with the lions, nor do I call them enemy."

Minotauro finally spoke up, his eyes wild with fury as he drove his fists into his thighs, "Queen! The wolves and lions feed upon my people! My *warriors!* Not the animals!"

Rebekah was taken off-guard by his sudden burst of emotion. Her eyes darkened. "What do you mean?"

"They are cannibals! And when they hunt, they cross into our lands to do it! My bull is more than likely their dinner tonight! He was captain of my guard!"

Rebekah's eyes darkened even more upon hearing this news. Byron saw them changing; the hair on his arms stood on end as he lowered his voice to almost a whisper as he cautiously added, "Our soldiers and clans are weak from starvation. They cannot defend themselves. We kings have been unable to help our people. If you sign a contract with us, the wolves and lions will stay away. The animals for them to hunt will return when nature decides, but nature needs a chance. My people also need a chance to heal and recover or it will be the end of us."

Byron looked down at the treaty. "We have nothing but our words, Queen Rebekah. Our fathers left us nothing to act upon. We have nothing...nothing but our word."

"And how do they hunt your warriors?"

"They come into our lands. It all depends on how much time has passed if we have not sent a sacrifice from each of our clans willingly."

Rebekah was horrified. There was no way these kings with their gaunt faces and starved looks would be much of a challenge for the den. It reminded her of when she was weak, barely healing when the lesser clans marched upon her gates. She could not imagine having to send one of her clan members to the slaughter for fear of further loss and repercussion.

"And the wolves?"

Byron looked her dead in the eye. "They cross over the borders when they have to."

She was angry.

Rebekah looked at all the kings' faces, wishing someone had stepped in to help and protect her and her clan when they needed it most. And the queen suddenly accepted the idea they were after: she *was* the one, the one who needed to step in. She suddenly felt ashamed of her emotions on wanting to distance herself from the rest of the realm, thinking only of herself. And it was in that moment when a deeply seeded anger stirred up the dormant fire in her heart that she had been trying to squelch. She took a deep breath, composing herself as she tried to still the wave of emotions swirling in her heart. She looked at the kings, her eyes swirling to a soft brown.

"I wish I had known you years ago, good kings. I will speak to the lion and wolf kings on your behalf — not only on this matter but also about the attack that occurred today. The lion king will not retaliate against your clans, but I will not sign a treaty against him — or the wolf king. It would undermine the power of my word if I did so. You do not need my signature to believe me. My word, too, means something here. Your people will be hunted no more."

Minotauro nodded, looking down at his strong hands again,

releasing his clenched fists. "Thank you, queen." Sebastian looked at her with wide-eyed hope. "Thank you." Byron's shoulders lowered as his body seemed to relax, drained of the pent up tension around his shoulders.

They stared at one another. Byron smiled faintly, "I don't want you to go, queen. I breathe easier with you here."

She watched him as he looked at her with his deep, brown eyes. It was a look she had to be mindful of, for she could see the deep admiration behind them — and a little bit more. She suddenly thought of Nathan and her gaze shifted from Byron's to all the kings sitting before her.

"I want you to know, kings, that I could have left long ago and you could not have stopped me. But I will leave you now and know that you can breathe easier all the same."

Byron looked confused. "I will call for my guards to escort you home."

Rebekah leveled her eyes at him and rose from her chair, "You'd better not. The Wolf Pack and Lion Guard will surely attack them. My raven and his squadron of crows will take me home. Poe..."

A cold breeze blew through the room as the queen looked to the shadows in the room.

"Tok...tok...tok..."

The raspy toggle startled the kings as they quickly rose the moment Poe emerged from the shadows of the library. The other two kings were equally taken off guard. Poe smashed the door of the library open.

Rebekah rose. "Remnants...the tide will turn in your favor." She jumped onto Poe's back as he ran down the hall toward a windowless pane. Byron and the other two kings ran after her. They watched as she soared into the sky. On Poe's wings, a legion of crows followed.

Sebastian was in awe, "My god..."

Minotauro finished his thought, "And those are only the crows."

XXIX

Rebekah jumped off of Poe's back and walked swiftly off of the balcony and into her bedchambers. Alexandra and Daniel were in the room with Reginald and Alexander. The two warrior birds stared at each other as their beloved queen was safely returned. Reginald bowed in relief the moment he saw her, "My queen!" Poe's eyes were burning hot; his entire body shook with the anger and hostility he felt for Reginald in failing to protect their queen.

Alexandra cried out in relief, "Rebekah!"

Rebekah was staring directly at Alexander when she said, "Alexandra, Prince Daniel...I shall have to postpone our meeting. I need to speak with the wolf king in private."

Alexandra looked at her father. He nodded for her to go. Daniel volunteered, "I'll walk you out." They left together, unsure of what had happened and what was about to happen.

The queen commanded her eagle, "Reginald, take Prince Daniel back to his den and let the lion king that I am well and safe at home. I was in the jungle. He is not to retaliate against the clans. If he does, I will send the Thunderbirds down against him. That goes for you too, Alexander."

Alexander's jaw clenched.

"My queen, I went to the den and did not find the king there."

"He's there. Tell Nathan he is to return the bull warrior to his clan. Is that understood?"

Reginald bowed, "I will do my best to carry this message, but the den does not always listen."

"If they don't, tell them I will cut off their food supply."

Poe's eyes glowed scarlet, but he remained unnaturally silent.

Reginald's feathers stood straight up. "Yes, my queen." He flew off the balcony. Rebekah turned her attention to Alexander.

"Don't look at me like that, Rebekah."

"Is it true!" She paced angrily back and forth across the floor with her hands on her hips. She stopped and shouted at him. "Have the Lion Guard and Wolf Pack become cannibals! Are they feeding off of the lesser clans?!?"

Poe swiveled his head in the wolf king's direction.

Alexander slowly sat down. He pounded his fist into the table. "Damn those monkeys!"

"Answer me!!!"

"Don't shout at me! People do things they normally wouldn't do when survival is necessary, Rebekah! My pack did what it needed to do in order to survive!"

"If your pack even takes *one* step into bull, gorilla or amphibian territories to hunt again, I will annihilate them and I will not think twice about it."

Alexander glared at her. "Don't you threaten *me* or my lair, woman! Demolition of my house is not so easily done!" A low growl rumbled in his undertone. "You look at me as if you didn't contribute to the current state the world is in!"

"Had Ice not frozen my kingdom, Alexander, we would not be having this conversation, for I would already be dead! What the wolf and lion clans have done is beyond the murders from long ago. There is no comparison!"

"Yes, there is! It's justified, Rebekah! What has made you so fired up over this now? No doubt Reginald wrote about it in that farce he calls a book!"

Poe clenched his talons together the moment Alexander spoke Reginald's name. Rebekah was glaring at him; her eyes were dark pools. "The kings of the lesser clans are what changed it."

Alexander narrowed his eyes. "Let me get this straight...they attack you, kidnap you, and you're turning your anger toward *me*."

"Alexander, make no mistake, I am not unforgiving when it comes to being attacked, but I saw the looks on those men's faces. Sitting across from them, hearing what they had to say, is a far different reality than reading about it in a *book!* I looked at them and saw *myself!* They were *me* in my darkest hour! When I needed help to come! And no one came!"

"*I* came! My mother and father came!"

But Rebekah was not listening. "The kings of the lesser clans have my utmost attention and greatest respect!"

"Yes, I can see the gorilla king has made quite the impression on you. If he hadn't, you would be out of that dress and burning it."

"Had he made the kind of impression you are insinuating, *cousin*, this dress would be off and I would be in his bed. Speaking of beds, get to yours!"

He held her stare as his eyes glowed silver.

Rebekah had had enough of his company. "Poe!"

Poe stooped forward. She threw a cloak on and grabbed her gloves. "I need some air." She jumped onto his back, and in an instant they were gone.

Alexander watched her go. "Since when do you ride with Poe?" He grabbed his cane and hammered it down on the chessboard. The pieces scattered all across the room. Alexander was furious with Rebekah. To see her looking so justified in chastising *him*. He had already been doing that to himself for years — he had made amends as best he could with what he could control. And he had resolved himself of the things he could not. It was not his fault the other side of the realm was eating each other to death!

He looked up and caught sight of Palimus' portrait hanging on the wall. When had that been placed here? Alexander stared at it for a long time. And the longer he stared, the look on the old king's face seemed to be changing. He was smiling more than what Alexander remembered. Staring at the portrait suddenly made Alexander's blood run cold.

Rebekah was with Poe.

A chill ran down his old spine. She was never with Poe; always

Reginald. He turned around and slowly limped to the balcony aided by his cane as he looked out over Bird Kingdom. Although Rebekah had sent Reginald to the lion's den, under any other circumstance, she would have waited for his return. Knowing she was riding with Poe made his heart slow to the rhythm of doom. He suddenly felt a cold breeze speaking its haunting tongues as he searched the sky for the queen and her assassin. He looked back at the portrait of Palimus.

What was going on here? And as he closed his eyes to listen to the sounds whispering in the night, he heard only an unnatural silence.

Poe was utterly silent as he and Rebekah soared over Bird Clan territory.

"You're angry with me."

He took a long time before answering. *"Yesss…you were supposed to wait for me…"*

"The time was right and you were not here."

"You were captured!"

"We knew it was a risk if I exposed myself in some way by stepping outside the realm. Besides, they followed my footsteps into Bull Valley like you thought they would."

"Because of the lion king…" His body stiffened the moment he made reference to Nathan. Rebekah could see Poe struggling to keep the feathers on his body from standing straight up.

"Where were you?"

He did not answer his queen.

"Poe…"

He could see the fortress in his mind's eye. *"I sssaw a place…a mountain larger than any I had ever ssseen. I sssaw land made of snow."*

"What are you talking about?"

"The eagle should have told you. There wasss a footprint on our land from a creature that doesss not live on our side of the realm. I went to find it."

"And did you?"

"No, my queen...I found sssomething else..."

"What?"

He craned his head around; his eyes glowed red. *"Purpose."*

Moments passed as the raven and his queen stared at one another, the weight of what this could mean was felt in both their hearts. "It never ends does it, Poe?"

He turned his head forward, *"No. It seemsss asss if it isss never meant to. Perhapsss that isss why we have been made exactly asss we are."*

"Tell me the plan."

"The crowsss and the ostrichesss will need to guard our bordersss to the north. I will gather the Thunderbird Guard and protect the boundariesss to the south. You, my queen, must stay within them to remain safe."

"You know I can't do that, Poe."

"Because of the lion."

"No. Because I am queen. I have agreed to feed the clans and have allowed for the rain to fall. Not to mention that I have been behind our borders for over fifty years. I don't intend on staying behind them again." She paused, feeling the heat rising up from his body. "You have not asked me about the three kings."

"Their actionsss speak louder than any wordsss you could utter."

"True. Their attempt in seeking an audience with me was not the wisest choice they could have made, but there is something you need to know about them. They hide behind the borders of their kingdoms. They hide in fear of the lions."

"From being eaten."

Rebekah looked out at the midnight sky. "Yes. And in order to stop that from happening any more, they asked for my help to set things right." She looked down at Poe. "That is why they risked what they did today. They knew no other way to help their own kind."

Poe was completely silent.

"Protect the borders, Poe, but know that I will be travelling past them. A new era is coming on the horizon. And with every sunrise and every sunset, we will make one small change for the better good...seeing as how I have been made exactly as I am to know that is what needs to be done."

"And what of the creature and the fortresss beyond on our realm?"

"If you find this creature, bring it to me…alive. Our kingdom is not the only one at stake if this creature and his clan mean harm."

"*Yesss, my queen…*"

And as they flew over Wolf Lake, Poe looked down at the water and smiled.

Reginald descended upon the Lion's Den. Just before landing in the courtyard, he let out a loud shrill alerting the warriors to his arrival. Tigers, jaguars, cheetah and lynx warriors stormed the courtyard just as Reginald descended.

Daniel jumped off of him.

Reginald said, "Young prince, I need to speak with your king."

Chester approached, "I told you, *eagle*, my king is not here!"

Reginald stood before the warrior confident and unafraid. "I must speak to him. My queen has a message for him."

"*Let him speak.*"

The warriors moved out of the way as their king approached. Reginald swallowed hard before saying, "My queen is safe inside her kingdom. She is unharmed." He could see Nathan's body slowly relax. "She wanted me to tell you that the bull warrior who attacked is to be returned to his clan…alive and whole."

Reginald waited as his words set in. He could see the warriors surrounding him shift and exchange glances between each other — all the while, remaining silent. Even Nathan's demeanor shifted from one of relief to one of anger. Reginald could see the tattoo around Nathan's neck slowly darkening.

"What else did she say?"

Reginald dreaded the next moment. He exhaled slowly and said, "If the bull is not returned as my queen has commanded, she will no longer send food to the den."

That did it.

The lion's den warriors erupted in roars, growls and shouts of rage. All the while, Nathan and Reginald stood silent amongst the outrage as they held each other's stare. Daniel remained dead silent during the entire exchange.

Nathan's voice was low and lethal. "I sent scouts to the valley and jungle to find her, so that war would not be waged amongst the clans on my side. I allowed my grandson to ride the falcons with the wolf princess as a means of bridging peace with those on your side. And *your* queen threatens the livelihood of my clan for doing what's right?!?"

Reginald lowered his head and leveled his eyes at Nathan. "Not when it comes to the bull."

The message behind that single phrase spoke volumes as Daniel watched for his grandfather's reaction. He could tell that his king was furious. His rage was evident in his body language as he stood rigid as he stared down the eagle. Daniel had never seen his grandfather's tattoo turn as black as it now appeared to be.

"Your queen does not rule here." His eyes had slit to a cat. "You tell Rebekah the bull will find its way home. And if she decides to step foot into the jungle or valley again, she's on her own."

And with that, Nathan turned and stormed back into the den. Daniel turned to Reginald, "You should go."

Without another word, Reginald vaulted into the sky, leaving Daniel to stand amongst a throng of roaring lions.

XXX

"*I will need your armies in the sky...*"

Palimus watched the bloodshed and slaughter down below. He hovered in the sky awaiting Luther's command. Damon craned his neck around to speak with his king. *"The lesser clansss will not survive thisss war..."*

"They'll survive, Damon, but without their kings."

The raven chief turned his attention back toward the battle down below. He had been following the lion king's path the entire time. And while the bird king watched from above, his heart was deeply troubled. Damon could feel his king's unsettled spirit deep within his own.

"My king...it may not be him. It may be an heir of hisss that we will never know..."

"And what if it's not? What if this war, Damon, is the sign foretold to me so I can end it now? My son would live on. Our clan would survive. Our realm would be at peace. Luther *is* that king. He is the ice in our sea, Damon, causing it to split and crack. That is what I saw in the fire. And I trust the vision, yet wish with all my heart, it were not so. I have never had cause to despise Luther except this one thing. An heir or not, if the lion king dies tonight, the poison in his blood is sure to be wiped out."

"And if he livesss, my king?"

"He won't." And Palimus watched as the buffalo soldiers ran into the haunted forest…and Luther followed. As Palimus watched the lion king walk into what could undoubtedly be a trap, he was glad. The bull king and his warriors would take the lion king down, and Palimus would finally be able to sleep.

"PALIMUS!!! SEND ME YOUR RAVENS!!!"

His heart was racing but he did not answer the lion king's cry.

"PALIMUS!"

He had hoped that he would not really have to decide, but life was making him choose. So he chose…to do nothing. It wasn't until he saw his eagles soaring toward the lion king's side that he issued the command. As he and the ravens descended, Palimus was only thinking one thing, "I hope you are dead, king."

And the lion king was. But what Palimus had not anticipated was how brutal a death it would be. Seeing the mound of flesh that was once Luther, not even Palimus could stop the horrified feeling he experienced when looking at what was left of the once great king. What was he feeling then? Gladness and sadness. It was over. The war had ended as swiftly as it had begun; and yet, Palimus felt a war still raging in his heart.

What had he done?

Nothing, some would argue. He could argue. But that was the problem. He had not answered when the lion king called. He knew that there were questions, and he could see them residing behind Brock and Feyedor's eyes as they looked at him.

Weeks later, it was their stares that still kept him awake at night. The peace he thought he would feel once the lion king had been done away with remained.

Yet, he had done…*nothing.*

Nothing wrong.

Nothing right.

Just…waiting a little too long to move, to jump into action.

But then again, he *had* jumped into action. He had done his part. The ravens had descended — even if it was a little too late. Besides, Luther was not *his* king. The lions were supposed to protect their lord and master — not him. Luther should have known better than to follow the buffaloes into the forest alone.

Who does that? Who thinks themself to be immortal like that?

Luther.

And on the Day of Justice, Palimus tried not to look down at Luther's grave as they all gathered in the den. Brock had just bludgeoned Cassius to death. The bull, amphibian, and reptile kings had been hurled into the fire while still alive; their bodies burned on a large pyre nearby. Palimus dared not look over at the fire for fear of what he might see in the flames. He could barely look at anyone for that matter — not even himself.

He had thought the moment Luther was killed that he would be affirmed with a sense of peace. But he wasn't. Instead, he was tormented. He was haunted. He was...regretful. The bird king looked up as Feyedor approached the lion queen Alana. Palimus stared as the wolf king knelt before the lion queen. As he rose and Brock took his place, kneeling in respect to the queen, Palimus felt as if he was going to throw up. He was next in line. And no matter how hard he tried, he could not rid himself of the look of shame and burden of remorse he carried with him as he approached the lion queen. This was not how he thought he would feel after Luther died. This is not the way he thought he would act. This was not the way he saw his future when he looked into the fire.

The bird king slowly lifted his eyes and searched for the sun. He could not find it. The clouds covered the sky tainting it with a hazy shade of gloom. He lowered his eyes and caught a glimpse of the large bonfire burning the bodies of all the traitors within its heat.

And that was when he saw it: one last vision. Palimus saw a young woman with dark, raven-colored hair. She was dancing amongst the flames. On her right was an eagle and on her left was a raven. Palimus did not know her but knew that she must be a descendent of his clan. Mesmerized, he watched as she danced. She swirled and moved rhythmically until keeling over, as if she were in tremendous pain. The eagle and the raven fell with her. That was when Palimus saw another being standing behind the woman. He wore the royal crest on his cloak...from the Lion's Den. It was a different king from another era. The lion king was smiling cruelly as the queen and her warriors went down. The lion king shifted his eyes and looked directly over the flames...at Palimus. The moment their eyes met, the lion king's eyes slit to a cat. Palimus watched in horror as the flames grew higher until it engulfed the lion king entirely and the vision ended.

Palimus turned away from the bonfire, rapidly deciphering what he saw.

He was wrong.

The vision he had was still going to come to pass.

He had played a part in killing the wrong king.

And as he approached the lion queen, Palimus could not stop his body from shaking. He knelt down before the queen, a penitent on his knees in prayer seeking forgiveness, hoping he would be able to right his wrong. And the moment King Palimus stood, finally finding the courage to look the lion queen in the eye, she lifted her hand and plunged a dagger straight into his heart.

XXXI

"Rebekah!"

Rebekah turned and saw Alexandra moving through the garden. She looked radiant. "I'm not disturbing you, am I?"

"Not at all."

Alexandra sat down beside her. "I had to share it with someone. My father is in a bad mood and refuses to come over. What happened the other night?"

"Nothing that cannot be mended."

"You met the other kings. What were they like?"

"You would like them. I will talk to your father about arranging a meeting with them."

Alexandra looked worried. "I doubt he'll agree to that."

"It's his duty and responsibility to arrange it — especially now that they have made themselves known. But that is not why you came here. What's on your mind?"

"Prince Daniel." She continued smiling.

"Tell me."

"Prince Daniel is so different than what I expected, Rebekah." The wolf princesses' eyes were twinkling as she spoke.

"And what did you expect?"

"Oh, I don't know. Someone more serious and grave."

"Like your father?"

Alexandra tried not to smile. "He is a bit of a grump, isn't he?"

Rebekah laughed. "Alexander was not so conservative as he is now. When he was your age, he was one of the few princes who could cross into all the other kingdoms without anyone making a fuss about it. He built quite a reputation for himself amongst the clans — especially amongst the females in the gorilla clan."

"Really?"

Rebekah nodded.

"What was my father like when you knew him?"

Rebekah smiled widely and shook her head. "Fun. Adventurous. Smart and witty. He was strong and could fight to the death with any warrior. And...he could dance."

Alexandra laughed in surprise. "No!"

"Oh, yes! He was excellent at it. And he was only passionate about one thing: his lair." Rebekah was lost in thought as she pondered those earlier days, feeling her current anger toward him lessening as she did so. "All the girls in the realm were in love with him — especially the Mariner Princess Lara." She paused and looked at Alexandra. "Did he ever tell you about her?"

Alexandra's fascinated look slowly dwindled; she shook her head.

"He never told me anything. I didn't even know he could dance. He's never danced with me."

Rebekah looked down at the ground, thinking carefully about what she wanted to say next. "I'm glad you flew over the realm with Prince Daniel, Alexandra. He is someone extraordinarily special...and not because he woke me."

Alexandra laughed softly.

"Even the Creators of this world could read his heart and found it to be worthy of a task unlike this realm has ever seen." Alexandra looked confused.

"The Creators?"

"Yes." Rebekah smiled softly but continued her train of thought. "I mention it because he is like your father in some ways, and so unlike him in other ways. And for you and your beautiful heart, that is a good thing."

Alexandra's eyes narrowed. "What do you mean?"

"There are some men in this world that may seem exciting in all their passions and bad habits — like your father was when he was younger — but there are also men in this world whose passions override the base desire of a man's heart to drive him toward a greater good, a more solid foundation. The kind of love that lasts an eternity rather than a fortnight. I know what I'm saying to you now may not make any sense, but one day you'll know what I mean." Rebekah smiled at Alexandra. "Are you going to see Prince Daniel again?"

Alexandra's entire face lit up. "Yes! I mean, I hope so. We talked all the way back here after we flew over the realm. It was as if we were famished for company and knowledge of knowing everything about each other and couldn't get enough of what each other had to say. He had...what am I trying to say..."

"Great words."

"Yes."

Rebekah smiled to herself. "Thank you for sharing this with me, Alexandra."

Alexandra's smile was rapidly replaced with a look of anger. "I didn't know the realm looked the way it did. I know Daniel and I never got to tell you what it was we saw."

"The look on your face tells me everything."

"What are you going to do now?"

Rebekah exhaled deeply. "I'm going to try and help rebuild it."

"How? None of the clans speak to one another except yours and mine."

"Correction. Yours, mine...and the lions."

Alexandra's eyes grew wide. "Oh...you're...you're going to see the lion king."

Rebekah nodded. Alexandra swallowed hard, trying to wrap her mind around what all of that could possibly mean. "Rebekah, if you did that, and King Nathan agreed...the world..." She looked up at the queen. "It would change."

"That, Alexandra, is why I believe I'm here."

Poe listened from the shadows in the garden; he was absolutely seething. She had not learned. She had not listened. She had not understood. She was making the same mistakes she had before, and now the wolf princess was a blind recruit about to follow in her footsteps.

He had to change what was about to happen. He had to try, for uniting the realm and sustaining it was not the purpose he had been born to fulfill. Joining hands with the lions was not an act he *could* fulfill. And the problem was his queen still felt her purpose was somehow aligned with his. It never was. It never would be. He never wanted his queen to sign Gunthar's treaty. He had never agreed they should feed the clans — not then and definitely not now. He knew that loving the lion went against everything that had even been born and bred into him as a member of the raven clan. It was never meant to be, and they almost lost their lives when his queen tried to make it so. They were lucky that the Elements had protected them from destruction all these years. Knowing his queen still sought to travel down the same path as before was a disgrace. It was embarrassing. It was a slap in the face to the Creators who had given them a chance to live. And it made him angry.

He could not take it. He would not take it anymore.

There had to be another way. Another way to sever his queen's heart from the clans once and for all. But how? His queen still needed an heir in order for them to survive. And once there was an heir, there would be no need for his queen anymore.

Poe suddenly caught himself, stunned by the thought that had just sprouted in his mind. He loved his queen, and yet…maybe he didn't love her anymore.

He looked out toward the garden gates and thought, Could it be done? Could he keep his queen inside the kingdom until she bore an heir? And if it could be accomplished, he would have what he wanted: life without the compromise. He could shut out the rest of the realm and live on. Let the rest of the clans die without the birds. His clan owed them nothing. Isn't that what Ice insinuated? Isn't that why Ice had spoken to him?

Poe looked up at the sun and suddenly felt a detachment to its fire. He had never had that feeling before. He couldn't even hear Palimus anymore — not even in his dreams. Only Ice. There was a reason for it. There must be. He only heard the old king's voice when his clan had been wounded, hurt and slowly healing. Now the voice was gone. Perhaps it meant they were getting stronger. And strong they were. The strongest in the realm. But they wouldn't be anymore if his queen had her way.

He looked back at Rebekah and Alexandra talking in the garden and suddenly felt a hatred for his queen that he never thought possible. Yes, he hated her. If not for her, his family would be alive. If not for her, he would not be the last raven left. If not for her, he wouldn't find himself forced to do the things he knew must be done.

Poe took one step forward and cried out in pain. He lifted his foot and found he had stepped onto a rose. A thorn had wedged itself under his taloned foot. He looked along the garden grounds and saw fallen roses and vines lying all across the path that led toward his queen — and they had not been there moments before.

His head began to pound as he stared at the roses.

"Poe."

Poe swiveled his head around toward an approaching crow warrior. "We have set up guards and traps along the borders leading to the lair."

"And what about the land in Critter Country and Reptile Desert?"

"The same. There's no creature that can cross into our lands from the south."

Poe looked up to the sky. *"So long asss they mean to cross along the ground. Summon Ume. I need to know hisss progress in the east."*

The crow warrior bowed his head and launched into the sky leaving Poe alone with his thoughts. He looked toward Rebekah, knowing the path he was going to travel down — with or without the roses and the vines. No clan member before had ever attempted what he was about to attempt. But he knew he could do it. And he knew how. The only issue was who would be the one to help his queen produce an heir?

Never the lion.

Not the gorilla. The idea made Poe's insides turn. The jungle king was weak, unable to protect his own people by using other warriors from other clans to help him carry out his purpose. Disgusting. The gorilla: he could not stand alone as a king should. And the other kings…they hid behind the gorilla king like cowards. They were always cowards. Loathsome beings that killed the members of his clan when they were sleeping soundly in their beds.

That left only the wolf. Alexander had never been able to pull off the act before, but then again…Poe looked at Alexandra. If the wolf had to protect his own, to help Poe protect his, could he be forced to do it? There was so much to lose otherwise. A cold wind suddenly blew across the roses and the vines. It was then that Poe had his answer.

He plucked the thorn from his foot and launched into the sky, pondering how to keep his queen inside her gates. He knew the scavenger birds were on his side, for he remembered their faces when the lion prince had first come knocking at their door. The vultures and owls always followed where he led, which meant that only left the ostriches, falcons, and hawks. He knew he could never recruit the eagles. They were far too loyal to Reginald.

And as he plotted the scene in his next act, he did not see his queen turn her head the moment she felt the cold wind on her back. He did not see her eyes shift from the roses and the vines up to the sky where he flew. And Poe did not see Alexander standing on his queen's balcony having witnessed the same thing.

"Hood."

The captain of the Wolf Pack stepped up beside his king.

"Dismantle the crows' nests along our borders. Gather the pack and rip their stations to shreds. Send them a message reminding them who rules the lair."

"It will be done before nightfall." Hood watched Poe fly toward the Great White Mountains. "What do you suppose the raven is up to?"

146

"Knowing Poe, he's plotting someone's death." He lowered his eyes toward Rebekah and his daughter. "Keep an eye on him."

"Yes, my king.

XXXII

"*QUEEN REBEKAH!!!*"

Rebekah turned and was surprised to see the gorilla king jogging across her fields toward her; he was carrying her dress. Five crow warriors were right on his trail but kept their distance.

"What are you doing here? Where are your guards?"

He slowed, a bit out breath as he answered, "I came on my own. I didn't think it wise to bring my warriors with me in case it caused your birds alarm." He extended his arm, "All fixed."

She took the dress from him and looked back at the crows standing guard silently in the fields and nodded to them. They faded away into the surrounding crops.

"So this is your kingdom." He looked out at all the land beyond. "I've only seen it in drawings in my books." He turned to face her. "Did you know that one of my ancestors was best friends with your king — King Palimus?"

The fields were eerily silent.

"No, I didn't."

"It's fascinating, really."

"What is?"

"The history of the clans. To know that a gorilla king was more friendly to the bird king than any wolf or lion."

Byron walked with Rebekah across the fields. He watched as her birds swooped in and out of the twenty-foot tall stalks of food. He was absolutely fascinated. "You know, Minotauro's bulls could help distribute the food so your birds don't have to do it all the time."

Rebekah tilted her head to the side, "Hmm...that's not a bad idea. However, it may take my birds a bit of getting used to seeing your bulls, but I'll speak to Reginald and Poe about it."

Byron whistled sharply to the sky and Reginald suddenly appeared; the eagle warrior bowed to the king in respect. "King..."

Byron spoke directly to him, "Queen Rebekah and I were discussing the possibility of the bulls running food to the other clans from the ground."

Reginald swiveled his head around to his queen. "The eagles would be grateful for the help, but the scavengers..."

Rebekah nodded. "I know. Perhaps, it's something to consider...over time."

Reginald nodded.

Byron smiled. "Good. I'll speak to King Minotauro about how best to tackle it."

Reginald nodded in reply. "I'd be more than happy to help with the plan, king."

A look passed between Reginald and his queen. "Thank you, Reginald." She handed him her dress. "Do you mind?"

Reginald took the garment from her and vaulted into the sky. She eyed Byron suspiciously.

"What?"

"Did Reginald bring you here?"

He nodded. "Is that a problem?"

"I'm just trying to figure out what this power is you seem to have over my eagle."

"What do you mean?"

"He answered when you called. He never does that for anyone but me."

Byron bowed dramatically. "I have what I like to call...*charm*." He grinned widely as he looked at her; his smile slowly dwindling as he saw the look on her face. "But it doesn't seem to work on queens."

"Correction. I have a feeling it's worked on many women who wish they were a queen. You have the voice of a true king. It causes people to respond. They listen to you. That's a very powerful weapon you wield...your words. I'm jealous of them. Reginald has never agreed to anything so quickly in all the time I've known him."

Byron's voice softened, "Well, I have nothing else to offer. My jungle is in shambles. I have no army but starving soldiers. I don't have a Reginald or a Poe." He reached for her medallion and lifted it in his fingertips. "I have no treasure. Not even a crown. All I have is my words: how I feel, what I dream, and what I desire. And if that stirs something in somebody...I'll take it."

Rebekah looked at his handsome face.

"Was this your father's?"

She looked down at her medallion. "No. It's mine."

"It looks like it's meant for a king." She snatched her medallion out of his hand and walked swiftly on; Byron followed. "Or a *queen*."

Byron tried to keep pace with her. "I've never seen anything like it. Did the critters craft it for you?"

At the mention of the critters, she slowed her step. "No." Rebekah turned and faced Byron. "There isn't anyone in the realm with this kind of skill anymore."

Byron continued, "Well, if there's no one to craft something like that for me, maybe I could wear yours once in a while. So I know what it's like to wear a king's medallion."

"It's a *queen's*. And I'd have to have a pretty good reason to let you borrow it. This medallion is my crown. No one wears my crown but me."

Byron took it in his fingertips once again looking at its intricate design. It suddenly ignited in flame. He cried out, dropping the medallion, *"OW!"*

Rebekah was stunned. "Are you all right?"

"Yes, but...didn't that hurt you?"

"No. I'm fine." Rebekah looked up at the sun. "It's never done that before." She held the medallion and looked down at it. "Maybe it doesn't like you." She smiled and lifted her eyes to find

Byron staring at her.

"Or maybe you don't like gorillas."

Rebekah's smile faded. "I didn't say..."

"My father didn't want you to die, you know. He wanted to marry you."

Rebekah paused. "What are you talking about?"

"When his army marched on your kingdom that night fifty years ago, Brutus sent them there to capture you and bring you to our jungle. He knew the lion king had poisoned you; that's why he killed him. He joined the mariners knowing they were after your lands. And he didn't want them to destroy you. He knew all the clans would perish without you and your clan. He was still a remnant at the time and wanted nothing more than to protect you. And by protecting you, he was protecting our people."

Her heart was pounding as images of the gorilla warriors filled her mind. "Then why march upon my kingdom to capture me?"

"My father knew your clan was weak. I cannot answer for why he did not communicate his will. Perhaps he did not think you would believe him after your poisoning. I suppose it was the same mistake I had made when I sent those warriors to bring you to my jungle. Perhaps, he did not think you would come or speak with him off of any invitation he had to offer."

"They were marching alongside the bulls, Byron. The bulls at the time had joined forces with Mar. So had the amphibians."

"He played his card, even if he did not play it well." Byron looked down. "When you disappeared from the realm, my father became a different man. He became a different kind of king. He hated himself for not being stronger. He regretted what he had done and the way he had done it. Time allows you solutions to all your problems once it has passed. Until the very end, he only wanted to protect his jungle. He realized later he should've joined with the wolves and the reptiles to fight against the lesser clans instead of with them. Then maybe they would've won and you wouldn't have had to build a wall around your heart that no one can touch."

She shifted uncomfortably.

Byron looked deep into her eyes. "There are many women in the realm, Rebekah, but there are very few queens. Because of you, it was the first time my father recognized the difference. A queen is no ordinary woman. It's a truth I've known and cherished all my life because of him and what he thought of you."

Rebekah moved away from him and looked out over her fields.

"I didn't mean to upset you. But I wanted you to know."

She turned around and attempted to smile. "In case I didn't like gorillas? Byron, I have much to rectify."

"You called me Byron." He grinned.

"I suppose it was bound to happen, king." She looked out over her fields once more. "It's a wonder to me that none of you kings hate me for what I've done. I'm just as responsible for the state the realm is in than any king who came before me."

Byron looked upset. "Hate you? We admire you. We kings wish we could protect our people the way you did if our clans faced total annihilation."

They started walking through the fields once again. She looked down at her medallion.

Byron kept stride with her. "You know, I've been thinking about it. Gorillas are more kin to your clan than any wolf or lion."

"And how is that?"

"We, too, can fly."

Byron grabbed her hand and turned, pulling her through her fields. He let go as they continued running all through her crops. He wound around a stalk and swung, picking her up by her waist and rapidly pulled her around him so that she was on his back.

"Hold on."

He swung all around the crops and stalks, faster and faster as he leapt and lunged with the use of his arms. One of the stalks he swung around broke and he and Rebekah went flying through the air; they collided onto the ground, sliding against the mud. Byron was horrified as he saw Rebekah slide face first. She landed flat out.

"Rebekah!"

Byron moved through the mud toward her as she pushed herself up. He saw several sets of large bird feet step up all around him from the surrounding crop. He looked up and saw Thunderbird warriors looking down at him and their muddied queen.

Kenuen lowered his large head and extended his taloned hand, "Queen...are you all right?"

She rolled over and burst out laughing. The birds looked at one another, half-amused at the sound of their queen's laughter. A serious look was on their faces as they stared down the gorilla king with a look of warning. They faded back into the crops once again.

Rebekah pointed at Byron, "You should see your face!" He stood and extended his hand to her to help her up. The moment he pulled, they both slipped back into the mud. Rebekah was on top of Byron. She was laughing. Her laughing slowed as she took in the look on his face as he stared at her. She immediately rose and helped pull him up. She looked at the straps on her dress. One was halfway ripped off. Byron stood. "Here, let me help you with that."

He ripped it off her dress and then ripped off the perfectly good one, leaving her strapless. He walked all around her and took in her appearance. "Now this, I like."

Rebekah shook her head as she adjusted her dress. "You and strapless dresses."

He threw his head back and laughed.

"What's so funny?" The moment she said it, she could feel the grainy texture of mud on her front teeth. She moved her tongue around and spat it out. "You weren't going to tell me. You were going to let me walk around with mud on my teeth, weren't you?"

Byron grinned widely and nodded his head. "Nope."

Rebekah put her hands on her hips and turned back toward her kingdom. "Real charming, *king*."

He jogged after her. "*Byron*. Does this mean you won't let me borrow your medallion?"

"You'll be lucky if I let you have a bath."

Alexander was sleeping in a chair beside the chessboard when Rebekah walked inside. She did not say a word as she walked past him as he sat up and turned his head to follow her.

"This is an interesting look. What happened to you?" Byron walked in; he saw the king's soiled appearance as well. "Oh...the *chimp*..." He rested back against his chair and eyed the gorilla king. "You're lucky, king. In my day, Rebekah was far too frigid to go rolling around in Gorilla Jungle."

Alexander immediately ducked just as Rebekah's shoe flew across the room at his head.

"Out! "She started unbuttoning her corset.

"Not on your life! If he gets to stay and watch you undress, so do I. I've been sitting here for hours waiting for you. I need a bit of entertainment."

"*Both* of you! Go show him where the baths are."

Alexander rose and followed Byron out. The gorilla king murmured under his breath, "Thanks a lot, king."

"You know, there are far quicker ways to get a woman out of her clothes without having to fling her in the mud to get her to do it."

Rebekah shook her head and muttered under her breath. "Dirty old dog..."

From the hallway, Alexander answered, *"I heard that, Rebekah."*

Rebekah unlocked the clasp around the chain on her medallion. She held it in her hand and took in its intricate design as she ran her fingers over the eagle and raven. The sun's rays shined down upon it. The sun emblem on the medallion ignited once again but it did not burn her. Strange that it burned Byron. Strange that it was burning at all. Rebekah looked out her balcony and up at the sun wondering what it could mean. The rays beamed down upon her and moved past her just as the wind began to blow. She turned to follow its path and saw them settle upon the portrait of Palimus. The eyes of the old king seemed to glow, but he was no longer speaking.

XXXIII

Alexander was reading the book Reginald had written, feeling his insides turn as he read page after page. The entire historical account was a reminder of all the past he had longed to forget. Reading it again made him feel as if he were living in that time and place all over again. He was suddenly exhausted.

A wolf howled in the distance and Hood, captain of the Wolf Pack, stormed inside Alexander's chambers. "The lion prince approaches."

He paused, feeling his heart sink at hearing that one simple phrase.

Two falcon warriors flew inside Alexander's chambers, one carrying Prince Daniel on his back. Alexander continued to sit by the fire engrossed in Reginald's book, completely ignoring the lion prince as he dismounted and stood there...waiting.

"I've been wondering when I'd be seeing you." He closed the book and looked at Daniel. "Well...what do you want?"

Daniel bowed to him. "Wolf King, I would like to formally introduce myself. I am Prince Daniel from the Lion's Den."

Alexander took a drink from his goblet of wine, examining the young man that stood before him.

Daniel coughed nervously, "I wanted to ask your permission to take Alexandra…"

"*Princess* Alexandra."

"Princess Alexandra…out flying tonight."

Alexander looked at the falcons. "I see Queen Rebekah has already given her consent on the matter. Annoying…"

"I asked for the use of her warriors, king, but you have the final say."

Alexander eyed him. "No."

Daniel stood there in shocked surprise; he had no idea what to do or say next.

Alexander continued, "My daughter has the final say."

Daniel stepped forward with a hopeful look on his face. "Well, I would like your permission all the same."

"Am I right in assuming you are more than fond of my daughter?"

Daniel froze and let out a nervous breath. "Yes, king, I am."

"And if I give my permission, am I to expect that there will be other nights you wish to go flying?"

"If all goes well, sir, that is my intent."

Alexander's eyes narrowed. "You do know that she's never flown with any other prince before."

Daniel lowered his head, "I'm glad to hear that, king."

Alexander tapped the top of his cane. "I will give my permission on two conditions: one, that you bring my daughter back in the same condition you took her, and two…that you protect her…at all costs. The realm is not at peace. The queen was just attacked. There are many enemies waiting in the shadows who would love to do me and my pack harm as well. You know my meaning."

"Yes, king. You have my word."

"Words are powerful, lion, but action is a weapon all its own. If you break your word to me, know that my kind of action will end you…noble heart or not."

"Understood, sir."

Alexander turned his head toward the door. "You can come in now, Alexandra."

Alexandra peeked her head around the door. "I wasn't eavesdropping." The moment she smiled at Daniel, the lion prince absolutely glowed.

"Well…would you like to go flying with the lion tonight?"

She flew through the door and strode over to Daniel, throwing her cloak over her shoulders. "Yes, I would." She kissed her father's cheek as she glided past him without even looking back. Alexander watched as they saddled the falcons and flew off the balcony. A myriad of emotions hit him deep within his heart as he watched them soar past the moon. "Damn lions." He turned his head toward his bedroom door. "Follow them from the ground, and watch for the raven."

Hood and another timber wolf burst through the doors and leaped off of the wolf king's balcony.

A deep sigh escaped him as his eyes moved from the night sky to the portrait of Rebekah dancing before the fire. As his eyes settled on the colors of the flames he himself had painted, he noticed their hue was a little more deep and a lot more vibrant. He continued to watch until it seemed the flames themselves began to dance before his eyes. It was then that he heard the whispered voices. He tilted his head to the side, listening ever so closely. He listened and heard the faintest sound of familiar voices: his father's voice…and his mother's.

Later that night, Poe watched from the shadows as Alexander slept. It was strange to see him look so old. Time at this moment was such a disappointment as he studied the lines on the old king's face, remembering the fiery passion of the man in his youth. This was the man Poe had wished would be king to his queen so long ago. He had the rage, he carried the darkness, he had the hunger, he had the ruthlessness required — but not anymore. Looking at Alexander as he slept, Poe knew the wolf king he saw lying in bed at this moment was not the king he needed. And with that thought, Poe was suddenly enraged. Why hadn't Alexander had a son instead of a daughter? Then there would be an option. A choice to consider, for he had suddenly reconsidered this one. Alexander was too old and suddenly looked more frail and skeletal than any other day before this one. Alexander would be lucky to last an hour in someone's bed rather than a month in this world. How very different everything suddenly seemed — and how ridiculous his plan to force an heir between the his queen and this king became. Poe looked out at the moon and suddenly felt extremely exhausted.

Defeated, Poe moved toward Alexander's balcony when he saw the portrait of his queen dancing before the fire. He stopped dead in his tracks feeling a sudden heat rising up from his chest. He was mesmerized by the image of Rebekah that Alexander had captured. He remembered that night in the lair when she had danced before the flames. He was the proudest of her he had ever been when she commanded the movement of the fire. That was the night her medallion appeared. Fire had given it to her, claiming her as his own. And Fire had been on her side ever since.

Poe lowered his head, remembering their darkest night. Remembering how she called upon Fire and the rest of the Creators to protect the clan. Had it not been for his queen, he would not be standing here. They would all be dead and the realm would continue to rot without them. And yet, he still wanted it to rot. He could not help it. His last memory was holding his son in his arms, and he had never been able to expel his vengeance on anyone since. And here he was trying to expel it on his own queen by capturing an old king who held no significance anymore in the world he had awoken to. The portrait was reminder enough how true that was.

Staring at the painting, he had no idea what he was supposed to do now. Protecting the borders did not seem enough. Protecting his queen was more than enough, however, since she continued to put herself in harm's way. Poe could not help but hate her and love her for it, for she seemed to remind him what it meant to be fully alive even when surrounded by the threat of death. She kept going — with or without his consent. She kept rising to the see the sun to make each day next different than the one before. It angered him yet excited him all the same. But he still felt that anchor in his heart that said, *Stand in her way. Make her think twice. Remind her of what happened before.* Looking at the portrait hanging in the wolf king's bedroom, seeing the look he captured in her face, he no longer knew how or why, only that he still should.

He continued to stand there, studying the portrait, absorbing the feelings he felt, and wondering what he was supposed to do with them. Poe felt the first pang of reconsideration the moment he saw the roses, and now this. Even Poe, in all his plotting understood when the world was trying to send a message. But what this one could possibly mean, he had yet to understand. All he knew was that the only voice that spoke out loud was the one he had been answering to. A voice he had never heard or followed before. Perhaps, he was listening to the wrong one. The signs were showing their faces, yet which ones to follow was the key.

Alexander began snoring behind him. Poe could not even find the energy to turn his head around to acknowledge it. He looked up one more time at the painting, studying the look on his queen's face. So many signs that said, Remember. Stop. Hold on. Trust. Protect. Kill. Destroy. Which sign to follow...he would wait to see which signs spoke louder...and more.

XXXIV

Feyedor stood over Palimus' grave. Staring at the king's name etched in stone, he did not weep. The thoughts that were swirling inside his head were one of deep regret. The realm had lost two of its greatest kings. The bird prince had lost his father. And more important: Feyedor had lost his closest friend.

"What is it, bird?"

Damon slowly approached from behind. *"I missss my king."*

"We all do."

"He made a choice, king."

"And he made a bad one."

"Then why did you side with my queen?"

Feyedor turned his silver eyes to the raven. "I didn't side with your queen, Damon. I sided with the clan. If there was one thing that Palimus and I agreed on, it was that the lions should never be allowed to be the most powerful kingdom in the realm. Had I sided with them, that's exactly what would have happened. That's the message it would have sent."

"Isss that why you gave your coat to the lion queen? Enemy but not."

Feyedor clenched his jaw. "Yes." He exhaled slowly. "The wolves and the ravens have always been kin to one another. They have always honored Fire together. And whatever vision Palimus had when he stood before it, he had it without involving the wolves — only you ravens. That was a dangerous thing to do — seeking an answer to a question with only your will in mind. You should have stopped him."

Damon looked down at his king's grave. *"What do we do now, king?"*

"You protect your prince. This isn't over yet." He turned and started walking out of the garden.

The raven lifted his head. *"What do you mean?"*

Feyedor stopped and looked back at the raven warrior. "The prophecy Palimus had has not come to pass."

"How do you know?"

"I'm still here." Damon absorbed his words as the wolf king continued. "But one day it will come to pass. And when that day comes, my clan will be ready. So should yours." He began walking again.

Damon flew over him and landed in front of him to stop him. *"What are you going to do?"*

"Whatever I have to, to make sure my house does not go down — *ever* ."

"The lionsss cannot be trusted?"

"That's for you to decide. But if they can't be, and Palimus' vision does come to pass, your clan will suffer, Damon. And when the birds go down, so do we. Unless…I can help it." He looked south.

Damon followed his gaze. *"The Amphibian Swampsss."*

Feyedor turned his silver eyes to the raven warrior; they seemed to glow as he said, "I'm going to see the Toad Chief."

Damon stared at him, trying to figure out his meaning.

Feyedor looked at him. "I'm going to make a deal with him. There's something his clan can do. It's an old ritual, but one that can be brought about when danger is near."

And with that, the wolf king left the raven to stand beside the grave of his king.

XXXV

Daniel and Alexandra flew over Wolf Lake. "So this is the lair..." Everywhere he looked, he saw nothing but barren trees reaching up to him as if their branches were the skeletal arms of the dead hoping to be resurrected once again. Seeing the dried-out land running between the trees, Daniel could not help but be reminded of a cemetery constructed of bones.

"It's better down below. Follow me."

Daniel had no idea how that could even be possible. As they rapidly descended, he wondered what it must have been like for Alexandra, growing up in such a desolate place. But hearing the excitement in her voice, he understood that this deserted bit of land she called "home" was all she knew. And she found it beautiful in her eyes.

Alexandra looked back at Daniel as they continued to descend. "How are you doing, lion?"

The moment she asked him the question, his thoughts shifted from the lair to the ground — and how quickly they were moving toward it. His face turned as white as a sheet. Seeing the ground coming closer into view, he clenched his eyes shut, gripping even tighter onto the falcon's feathers. "Fine! I'm fine!"

As the lion prince and wolf princess descended, the falcon

warriors glided over the moonlit water of Wolf Lake. They landed gently atop the surface, floating just above the water like swans wading in the water. Alexandra could not help but laugh the moment she saw Daniel's face. He was as pale as a ghost; sweat trickled down his brow. He looked so strong and so vulnerable all at once that Alexandra's heart softened; she liked him even more. Daniel finally opened his eyes once he realized they had stopped flying.

"You're amazing, Daniel. No other clan member has ever ridden falcons before other than Queen Rebekah and me."

"Not so, princess."

Alexandra turned to the falcon she was riding, "What do you mean?"

"Your father has ridden with my queen many times before."

Alexandra was stunned. "Really? He never told me that."

"I'm sure he was better suited to this than I am," Daniel replied.

"No, lion. He too looked like a ghost from the moment we took off to the moment we landed."

Daniel laughed in relief. "That makes me feel a whole lot better."

Alexandra noticed a feather sticking out of Daniel's hair. "Here." She leaned over and pulled the feather from his head. Daniel was watching her face the entire time. It was the closest they had ever been to one another. Alexandra knew it too. She quickly pulled back and twirled the feather in her fingers. "You know, you have to make a wish now."

"I do?"

She nodded. "We both do." Alexandra took his hand and placed the feather between their palms. "Now, close your eyes. Make a wish and push against my palm as hard as you can. When we pull our hands apart, whomever has the feather stuck to their palm...well, that person's wish will come true."

Daniel smiled. "Okay."

They closed their eyes and pressed the feather between their palms. But instead of keeping their hands palm to palm, Daniel closed his fingers around Alexandra's and held her hand tight. Alexandra tried not to smile even wider, but found she could not help it. "Okay, on the count of three, let go. One...two...three..."

He didn't let go.

Alexandra laughed. They both opened their eyes. "Daniel, you have to let go or your wish won't come true. One…two…three…"

This time, he released her hand. They both looked down at their palms. Alexandra shook her head, "Beginner's luck."

Daniel smiled widely. "Well, it's a good one."

"Don't tell me or it won't come true!"

Daniel grabbed her hand and held it gently. "Now what?"

"Now you let the feather go so it blows away, carrying your wish into the sky and out into the universe."

The falcon warrior Daniel was sitting on craned his neck around and blew on Daniel's hand, causing the feather to float away.

Alexandra burst out laughing. Daniel was shocked. "Why did you do that?"

"You were taking too long. Now, prince, it's done." He turned his neck back around without saying another word.

Daniel watched Alexandra as her entire face lit up with laughter. Still holding her hand, he pulled her close, leaned in and kissed her. He slowly pulled away, still holding her hand; their faces were inches apart.

"My wish just came true."

He leaned in again and kissed her softly on the lips. When he pulled away the second time, he saw glowing insects swarming all around them. His eyes went wide in wonderment as he watched in amazement as they lit up the water and surrounding sky. "What are these?"

"Fireflies." Alexandra turned her head and looked out across the water. The moment Daniel turned his attention from the insects back to Alexandra, he noticed a serious look on her face as she stared across the lake.

"What's wrong?"

"There's something in the water." She commanded the falcon, "Knack, swim to the north shore."

The falcon warriors immediately paddled in that direction. As they did so, the fireflies followed them, lighting the way. Alexandra searched the waters, listening for the sound she thought she heard. Her eyes narrowed the moment she saw an object up ahead floating in the water.

"There!"

She pointed to it; the falcons swam even faster. The fireflies swarmed all around them as the object came into view. Alexandra's heart stopped and her eyes went wide as she gasped, "It's a body!"

"Move!" Daniel immediately rushed in front of Alexandra, leaned over the falcon warrior and pulled the body from the water, turning it over. The man's face was so bloated, Daniel was barely able to make out the man's features. His eyes roamed over the man's wardrobe. That was when he saw it: the riding gear, the small pocket that held his monocle…

His eyes slit to a cat as he shouted, "Marcus!"

"You know this man?"

Daniel stared at her in stunned silence as he held onto the body. He could barely speak. "It's my uncle."

The falcons whispered in unison, "Young lion…"

Daniel clutched onto Marcus' body, trying to wrap his mind around what he was seeing. That was when he saw the large gaping wound in Marcus' chest. Alexandra saw it too. His heart…it had been ripped from his body.

Daniel looked up at Alexandra with such anger and rage, the young princess flinched as if she had just been physically struck. *"WHO DID THIS?!?"*

Alexandra shook her head, barely whispering the words, "I don't know."

Daniel looked all around the lake and back at the shoreline where he could see the shadows of the trees. *"WHO DID THIS?!?"*

Alexandra was shaking, completely taken off guard by his ferocious cry. She tried to calm him down. "Daniel, wolves don't rip hearts out. I don't know who did this, but my pack…it wasn't them. He wouldn't be in the lake, Daniel. My wolves hate water. You have to believe me."

"I don't know what to believe!" Daniel looked at her with utter rage; his chest rapidly rose and fell as he tried to contain the fury he felt. He shouted to the falcon soldier, "Bird! Take me to the den!"

And without another word, the falcon warrior launched into the sky with Daniel carrying Marcus' body. Alexandra watched them jetting across the sky.

"You are right, princess."

She looked at the falcon warrior.

"Wolves don't rip hearts out of their victims. But gorillas do."

Alexandra was speechless. She looked across the lake to the outline of the trees and saw their yellow eyes mirroring in the distance. The Wolf Pack was watching her from the shoreline. They had been watching the entire scene play out, and they had been eerily silent.

"Ask your pack what happened here. They see and hear everything in the lair."

She watched as their mirroring eyes faded back into the shadows of the trees until all she could see was darkness. Alexandra turned her head to the south.

"What is it, princess?"

"There..." she looked down at the water, unsure of what she was hearing. "It's the water."

The falcon swiveled his head around to look at her. Alexandra continued to stare at the water below. She reached her hand out and gently touched its surface with her fingertips.

"Whoever rules the sea, rules the realm..." She spoke in a whisper, wondering where she had heard that phrase and why the thought came to her now as she stared at the water. Was it something her father had told her? Or was it something Reginald had said once? But as she looked at the dark waters beneath her fingertips, she felt as if it were somehow alive — breathing and speaking to her — as if the water itself were watching her and studying her.

"That's not true." Alexandra looked at the falcon warrior. He continued, "Whoever rules the sea commands it. The ruler of the realm...is beyond this world." He swiveled his head back around and said nothing more. Alexandra removed her fingers from the water as if she had just been burned.

"What is going on?" She asked the question to herself.

Remembering the warmth of Daniel's hand in hers, she looked to the sky again where he had taken flight. It was then she noticed her body was still trembling. She was deeply shaken at what had just occurred. It was her first kiss and, unfortunately, it was the first time she had ever seen a dead body with its heart torn out. Knowing it was a prince from the den, Alexandra knew that whatever was going on, it was going to get much, much worse. "Take me to my father. I need to speak to the king."

XXXVI

Reginald looked up the moment the falcon soldier landed inside the den carrying Daniel and...*a body*. Reginald rushed forth to help him carry the body off of the bird warrior. He gasped the moment he recognized the face even in its bloated form. "Prince Marcus..."

SinJin burst inside the courtyard. The moment the old lynx warrior saw the prince, he roared in agony. He ripped Marcus' body away from Reginald and held him close. A low growl of woe emanated from the warrior's chest.

"Where is my grandfather! Where is the king!"

Nathan stormed through the gates and into the courtyard followed by a squadron of warriors. "What's going on?" His steps slowed the moment he saw SinJin holding his brother in his arms. Nathan looked at Daniel. He could not believe it. His eyes spoke volumes as tears filled them; he stared at the young prince, searching for answers. Daniel had never seen the look of such grief on his grandfather's face before. It nearly broke him to have to tell him the news.

"I found him...in Wolf Lake."

Roars and howls echoed all throughout the den. Daniel watched as Nathan's eyes slit to a cat. As dark as Queen Rebekah's eyes had gone upon that first day of awakening her, they were not as dark as Nathan's at that moment — even the tattoo around his neck turned black.

"Princess Alexandra swears it wasn't the wolves."

Nathan walked over to SinJin in silence. He looked down at Marcus' chest and saw the gaping hole where his heart should have been. No one spoke a word as they watched their king take it all in. Nathan slowly turned to Reginald. "Have the gorillas been traveling through the lair?"

Reginald chose his words carefully. "Only their king."

"King Alexander has been conversing with their king?"

Reginald could barely breathe as the lion warriors stared him down. "No, king. He has been conversing…with my queen."

Whatever reaction Reginald thought would be coming, could not prepare him for the one he saw on the lion king's face. The tattoo marking on King Nathan's neck turned as black as the darkest night. Nathan pulled his sword from his sheath, staring at Reginald with such hatred that the eagle captain knew he was in danger. *"LIONS!!!"*

Nathan's enraged shout echoed across the plains. *"TO THE JUNGLE!!!!"*

The lion warriors erupted in deafening roars. They raced out of the den ahead of their king. "You tell Rebekah, *bird*, that there will be no truce amongst the clans! Not today!" Nathan turned and raced out of the den with his warriors on his heels. Daniel pulled his sword from his sheath and turned to follow when Reginald put his taloned hand out and onto his chest to stop him. Cheetah jumped between them, coming out of nowhere to protect his prince. Cheetah's claws swiped at Reginald as the eagle dodged and weaved the oncoming blows.

"Prince Daniel! I do not mean you harm!"

Cheetah pulled his dagger from his armor. "Do not speak to my prince!"

"Daniel! It wasn't the gorillas!" Reginald dodged Cheetah again as he continued to swipe at him with his blade.

But Daniel was so upset, he did not say a word.

"It wasn't the gorillas, prince!" Reginald had had it with the warrior. He ducked just as Cheetah swung his dagger at Reginald's face. He swung and punched Cheetah in the liver; the warrior went down. Reginald stepped toward the lion prince, his pupils the size of pins. "Are you listening to me, prince?!?"

Daniel's face was one of rage. "How do you know?"

"Gorillas don't cross into the lair. They never have!"

"What about their king?"

"He did not bring his warriors with him. He is smart, prince. He knew what it would mean if he did. *I* brought him to my kingdom!"

"Then what are you saying? That the *wolves* killed him?"

"No, I don't know who did this but it wasn't..."

"Get out of my, Reginald!"

Reginald stepped in front of him. "No, noble one! *THINK!* My queen is safe! They did not harm her! They asked for help against you lions! They would not risk exposing themselves to gather the den to their jungle! It would be suicide!"

Daniel walked forward but Reginald stepped in front of him again. "*LISTEN!* If you do this, you will be responsible for the slaughter of innocent lives! *You*, prince! A genocide far worse than the one your king brought about when he annihilated the Mariners and brought down an entire clan! Do you want to be remembered that way? You don't have all the facts and evidence. Find them!"

"He was my *uncle*, Reginald! He was not a creature penetrating borders! How much evidence do I need to know that it was the wolves or gorillas? They would never admit it!"

"Your uncle was not a creature, prince, but he went to the Lair all the same."

Daniel stepped to Reginald, glaring at him with his cat-like eyes. "He did *not* bring this upon himself!"

"No, but someone knew he was there. They knew who he was and they killed him anyway."

"*Why?!?*"

"That, noble one, is what you must find out before your king burns the jungle down!"

Daniel gritted his teeth, staring at the eagle captain with emotions of hate, anger and sadness. Tears of anguish streamed down Daniel's face as he tried to gather his emotions. He turned and punched the wall over and over again, trying to expel his rage, crying out until he exhausted himself. He laid his forehead against the wall and closed his eyes. "Go to your queen, Reginald. Tell her...I'm going to need her birds."

"You look tired, Alex."

"I am tired."

They were playing a game of chess in the bird queen's chambers. From the time Rebekah had awakened until now, Alexander seemed to have aged that much faster. He was walking slower, sleeping more. She reached across the board and held his hand. "I'm sorry."

He looked up at her, "For what?"

"For not taking you with me."

Alexander stared at her for several moments. "What would it have mattered?"

"I'd have had more time with you in this world."

He let out a long breath. "But then, I would not have had my daughter." He squeezed her hand, holding it tight. "I was not meant to be where you are, no matter how much I wanted to be. My life has worked out the way that it was supposed to — with all of my mistakes included. And I have come to know, as all we elderly people do, that what you want in this world, what you wish to seem to be and become, can only happen if you make a decision. And I, too, made many decisions to be in places I should never have gone, but it led to where I needed to be. Right here. Which is where I wanted to be all along — with you in your kingdom and the cornerstone in my house. I have the best of both worlds with you and Alexandra." They smiled at one another. "But I need to talk to you about Poe."

Before Rebekah could answer, Alexandra swooped inside the queen's chambers. She jumped off the falcon soldier and shouted, "FATHER!"

Alexander stood up in alarm the moment he saw the look on his daughter's face.

"Father, something awful has happened! Prince Daniel and I found his uncle's body floating in our lake!"

Rebekah rose from her seat. "What! Prince Marcus?"

Alexander was dead silent.

Alexandra nodded.

Rebekah's voice was barely a whisper, "Young lion..."

Alexandra turned to her father, "His heart was torn out. Daniel took his body to the den to inform the king. He thinks the gorillas may have done it."

Reginald suddenly flew inside. "My queen...the lion prince needs your help. He is flying to the jungle to thwart the lion king."

Rebekah's eyes grew wide, "Nathan went there?"

Reginald nodded. Alexander and Rebekah looked at one another. "Nathan will slaughter them, Rebekah."

Rebekah was immediately thrown back into the memory of the night her kingdom was marched upon and how she felt the moment she realized that if she did not do something, her clan was going to be destroyed. She thought of the three kings and how weak their clans were. *Just like hers.* She jumped into action. "Reginald, summon the Thunderbirds and then circle back for me. We're going to the jungle."

Alexander commanded his daughter, "Go back to the Lair. Stay there. You'll be safe."

Her eyes were wide with fear. "What's going to happen?"

"Hopefully nothing. Now go!"

She nodded and raced down the hallway.

Rebekah was shaking her head in disbelief. "It can't be the gorillas, Alex. I don't believe it."

Alexander was exasperated with her. "But Nathan does. If you don't stop him, Rebekah, the gorillas are as good as dead."

XXXVII

Byron watched as the Lion Guard marched toward his kingdom armed for war. Minotauro and Sebastian were nearby; they, too, had gathered an army to battle it out with the den to protect the jungle — and their friend.

The three kings watched from the trees as the lion king stepped forward. They watched helplessly as Chester dragged the bull warrior by the tail. He hurled its body toward the trees; it collided into a nearby trunk. It was dead. Even from where they stood, Byron and Minotauro could see the marks of torture etched all over the bull's body, imagining the pain he must have endured before he died. Minotauro's eyes shifted to a far-off place Byron had seen him go to before. It meant detachment. And in battle, that was Minotauro's weapon. When Byron saw the bull king's eyes move from the bull warrior to the lion king, he could have sworn he saw a shadow cast itself across Minotauro's face.

Whatever fight was about to break out, Byron knew the battle was going to be both brutal and personal — the worst kind. The bulls and buffalo soldiers stamped their hooves and lowered their heads in the den's direction, while the toads and frogs gripped their weapons tight. They were ready.

Nathan continued to watch the movement amongst the trees —

or lack thereof. He knew they were there. He stared straight ahead and commanded, "Smoke them out. Ready your swords."

Chester roared and turned to the Lion Guard. Their arrows ignited in flame.

Byron whispered to the armies behind him, "Get ready for it." He clutched his bone scepter, Bane, as he braced himself for attack just as the Lion Guard took aim. Just as they were about to fire, a large wind blew through the trees, causing the flames to flicker and die out. From the sky, the Thunderbirds dove down slamming onto the ground. They lined up side by side — each standing over nine feet tall. They faced the lions, creating a barrier between the den and the jungle.

Kenuen, captain of the Thunderbirds, cried out, "Lion! You will not attack this clan in the name of the queen!"

Sebastian looked hopefully at Byron. He could see the lion king's reaction. Nathan was absolutely furious. "Your queen does not rule this land, *bird!* Move before you get shot!"

"WAIT!!!"

The three kings watched as a young man raced over the hill weaving his way to the front of the Lion's Den army.

Minotauro asked, "Who is that?"

Byron answered, "I don't know. It may be a prince."

They continued to watch as Daniel ran through the army and joined the Thunderbirds. "My king! It wasn't the gorillas. They didn't kill Marcus." He was breathing hard. "Reginald swears by it."

Sebastian looked at Byron. "What is he talking about? I thought they were here because we kidnapped the queen."

Minotauro added, "And attacked the lion king."

Sebastian exhaled deeply. "I forgot about that."

"He didn't. He just killed my bull."

Byron whispered, "Quiet! I'm trying to listen."

They turned their attention back to the scene ahead.

The Lion Guard roared as Nathan stepped toward his grandson. "Get out of the way, Daniel!"

Daniel protested, "Please! You must listen to me…"

"There's nothing to say!" Nathan's face contorted in rage; he whirled around and shouted to the den, "On my command, advance!"

Daniel stepped in front of him once more and tried to hold him back. Nathan shoved Daniel out of the way but Daniel quickly moved in front of him again. "Grandfather! *Please!*"

Nathan grabbed hold of Daniel by his shirt and pulled him close, "You defy me in front of the entire pride! They killed my *brother!* They murdered a prince!"

Sebastian and Minotauro looked at one another.

"No, they didn't! Listen to me…"

Nathan did not say a word.

Daniel continued, "I've seen these people's lands. We've done them a great wrong, my king, but they did not retaliate because of it. They are not responsible for Marcus' death. I know it in my *soul.* Someone is trying to make it look like it was the gorillas. I swear to you that I will find who is responsible for my uncle's death. If I'm wrong, and it is this clan, I will burn this jungle down myself."

Nathan stared at his grandson for a long time. The only thing he wanted to do at this moment was destroy. If not for the pleading look on his grandson's face, he would have done it. Instead, he slowly loosened his grip on the prince, trying to simmer his rage. "You have three days." Several moments passed where Nathan held onto Daniel as he attempted to gather his emotions. He released his grip on the prince and shouted to the trees, *"THREE DAYS!!!"*

Nathan turned away from the jungle border and came face to face with Rebekah. The look on his face was one of pure fury. Without a word, he walked past her and back toward his den. Only Daniel and Cheetah remained.

Reginald stood beside his queen as Daniel approached. The prince was deeply distraught. "Tell me that it wasn't the gorillas. I know the king is hiding in those trees, and I can't bear the thought of turning my head in his direction. If I do, I will end him. I want what my king wants. It took every ounce of strength not to stand beside my king and watch him burn this place down. I've hurt him. So tell me, queen. Tell me it wasn't them."

Byron, Minotauro and Sebastian continued to watch and listen from the trees.

Rebekah answered, "I don't believe it was the gorillas who did this."

Daniel stared at her, unsure as to whether or not he believed her. "Then help me find who did." He walked on with Cheetah at his side.

Rebekah turned and watched him go. "Oh, Reginald…"

"The king will forgive you, my queen."

She shook her head, remembering the look he had given her. "Daniel's not the only one who's hurt him." She sighed deeply. "Take me home."

"Yes, my queen."

She mounted her warrior and flew back to her kingdom with the Thunderbird Guard at her heels.

The three kings sat silently amongst themselves in the shadows of the trees. They were still in shock trying to comprehend what had just transpired. Sebastian finally asked, "What was that all about?"

Byron stared at the arrow of flame sticking in the ground that the Lion Guard had left. "I don't know."

Minotauro replied, "They were talking about murder…one of their own."

Byron shook his head. "It doesn't make sense. Who would murder a member of the den?"

Sebastian answered, "Whomever it was is no friend of yours, Byron. The den was here to annihilate you and your jungle."

Minotauro jumped in, "Not just the jungle, Sebastian. *All* of us. They threw my warrior down at my feet as if I were standing right in front of them. They knew I was here…as well as you."

"Why would someone try to start a war using us as bait?"

"Do you think it's the wolves?"

Byron and Minotauro looked up simultaneously and stared at the amphibian king. It was Byron who answered, "I don't know but I'm going to find out."

"How?"

"I'm going to see the queen."

From the shadows in the trees, Poe listened. His heart was beating rapidly at what had just transpired. It was a sign as to where this night could lead, and it was leading to someplace good. He vaulted into the sky and silently flew across the realm. He watched as the lion king stormed inside his den — without his queen. He could see the lion prince through the library windows staring at a large empty desk — without the wolf princess. He looked back at the jungle and understood that an option was trying to present itself in the form of a king, but not one that would ever come to fruition, for weakness was disease and the gorilla king carried it with him. One must rid itself of the disease before its infection spread. A task the raven assassin would gladly undertake.

Poe smiled to himself, suddenly feeling more alive and at peace than any other night since he had awakened. To wait was working out to be a good thing, for it was helping Poe see the signs leading to a better tomorrow — and an even greater night.

XXXVIII

Daniel sat in Marcus' large chair in the Great Library staring out through the large glass windows. It was raining again. Watching the water hit against the glass and roll down the pane, he suddenly realized how much rain resembled the act of crying. But sitting in his uncle's chair, Daniel did not feel like weeping. He was angry. Someone had murdered his uncle, killed him as if his life meant nothing to anyone that it could be so easily claimed in so violent a way.

Why?

Why kill Marcus? Who had he ever hurt? What had he ever done but try and do something better by trying to find a way to helping the realm survive. Such a thankless act that only the members of the den knew anything about.

He hated the rest of the realm at that moment; the undeserving kind. The ones who didn't realize they had just killed off their only hope of surviving without the birds. Whoever did this deserved to die.

Daniel continued to stare out at the rain, feeling his body tense; his breathing sped up the more he thought about his uncle's murderer. He had never felt rage like this before. He suddenly understood his grandfather's position in wanting to burn the entire jungle down. Part of him wished Nathan had. But what if Reginald was right? Then what? Then he was no better than the generation before him who had answered all their problems with a sword and a fight.

There were no other clues as to who was responsible for what had been done, and Daniel felt his anger shift from the unknown assailant to his uncle instead.

"Why were you in the lair? Why would you go there knowing there was danger to be had?"

Thunder rolled across the sky, almost as if the thunder itself were replying to the question in angry tones. Daniel sat there trying to figure it out with nothing but a desperate hope and a raging motivation to drive him forward, and yet…he couldn't move. He just continued to watch as the rain fell outside.

And then he remembered — *the letter.*

He shot out of the chair and walked as fast as he could to the hearth; it was still there. He reached for the letter SinJin had given him the day Marcus had left the den. He had forgotten all about it.

Daniel ripped the letter open and heard something fall to the ground directly beside his feet. He knelt down to see what it was. It was a tiny gold compass. Marcus' compass.

Daniel exhaled deeply the moment he recognized it; feeling all the pent-up tension completely drain from his body. He picked up the tiny compass and, clutching it in his strong hand, the lion prince began to weep.

He looked at the letter and saw Marcus' familiar handwriting:

My dear nephew,

You're probably wondering why I would go on another adventure without the most important tool to guide me: my compass. It was never really mine, you know. It belonged to the critter warrior I had killed long ago. I used to stare at it for hours, wishing that I didn't have it, willing that the creature who owned it still did, and angry that he had crossed into the den on that particular day at that exact time that I was out hunting with SinJin. The compass evolved with me over the years as I grew into the type of man I have become. It was the symbol of guilt and a constant visual punishment that I brutalized my conscience with as I went from a young, naive boy without a care in the world, to a boy who came to understand that there are those who care. As I grew, I kept it in a locked box under my bed so I would no longer have to look at it and be reminded of what I had done. I was hiding from myself, really, but the box didn't remain locked for long. I eventually accepted the compass into my life — not as a curse or shameful branding — but as a comfort. It helped me find my way through this world and in this life.

You see, Daniel, there will be people that come in and out of your life. Some of whom you'll forget and others you hope you'll be able to hold onto. But you need to always remember the goal, Daniel, the objective you have defined for yourself on how you will use your time in this world. You need to hold on to the anchor that is you. The one that you will need to remind yourself of from time to time, because it is so easy to forget the goal. It is so easy to get distracted from the one thing you are trying to do in this world — especially when you are king. Love may cripple you. Anger may drive you. Woe may destroy you. Greed may overcome you. Envy will enslave you. And ambition may undo you.

But then again. . . maybe not. It depends on who you are at your core, Daniel. And should I never return from the one thing I have been trying to *do, I leave you with one bit of advice: Remember your compass.*

So what was mine is now yours. May it be your guide, reminding you of where you are and where you want to be.

Until we meet again,

Marcus

Daniel read the letter several more times before folding it back up again. He looked down at the tiny instrument resting in the palm of his hand, comforted by the unexpected gift. He suddenly felt an overwhelming peace that he so desperately needed. It was only then that he turned his head toward the windows that overlooked the den down below and realized it was no longer raining.

Nathan stood inside the enormous mausoleum. Like the portraits hanging in the Great Library, the markers of the dead lined the marble walls, flooding the lion king with history, memory and the overwhelming feeling of deep loss. His eyes scanned the names carved in gold: Leopold, Gastar, Luther, Midas, Logan, Darfur, Gunthar, Marcus, until he finally reached the name that brought him the most pain — Matthew — his son. He lifted his hand and gently touched the engraved name against his fingertips.

A low growl of woe rumbled deep inside the lion king's chest. He stood there, barely breathing, barely moving, as he thought of all the tragedy he had seen in his lifetime — and it was not over yet. His eyes moved to Marcus' newly engraved nameplate. Still touching his son's name while looking at his brother's beside it, Nathan could feel the sprouting of a deep-seeded anger slowly growing deep within his heart. Their names were not supposed to be here — not yet. And he was not supposed to he there burying them, left here to remain in a life and in a world that continued to bring him pain, reminding him that he was not of the favored, had less control of what he wanted, and belonged to the prison of the damned.

And that thought was what stirred his anger into absolute rage as he stood amongst the markers of the dead. He had shut the doors of his den long ago to protect what little he had left, but now the doors had swung wide open. He was going to annihilate any further threat remaining so there was nothing more left to chance.

Chester, captain of the Lion Guard, approached. "My king…" He bowed respectfully.

Nathan was still touching the name of his son, remembering how he brutally died. "In two days, gather the den. Kill the three kings, and burn the jungle down."

Rebekah had not slept the entire night; she was too busy thinking about Marcus and who could have done something so horrendous. Whomever it was, was trying to destroy the other side of the realm. Which could mean one thing: it was someone from her side of the realm. To leave a body in Wolf Lake would the most foolish act a murderer could or would do if the it were the pack, which left only one other clan — *hers*.

"This is where you saw the footprint?"

"*Yesss, my queen…*"

She stared at him, noticing he seemed to distance himself as he stared off to the north. She followed his gaze. "And is that where the mountain fortress resides?"

"*Yesss…*"

"You saw something else when you were there. I can tell."

He craned his head to look at her.

"What did you see?"

He hesitated.

"Tell me."

"Ice…"

Rebekah narrowed her eyes. "What do you mean?"

"He spoke to me. He spoke of our king." He swiveled his large ebony head around and looked at his queen. *"He said, 'Finish what he started'…"*

Rebekah continued to stare at Poe.

"We not only have Fire on our side but Ice…"

"He's lying to you, Poe."

Poe's eyes narrowed in confusion.

"Ice is not on our side. He is the Lord of the Sea. A sea that no longer flows."

"Because of your lion…"

"No. Because of me." Rebekah paused, knowing that what she was about to say next was going to upset Poe. "I went to the Lair while you were away. I summoned the pack, and I danced before the fire…just like that night long ago."

Poe was stunned. *"Without me?"*

"Yes. You were nowhere to be found."

Poe's eyes rapidly dilated as he reacted to her news.

"I went there because my medallion caught fire one afternoon, and yet it did not burn. I knew Fire had something to say. Something more important than what the whispers of Palimus were speaking. And I could not hear Palimus speaking anymore." Rebekah looked out at the sun, feeling the gentle wind on her face. "I saw Palimus' vision once more. I saw his fear. I felt his anger." She turned and looked at Poe. "And I heard what it was he has been trying to say for so long." She looked him dead in the eye. "I was wrong, Poe. What Palimus has to say does matter."

Poe's feathers were rising and falling with each breath he took as he hung onto Rebekah's every word.

"'Protect,' he said."

Poe stopped breathing.

"'Protect like the ravens of old. Protect the lives of those you love. Protect the legacy you have built. Protect them…from what I destroyed'." Rebekah watched Poe's reaction as he tried to decipher her words. "He is no longer speaking because he finished what it was he had to say."

"*Ice...*"

She reached out and touched the side of Poe's face, "Ice mourns for a people and a sea that no longer lives! Ice does not hold claim over our clan. Only Fire. Ice rules the sea. And we have never lived there, Poe. We rule the sky and will be bound by no other master. Ice speaks to you because he knows your hate for the lions. But the king that ruled the den is gone, Poe! Nathan is not that same king! He raised a prince out of the sufferings of the realm to be the best of the ones who came before them. That prince was the noble one. The one who was born to awaken us to save the realm — not destroy it!"

Poe's eyes shifted to the medallion resting against his queen's chest. He stared at the burning sun etched in gold with the eagle on one side and the raven on the other.

"The vision I had in the fire reminded me that the hearts of the wicked thrive in the cold, in the lonely and in the dark. The pendulum swings both ways. Palimus has been in the dark where our clan has lived for so long under his the shadow of shame. It is time we stood in the light. For it is in the sun, Poe, that we shine best."

He moved away from Rebekah, trying to wrap his mind around what she had just said. "*Palimusss...*"

"Palimus wants us to be at peace. He wants the last remaining raven to protect all that was lost, for we are unbalanced, are we not? One foot in the dark and one in the light. Ice is trying to keep the balance shifted, Poe. Why, I don't know. But I need you to look to the clan once more. I need you to step back into the world of the living and stand alongside me as a shield rather than as a sword."

He looked at her, stunned.

"I know you are angry with me. I see it in your face. I hear it in your words. But I was not the one that marched on our kingdom to bring it down. I didn't ask for anyone to visit us here. I never opened our doors to offer that kind of welcome. And I still haven't." Her eyes were dimming. "I asked you to do what you thought best when it came to the unknown that has come down from the north." She pointed to the land beyond. "I agreed that you should set watch to the south. But what I did not agree to, Poe, was for you to have free reign to decide what is best for our clan. You are not king!"

Her eyes grew even darker. Poe had never seen her look at him this way before. "You can despise the lions all you want, Poe, but they are the only clan left that can help us survive. The den despises us too; they always have. But not their king! And definitely not this queen." She looked him dead in the eye. "You forget that I have stood before kings who wished me dead and almost accomplished it. I recognize the same desire behind your eyes, Poe."

Every feather on Poe's head stood on end.

"I don't fear you. I can end my own life faster than you can take it. And we both know how."

Poe could barely breathe.

"We are bound to one another. Never forget it. You feel what I feel, and I feel what you feel. But there is a third part to this that balances us out to make sure that the path we are on is the same one."

She lifted the medallion. Poe could not help but look at the eagle engraved on it.

"Look at me, Poe."

Her eyes were dark pools of black.

"We cannot live where your heart is living. It will destroy us. And just like you have vowed not to let our clan be destroyed, neither will I."

Poe's feathers were rising and falling with each breath he took.

"Did you kill the lion prince?"

He looked down.

"Did you?!?"

He lifted his large ebony head, feeling the anger rising up to overcome the shock he was feeling. He leveled his eyes at her. *What if I did?*"

"Why? Why would you do such a thing?"

"To bring them pain."

"You almost brought down the houses of three clans because of your pain!"

He grew even angrier. *"Good! I'm glad, queen! They all deserve to die! Their king deservesss to die!"*

"WHY?!?"

"Because you said so."

"I never said to kill those kings or the old lion prince!"

"I only live on because of your promise to us, 'I promise you, all of you, that for the rest of my days, I will never allow my heart to stand in the way of my head when it comesss to you, my clan. Your livesss are all that matter now. Yours alone....if anyone marches on our kingdom...attack.' I live on to carry out your promise. Even the lion king wishes to destroy the other clansss. The gorilla king hasss one day left."

"No one has marched on our kingdom!"

"But they will. The old lion prince was the first to do it. He paved the way. I was sending a message to those inside our realm and beyond, 'Don't...come...here'." He stepped toward his queen and glared down at her. *"I wasss wrong about you, my queen. I thought you were just like Palimusss. You are nothing like him. You have misunderstood his message. You do not see what he seesss from the fog of the dead. You will bring down our house once more by allowing the enemiesss in with your kindnessss and your grace and your mercy! It brought usss nothing but pain, queen! And I will not let you do it again. I will tear the heartsss out of every single one of them so that you may see...that it isss not in the sun that we shine best. It isss only in the dark where you can see the light..."*

He vaulted into the sky and flew north toward the fortress. Reginald landed directly behind his queen. They both stood side by side as Poe flew to the land beyond.

Rebekah was furious. "Why would Ice tell Poe to destroy the realm!"

"I do not know, my queen." He watched her face as she continued to watch Poe in flight. "But just as we are unbalanced, so must the Elements be."

Her eyes began to lighten as she calmed herself down. "Poe murdered Prince Marcus. You were right." Reginald's face seemed to darken at the news. "He almost started another war. He will not stop until he starts another one." She turned and looked at him.

"There is only one thing left to do. Capture him. And in the meantime, I will inform the kings of Poe's actions."

"Do you think that's wise, my queen? If he returns and crosses over into their territories, they may kill him. He is the last of his kind, the balance between us."

"And he knows it, Reginald. But he cannot be allowed to continue down this path free from the knowledge or feeling of repercussion. We would be just as guilty as Poe if we allowed that to happen."

Reginald nodded in reply.

"If Poe is foolish enough to invade another territory, then he faces the consequence of that choice." She looked down at her medallion. "And if that shifts the balance between us to one side…" She looked up at Reginald, "What better side to be on than yours."

Reginald smiled softly. "I wish we did not have to think this way."

"Reginald, I wish sometimes the world was not this way."

"I want you to know that the gorilla king has been calling for me. Shall I bring him here?"

Rebekah exhaled slowly. "No, I need you to keep an eye out for Poe with the Thunderbird Guard. The scavengers will need to be watched in particular. Send a falcon warrior to the king instead."

"As you wish, my queen."

Reginald launched into the sky leaving Rebekah alone with her thoughts. She looked up at the sun and silently prayed. It was a long day, and little did she know, it was going to be an even longer night.

XXXIX

Byron rode atop a falcon warrior as he made his way from Gorilla Jungle toward Bird Kingdom. As they flew over the Wolf Lair, the gorilla king felt uneasy. He was looking at the shadows moving amongst the trees below. He shifted his eyes to survey the landscape, catching a glimpse of the lake. "Warrior, is that where the lion prince was found?"

The falcon looked down toward Wolf Lake. "Yes, king."

"I'd like to take a closer look."

"My queen commanded that I take you directly to her kingdom. It is not safe here."

"I just want to…"

BAM!

Before Byron could finish his thought, he and the falcon collided into a massive object. The falcon cried out and spun sideways causing Byron to fall from the sky…and down toward the lake.

The gorilla king plunged into the darkened waters below. He swam to the surface, feeling the water temperature grow colder and colder with each passing second. He swam as fast as he could toward the shoreline. With each stroke he took, the water around him began to freeze over. Bits of ice began surfacing around him; he swam even faster. By the time he reached shore, the lake had almost completely frozen over. Byron could not believe his eyes as he watched the water hardening to solid ice.

Byron was freezing. He searched the sky for the falcon warrior, but he was nowhere to be seen. His head was throbbing, still feeling the impact from the bludgeon he had just received. He took in his surroundings. All he could see were skeletal trees reaching out to him from all sides as if the branches themselves were outstretched arms. Byron had no desire to stay in the lair any longer. He was about to whistle for Reginald when he heard the sound of twigs breaking behind him. Byron whirled around, jumping onto one of the trees. He hung onto the branches, searching for the source of the sound but saw nothing. He reached for his bone scepter at his side and realized it was gone.

Byron heard the sound again. It was behind him. Byron quickly swung to another tree, searching for the source of the sound. He could barely make anything out.

"Tok...tok...tok..."

Byron slowly turned around and came face to face with Poe.

Rebekah and Reginald were flying over the northern side of the realm.

"Do you think Poe would have come back this way, Reginald?"

Reginald replied, "It's possible, my queen. I knew he would return, but I did not realize it was going to be this soon."

"I don't think he ever left. He only seemed to." They rode swiftly through the night, feeling the urgency in finding Poe. One of the Thunderbird Guards had seen Poe flying across the fields the moment the sun set. "This is the only other place I thought to look other than Raven Territory."

"There is one other place he would be."

Rebekah answered knowingly, "The Wolf Lair. But Kenuen already searched the lair with Hood."

Reginald had already changed directions, "Poe has many places to hide inside the woods. He is there, my queen."

As if on cue, Rebekah and Reginald heard wolves howling in the distance. Their cry grew so loud the closer they came to the forest, that Rebekah almost went into a panic.

"What's going on?!?"

"I don't know, my queen."

Rebekah and Reginald descended and landed on the shoreline to Wolf Lake. The moment Rebekah dismounted, a chill surged down her spine. The entire lake had frozen over.

Ice…

Reginald called to Rebekah, "My queen, the wolves approach."

Rebekah turned and saw dozens of yellow eyes mirroring through the shadows of the trees. Hood slowly approached them. "Come with us, queen." He dropped to all fours. Rebekah quickly mounted Hood. They took off into the darkness of the trees.

As they wove their way through the darkness, Rebekah's mind was on overdrive. The wolves continued to howl as they moved deeper into the forest. Hood slowed as they approached a group of wolves and hyenas gathered around a large object. Rebekah jumped off of Hood and raced over to the pack. She moved past them and saw her falcon warrior on the ground. His body was bloodied and mutilated — dead.

"This way, queen."

Rebekah followed Hood a few more feet when her legs almost fell out from underneath her. *"NO!!!"* Her scream echoed across the realm as she ran toward the gorilla king. She dropped to the ground and scooped him up in her arms. *"BYRON!"* There was blood pouring out from multiple wounds all over his body. His face was deathly pale as she lifted his head between her hands. She shouted at him, *"KING! OPEN YOUR EYES!"*

He opened his eyes, coughing up blood as he tried to speak.

"Keep your eyes on me, Byron! Don't fall asleep!"

Reginald was beside her. "My queen…"

"Not now, Reginald!"

Rebekah looked up at the moon, angling her body in the direction of its light. She ripped her gloves off and placed one hand over Byron's heart.

He stepped in front of her. "It will be too much for you. He has too many injuries!"

"MOVE!" She reached up to the moon with her other hand. Both Rebekah and Reginald braced themselves for what was coming next.

SNAP!

Rebekah cried out as the light shot through her entire body and down into Byron's heart. Reginald shrieked in agony and was knocked to the ground beside his queen.

Byron gasped as the light shot through him — electrifying him. Several moments passed. Silence filled the woods, almost as if the world itself were waiting on a hope and a prayer. It was then that the gorilla king slowly opened his eyes. He laid there, trying to orient himself to his surroundings. He could not remember where he was or what had just happened. He slowly turned his head and saw Rebekah lying on her stomach beside him. Her hand was still on his chest. He laid his hand over hers and looked into her eyes. The wolves and hyenas were surrounding her; they were absolutely still.

"Queen…what have you done?"

Rebekah was breathing hard; she was in tremendous pain as she whispered, "You…are supposed to have…your many sons…" She smiled weakly. "Have Hood carry me and my eagle home."

Byron slowly sat up and saw Reginald on the ground a few feet away. He was breathing in the same rhythmic pattern as his queen. He looked down at his bloodied shirt, wondering how it was that he still lived. His scepter was gone. He couldn't remember what had happened — only that he had fallen from the sky. The rest was all a void. Seeing the queen and her eagle in pain, whatever had happened, she had helped him once again. He looked down and saw severe burns all over the back of her neck and on her hand.

"Queen…" He pulled Rebekah's body into his, cradling her in his lap. She had passed out. Hood approached the king and reached out to pick up the bird queen. Byron shook his head.

"No, wolf. I will carry her home. Carry her eagle."

Hood turned and saw Reginald on the ground. He barked to the pack; two hyenas moved forward. They stared down at the queen as the wind silently blew past them. They growled lowly at the surrounding trees, sensing a threat to their domain. Byron watched them as they sniffed rapidly around.

"What is it?"

Hood dropped down on all fours. He turned his large head in the gorilla king's direction. "Fire, king…she called to him. And he answered…"

As he continued to breathe, his breath fogged on the night air. "Ice is here…"

One of the hyenas lowered his head like a bull in the direction of Wolf Lake. "What does this mean?"

Hood stared straight ahead, listening to the movements in the dark. "The birds are not the only ones unbalanced." His eyes glowed. "Follow me. The raven is near. And if his captain and queen are hurt, so is he."

They took off into the darkness.

XL

Daniel could see the warm glow of firelight emanating from beneath the doors that led into the Great Library. He entered the large room and was surprised to find Nathan sitting in Marcus' chair behind the wooden desk. He was sifting through a pile of papers, focusing on a few words at a time before moving on to the next one.

"Grandfather..."

Nathan did not look up. Daniel walked over to him. "I'm sorry about what happened last night."

Nathan continued to read through the papers. "No, you're not. If you end up being right about Marcus' murder, you did an honorable thing. You saved those people's lives. There have been too many deaths, Daniel. But if we have to fight, then the den fights to win. There can be no dissent, understood?"

Daniel nodded. "Have you heard from Queen Rebekah?"

Nathan went back to the papers. "No, I haven't. And I don't expect I will for some time."

"Why not?"

Nathan shifted his eyes to his grandson. "Because she's a queen, Daniel. There's a certain protocol to territories and politics than mere letters and personal visitations to solve them. This particular issue of the jungle and my brother is a complicated one."

"What are you reading?"

"Notes. Marcus had so many damned notes on everything."

"What are you looking for?"

Nathan sat back in the large chair; he looked exhausted. "A trail. Marcus always kept notes on where he had just come from and where he was going. I'm trying to figure out where he went. I don't know why he'd ever go through the Lair — not after what happened the last time, anyway." Nathan rubbed his eyes.

Daniel sat down in a chair opposite his grandfather. "He didn't even tell SinJin, you know. He's devastated."

"As he should be. He was Marcus' guardian — swearing an oath to never leave his side. And he never had."

Daniel looked at the large collection of papers piled up on the desk. "For whatever reason Uncle Marcus went to the Lair, it would seem he was going through it to go past it."

"To do what?"

"What he always did: to find a means to sustain the water source in the realm — with or without the birds. I think he wanted Mariner Sea to flow again."

At the sound of Mariner Sea, Nathan shifted uncomfortably in his seat. "It would take a miracle to resurrect that sea, Daniel. The rain would have to fall for years. And if it did, flooding and mudslides would destroy the surrounding landscape. There's no way it can be done." He shook his head. "He should have known better. And now he's dead. And someone from another clan did it. What am I supposed to do with that? To do nothing would send the kind of message that no member of the den would stand behind. It puts all of our lives at risk to let this one go."

Daniel knew his king was right, but without proof of who was responsible, what could be done? "I think we should summon the four kings and bird queen to the den. Rescind the three-day threat on the gorilla king and let each clan do the work for us to find who did this. It would send a greater message to the entire realm if we banded together. The way I see it, the one who killed Marcus is the one who's trying to keep everyone apart. Send a different kind of message. One where we're not sitting separate in the dark, but one where we're bonded in the light."

Nathan sat there listening to his grandson speak. He was suddenly reminded of himself in his younger days where he wanted to do the same and unite the realm as one. And here was a young man, his grandson, sitting opposite him saying the same thing in the same way but for a different reason. For all the wrong Nathan felt he had done in his life, he suddenly had the realization that he had done something right. His heart ached at that moment; with a beat of pride, a pulse of hope, and a surge of relief. Daniel was right. And in that realization, Nathan knew that long after he was king, the den would live on because of the kind of king that would one day follow him. The weight Nathan had carried on his shoulders all these years suddenly lifted as he looked at his grandson.

"You're right, Daniel."

Daniel breathed in deep, feeling a surge of confidence and pride at hearing his king's words.

"On behalf of the den, I want you to summon the kings and queen here for a new treaty to be written. What the details will entail, I leave to you, our prince. In this, we honor Marcus, our people and those who will live inside these walls long after we are gone."

Daniel could feel the emotion welling up inside him as he understood what the king was truly saying. He nodded in respect to his grandfather and his king.

"It would be my honor to carry out your command, my king."

Nathan chuckled softly to himself.

"What?"

"I was just thinking about my father and what conversation he must have had the moment he summoned the kings and queen to the den. Whatever it was and whomever he had it with, it wasn't me."

Daniel looked across the library at the large portrait of Gunthar. "Perhaps, he had discussed it with his queen." He looked back at Nathan. "Go see her, grandfather. Not for politics, treaties or territories, but because you want to. Because you love her. Marry her."

Nathan exhaled deeply. But before he could answer, Daniel stood up. "Let's go."

"Right now?"

"Absolutely." He moved toward the door. Daniel turned back around and looked at his grandfather. "Well, are you coming...or are you too old to run?"

Nathan growled lowly. Daniel smiled and raced out the courtyard.

Rebekah was lying on her stomach in her bed; she was fast asleep. Byron was sitting in a chair beside her watching her as she breathed. Reginald walked up beside him and placed his talon on the king's shoulder.

"My queen will be fine, king. She needs her rest in order to heal. Your clan will want to know that you are all right. I shall carry you home."

Byron moved a strand of hair from Rebekah's face. "I love your queen, Reginald."

Reginald studied the look on the gorilla king's face. "As do I."

"Is it true that the lion king still loves her?"

"Yes, king. It is."

"And does she still love him?"

Reginald looked at the gorilla king and lowered his voice, "Yes, she does."

"I don't know that I believe you, Reginald."

"I do not lie, king."

Byron looked up at him and said, "I don't know you well enough to believe otherwise. I don't mean to insult you either. The eagles have always been known for their strength, bravery and courage. But they've also been known for their fierceness in protecting their kings and their queens."

"We have nothing to fear from you, king, for we see. We see far and wide. We see the small and the near. My queen sees it too; you have a king's heart. One that champions his people…and his friends."

"Your queen needs an heir. As do I. I almost died tonight, Reginald. I was attacked in the sky — not even the falcon saw it coming."

Poe.

Every feather on his body stood on end. He tried to calm his mind before the gorilla king saw his reaction.

Byron stood. "If the lion king does not make his move, I will. And it will be for all the right reasons."

Reginald did not reply.

"Even if she loves the lion as you say, perhaps she can love me anyway — in a different way. I'm not that bad a guy." He leaned over and kissed Rebekah softly on her forehead. "Take me home, eagle."

As Byron moved toward the balcony, Reginald pulled the king's bone scepter out and extended it to him. Byron immediately grabbed it and clutched it tight. "Where did you find it?"

"Fire melted Wolf Lake. It was there."

"Fire…"

"There is more to this life, king, than what we see." He bowed to the gorilla king as they moved toward the balcony and dove over the field below. From the shadows in the corner of the room, Poe emerged. He stood on the balcony watching them fly over the kingdom he called his own. *"You will not undo what I have done…"*

"That's treason, Poe."

Poe whirled around and stared into the dark corner opposite him. He saw silver eyes mirroring in the darkness. Alexander slowly emerged from the shadows. "This is one of those rare occasions I've longed to see: a wolf taking a raven by surprise."

"Tok…tok…tok…" Poe's eyes burned red. Alexander could see his chest rising and falling rapidly from having been taken off-guard.

"I hear many things, Poe. Howls in the distance. Cries of the weak. Intruders in the trees. And ravens attacking princes and kings. You're not so clever, bird."

Poe slowly stood so that he towered over Alexander. *"It wasss sssuposed to be you, king. You were to be king over my clan. But you failed usss…the ravensss and the wolvesss."*

Alexander clutched his cane tight.

"Now you're old, king. You have no sssay. For your influence isss non-existent in the realm of thisss day…"

The wolf king leveled his eyes at the raven assassin; they seemed to glow even brighter. "You're only still alive, Poe, because you're the only one left."

The feathers on Poe's crown stood on end as if a chill had run down his spine.

"My pack does not know you, nor do they care whether you live to see another night. They wanted to tear you to shreds when they saw you murder the lion, when you tried to kill the gorilla king, and when you slaughtered your own kind. You are a threat to their peace, and they will not bow down to the will of your war. You are only a bird without a home to make his nest. And you only live on because of me. And that can end at any moment."

Poe was breathing fast and hard.

"You are not the wielder of the flame, bird. You forget that I, too, have stood before the fire and have had a vision all my own. And I have lived my life to make sure that my vision comes to pass." He stepped closer to Poe. "Now that I know what you've done, rest assured I know why. Step into the lair one more time, the shadows in the trees will be the last thing you ever see. Leave this place. Fly to that fortress of yours and build your nest. Stay there. Die there. Step foot anywhere else again, and know that it will be the last step you ever take." There was a low growl in the undertone of his words.

Poe shifted his eyes to the shadows in the room where Alexander emerged from. There he saw two sets of yellow eyes mirroring against the candlelight that lit the room. Hood slowly emerged along with a gray wolf beside him. Their teeth were barred; their growls were low and lethal. Poe shifted his scarlet eyes back to Alexander.

"It should have been you, king…how you have disappointed me." And with that, Poe raced toward the balcony and vaulted into the sky. The wolves approached their king as all three watched the raven

assassin in flight.

"Will he listen, my king?"

"No. Kill him if he steps foot in the lair or Bird Kingdom again. Shoot him down from the sky if he hovers near." Alexander turned and looked at Rebekah sleeping. "Come. The queen is going to need her rest to receive the guests that will soon be coming."

Alexander headed down the hallway king with his warriors just as the lion king and prince had arrived.

XLI

As Nathan and Daniel approached Bird Clan gates, they stopped dead in their tracks the moment they saw a pair of yellow eyes mirroring in the darkness. Nathan put his hand in front of Daniel to protect him while reaching for the hilt of his sword.

Hood, the captain of the wolf pack, crept slowly toward the lion king and prince. "Lion…" He stood on his hind legs, rising to over seven-feet-tall. "My king wishes to express his deepest sympathies to the loss of Prince Marcus."

Nathan nodded. Hood continued, "He did not come to seek an audience with you, for he said he likes to keep his promises." Daniel looked at his grandfather wondering what it meant, but Nathan seemed to know as a faint smile crept onto the lion king's face. "My king had one last message he wanted to share. He said to watch for the shadows. It is there that darkness lies. And you will not find it in the jungle." With nothing further, Hood dropped down on all fours and raced back toward the lair.

Daniel spoke first, "They know. They know who killed Marcus."

Nathan continued to watch the path of the timber wolf as he raced across the fields. He said nothing more as he turned and walked toward the Bird Kingdom gates.

"Grandfather?"

"Not tonight, Daniel. We have tomorrow to break it down and discover the meaning behind the wolf king's message. But not tonight."

Daniel nodded and walked through the courtyard beside his king. It was strange to see the guardians simply nod to his grandfather, allowing them to pass through the gates and into the gardens without stopping them — almost as if they were expecting them.

A cold wind blew. Nathan looked up at the queen's balcony. "Something is wrong."

Daniel looked back at the crow warriors staring at him with their dark eyes as they walked toward the main tower. They were eerily silent, barely seeming to move; it crept Daniel out. They were not anything like the eagles or the falcons as they continued to stare at him. One thing was certain: they had no fear.

They ran toward the gate. Reginald dropped down from the sky and bowed to his guests, "King..." When he lifted his head he smiled the moment he saw Daniel. "And prince. My queen is not well."

Nathan's face paled at the news. He looked up at her balcony. "What happened, Reginald?"

"The gorilla king was attacked in the lair."

Daniel was shocked, *"WHAT!"*

Nathan locked eyes with Reginald. He spoke slowly, "Are you going to stand there and tell me that it wasn't the wolves who attacked my brother and the gorilla king?"

"No, king. I'm standing here to tell you the news, and to tell you that my queen saved the gorilla king's life — as she did for Prince Marcus once before. You know my meaning."

Daniel watched as the realization as to what Reginald was saying to his grandfather sunk in. "I want to see her."

Reginald nodded. The three of them walked swiftly toward her tower; Nathan led the way. A cold breeze blew past them, causing Reginald to stop dead in his tracks. The feathers on his crown stood on end as he slowly turned to face the wind. His gray eyes searched the darkness, knowing he was being watched. He turned back toward the tower and walked inside, but not without gripping the hilt of his sword tight.

The crow cocked four times as Daniel and Nathan walked inside Rebekah's chambers. It was quiet inside. Only the faint glow of candlelight lit her room, giving it a warm glow. She was fast asleep. Daniel came around her bed and sat on the chair beside her. She opened her eyes at the sound of the chair moving against the floor. The moment she saw him, she smiled.

"Young lion..."

Nathan kept his distance, not wishing to intrude upon her in this state just yet. His heart ached as he watched her lying there. He knew she was in pain. It reminded him of when he stood in the shadows long ago watching her clinging to life as the old toad chief tried to save her from the poison his clan had given her. It was one of the longest nights of his life. He had almost lost her then, and he vowed that night he would never lose her again.

"You look well."

She laughed softly. "You're just like Nathan...I don't look well at all." She struggled to keep her eyes open. "I didn't hear my birds announce you."

"I arrived with Reginald. He told me that the gorilla king was attacked at Wolf Lake. Just like Uncle Marcus..."

She exhaled deeply. "I know what you must be thinking. Was it the wolves?" She inhaled slowly. "Long ago there was a great mystery that had yet to be solved; just like this one. Bodies from the clans on your side of the realm showed up dead at each of the borders on our side. It was a ruse to cover up a more sinister plot. Your uncle and King Byron's attacks follow the same pattern."

"But why would someone do this?"

"Why did they do it before?"

Daniel thought about it a moment. "To start a war."

Rebekah smiled softly, "Not everyone wants peace, young lion."

"You and my grandfather did."

Her smile slowly faded. "Yes, we did."

"If what you say is true, queen, it would seem that whomever is behind all this wants all the clans to remain enemies — especially yours and mine." He weighed his words before he spoke next. "If my logic is as sound as it seems, there is only one way to ensure that that doesn't happen."

"And what's that?"

"Unite the realm. The way you and my king wanted to before."

Rebekah closed her eyes and exhaled deeply. "I don't think so."

"Why not?"

"Because. Your grandfather despises me."

Daniel shook his head, trying not to look behind him at Nathan's reaction. "No! He doesn't!"

She opened her eyes. "Yes, he does. He thinks I betrayed him by protecting the gorilla king. He believes I undermined him that night at the jungle. Believe me, he does not want to speak with me...and I don't have the energy at this moment to speak with him. We would just end up either arguing or staring at each other in silence. I've had enough silence, and I've been in too many verbal battles since I've awoken. I need my rest."

"Better to have a verbal argument than a physical one, don't you think?"

She glared at him. "You just wait to have your first fight with Alexandra, and then we'll see if you're exhausted after you have one."

Daniel did not know what to say in reply. Rebekah noticed his look. "Did you have a fight?"

"Sort of. When I found Marcus in the lake, I took my anger out on her. We haven't spoken since."

"Then why are you here? Shouldn't you be at the lair?"

"I don't know about that." Daniel looked behind him slightly, "I came to ask you something."

"What?"

"Do you still love my grandfather?"

Rebekah looked at him with his mariner-colored eyes and started laughing. She slowly pushed herself up and rolled over in order to sit up. "That's not up for conversation." She flinched in pain.

"Here. Let me help you." It was then that Daniel noticed the deep burns on her neck and chest. He gasped. "Queen...what happened tonight? Reginald said that the gorilla king was attacked, and that you helped him the way you helped my uncle long ago."

"Don't fret, lion. I will heal. The scars are not permanent, although the memories are. There is a gift I have been given that allows me to help others heal. But when I use that gift, I get a little burnt in the end." She let out a gentle laugh. "The gorilla king is alive and well and back in his jungle."

Daniel did not completely understand what that meant, but it did not matter. Knowing that she was willing to sacrifice her own comfort for a greater good, made him look at her with a new admiration. He understood why his grandfather could love her for so long over so many years. She had something within her that he had never known in anyone before. His respect for her grew a thousand times more in that single moment. Marcus. Rebekah. The realm had no idea what extraordinary people ruled within it, and what lengths they went to for others they owed nothing to and gained nothing from.

He sat down in the chair with a completely different point of view. "Tell me. Do you love him?"

She studied him. "You first. Do you love Alexandra?"

Daniel's face turned bright red.

"Not such a fun question to be asked, is it, prince?"

He cleared his throat and moved his chair up. "Yes, I do. She *sees* me."

"And do you *see* her?"

"I do."

"Then you deserve her. And she deserves you."

He smiled. "Your turn."

"Oh, get out. I'm tired."

"Nope." He leaned back in his chair and crossed his arms over his chest.

Rebekah let out a loud sigh. "I have been alone all my life, lion, and I could have lived that way forever. I could have, but then Nathan came along — so unexpectedly. Like it were a gift from the heavens. And for the first time, I realized that I didn't have to live alone and that I didn't want to. As queen I have been a strong female, but with him at my side I was suddenly a strong woman — and I was complete." She looked down at her hands. "I thought he'd be dead by the time I had awoken again. And now he is older and lived his life. Yet I see his face as he was and I am no different than before that last moment when I remembered him best. And my feelings don't match the time, my memories don't match this place. And yet, fifty years may have passed for him, but my love is just as new as the night our hands touched on that dance floor long ago. His eyes...his heart...they are the same to me now as they were then. And I cannot help but desire him all the more no matter how much time passes." She breathed deeply and looked up at him. "Does that answer your question?

He nodded.

"Why did you ask me that?"

"Because I think he needed to hear it."

He turned his head around and looked over his shoulder. She followed his gaze and saw Nathan standing on the other side of her bed. In his hand was a single rose. Nathan moved inside the room and sat down beside her.

"Nathan..."

Nathan touched her face. "I did need to hear that." He gently pulled her into his arms and kissed her long and deep. Daniel waited for them to finish, but they did not. He slowly stood to make his way across the room.

"I will...leave you two..."

Daniel was almost to the door.

"Young lion..."

He turned back around.

"The moon is beautiful tonight. You may have my falcons for the evening. There may be some things that Alexandra needs to hear...from you."

Daniel smiled and raced out the door. Nathan turned Rebekah's face back to his with the crook of his finger and kissed her again.

XLII

Byron jumped off of Reginald and landed on the footsteps of his fortress. He swiftly walked the stone stairway as the drums echoed throughout the jungle, signaling his arrival. Minotauro burst through the doors and charged down the steps toward Byron.

The gorilla king looked up and saw him barreling straight towards him. Before he could move out of the way, Minotauro collided into him, picking him up by the waist, squeezing him tight. "You're alive!"

Byron could barely breathe.

Minotauro dropped him and grabbed Byron's face with his two strong hands and butted his forehead against his friend's. "Don't do that again." He leveled his eyes at him.

"Minotauro, you're squeezing ma facthe too hrrrd. Leggo…"

Minotauro smacked both sides of Byron's face before he stepped back. Sebastian slowly descended the stairs. He moved past the bull king and stopped the moment he was in front of Byron. They stared at each other in silence. Sebastian had tears in his eyes — tears of anger and relief. Byron smiled faintly, understanding how upset his friends were with him. He was about to say something when, out of nowhere, Sebastian decked him across the face. "Don't *ever* do that again!"

Byron grabbed his jaw; he was in pain, and now he was angry. "He already said that!"

Minotauro replied, "I didn't say 'ever'."

Sebastian continued, "You have no idea what it was like seeing the gorillas go down! Your warriors were falling from the trees!"

"It wasn't my fault. I wasn't *trying* to die, Sebastian."

"Oh no? You just had to go see the bird queen without taking any of your warriors!"

"If I had taken any one of them, we'd have been slaughtered by the den before making it past Bull Valley. I was safe with Reginald."

"Then what happened?"

He looked between his two best friends. They were angry. "I was attacked."

"Obviously."

"At Wolf Lake."

The weight of what that meaning hit Minotauro like a ton of bricks whose master was named "Doom"; his eyes darkened as if a shadow had suddenly cast itself across his face. He crossed his arms over his chest. "Then it *is* the wolves who are behind the attacks."

"I don't think so."

Sebastian narrowed his eyes. "Why not?"

"Because...the wolf king would have showed his hand and brought war onto his side. They're just as weak as we are. There is no way he would command something like this. It wasn't the wolves. I know it wasn't."

"I don't understand."

Minotauro put his hand out to stop Sebastian, keeping his eyes the entire time on Byron. "I want to know what happened...then maybe we'll understand."

Byron took a deep breath. "I was on my way back home." He shook his head. "That's all I remember. It's all a blank. I remember everything up until that moment when I was attacked. All I saw was black."

Minotauro moved closer toward him. "You were *flying* when you were attacked?"

Byron nodded.

Sebastian finally understood. "You don't think…"

Minotauro was staring directly at Byron when he said, "Yes, I do."

Byron shook his head. "No. The queen saved my life."

"I wasn't referring to the queen. All you saw was black." Minotauro and Sebastian looked at one another. "It was him. It was her raven."

Byron's face went pale and his body began to shake. He could see Wolf Lake in his mind's eye. He could hear the falcon shriek just as something dark collided into them. "You…" He looked between both Sebastian and Minotauro. "Why would…" He saw them. The red eyes. He could barely breathe. "Why?"

The bull king looked north to the Great White Mountains. "Isn't it obvious, Byron? We slaughtered his kind. And for that…" He looked at Sebastian. "He wants his vengeance."

Sebastian's voice was barely a whisper, "The gorillas didn't slaughter the ravens."

Minotauro looked at the amphibian king. "They didn't stop the bulls and amphibians either."

The three kings turned and looked toward the mountains. Sebastian asked, "What do we need to do?"

"Kill the raven before he kills us all."

"But what about the queen?"

"What about the queen!"

Byron remained silent the entire time, feeling a large shadow consume him before all went black. His body continued to tremble.

"He's the last of his kind; the balance in her clan. We all have the light and the dark in each of our kind, in each of our clans. To kill the raven would shift the balance."

"To shift the balance, Sebastian, might be the best thing to happen to us all. We've had too much darkness…and the raven seeks to bring even more. We have to kill the raven in order to turn our darkness into light."

"Then there's one other thing I need to do before we take him out."

Sebastian asked, "What?"

"Go see the lion king."

Rebekah was laying in Nathan's arms when he took her hand and placed a small box in the palm of it. "I've been holding onto this for fifty years. I asked the critter chief to craft this for you. I remembered you saying how each clan had a special gift. It was the first time I ever saw you. The moment I heard your voice. I knew you were destined to be mine. I had this the morning my father made me marry the mariner princess. I was on my way to you...that's when it all changed."

Rebekah was shaking; she opened the box. Inside was a ruby molded into the shape of a rose. Emerald gems formed its leaves, and the gold band was perfectly crafted around it.

He looked at her. "I know I'm an old man now, but I still have a young man's heart. I love you. I have always loved you. Would you do me the honor, Queen of the Bird Clan...and marry this old lion from the den?"

Rebekah took his face in her hands and kissed him. When she opened her eyes, she noticed Nathan's face had changed. "What is this look?"

Nathan breathed deeply. "Peace. With you in my arms, I have finally found my peace." He rested his head against her shoulder. His chest rumbled lowly. She kissed his forehead. He looked up at her and asked, "What?"

"I'm just looking at your wrinkles."

"There aren't that many."

"There are a few. And each one of these lines tells a story for all the moments I was not there. No more lines without me, lion. I don't want to miss another one."

He took her hand in his and clasped his fingers around hers. "Do you remember the night we first met?"

"Yes. It was the night your father had a heart attack over seeing you dance with the enemy queen."

He rested his head against hers. "Dance with me, woman."

She took his hand and placed it over her heart. "Tomorrow."

Nathan lifted his head and looked at her. "You're in pain. I should've known better." She smiled through her tears and nodded. He moved away from her so that he could arrange her pillows for her to lay down. He touched the tears streaming down her face, wiping them away. "You did something good for that king. You saved his life, took away his pain. You saved an entire clan from becoming extinct. You two have a lot in common." He paused. "Are you sure you don't want to marry a young man like him?"

She reached for his hand and held it tight. "Nathan, there are many pathways to my heart, but you had the straight arrow. I'll dance with you, lion. I will sleep and I will rest. And when the sun rises, awaken me, and I'll dance with you forever. Now come and lay beside me. I want to stare at my ring."

He cradled her in his arms, stroking her hair, and held her until she fell asleep.

XLIII

Daniel landed with the two falcon warriors in the middle of the lair. "Hello?" The lion prince looked all around the empty courtyard. If it weren't for the burning torches lighting the corridors, he would have thought the lair was abandoned. "Are they even here?"

"Yes, prince. The pack is always here."

As if on cue, a low growl could be heard echoing throughout the courtyard. Several pairs of yellow eyes appeared.

Daniel swallowed hard, "I've come to see Princess Alexandra." A large hyena warrior slowly crept forward. He was on all fours but slowly stood on his two hind legs the moment he reached the prince. "Cats and dogs don't mix, prince."

"Oh stop it, Igor." Alexandra approached. "What are you doing here?"

The moment Daniel saw Alexandra, his stomach plummeted to his feet. He could barely speak. "I came to apologize...for the other night. I didn't mean to yell at you. I'm sorry."

Alexandra reached out and took his hand. "You don't have to apologize. I would've done the same thing if it were my uncle that was found murdered in your den."

Daniel looked at her appreciatively.

"How are you doing?"

"Okay. Actually, I'm not okay. I miss him."

Alexandra squeezed his hand. "My father told me what you did in the jungle. That was a very brave thing to do."

"Or very stupid. I'm no closer to finding Marcus' killer."

Igor started to creep slowly back into the shadows. Alexandra caught his movement out of the corner of her eye before he disappeared into the darkness. "They'll find him, Daniel."

"Does your pack know anything?"

She shook her head. "I see you brought the falcons." She moved toward them, trying to change the subject.

Daniel's face seemed to brighten. "Would you like to go flying tonight?"

She nodded. "On two conditions."

"What?"

"One: that you show me your den. And two: we watch the sun rise over Bull Valley — like your grandfather always does."

Daniel smiled widely. "Your wish is my command."

They mounted the falcons and took off into the night sky. The yellow eyes appeared once more. Igor growled to another hyena warrior beside him. "Our king is not going to be happy."

"And he is not the only one."

A bark rose up from the hyena and other yipping howls answered until the sound of wolves howling drowned out their cries. The Wolf Pack gathered in the empty courtyard and looked to the sky where their princess had fled. "Summon the king."

Reginald had been searching high and low for any sign of Poe. He flew as high into the sky as he possibly could, knowing that was the only way to clearly see the movement amongst the shadows. He had soared over the Wolf Lair several times over, descending now and again to confer with Hood and the rest of the Wolf Pack. Everyone was searching for him, fully aware of the crimes he had committed; fully comprehending that his actions meant to undo all others outside Bird Kingdom — even the wolves.

Kenuen and the Thunderbird Guard had been ordered to remain behind and guard the lion king and bird queen. It had been the first time such an order had ever been given, but these were not ordinary times.

Poe wasn't the only one missing — so were all the scavengers, vultures and owls. Knowing they outnumbered all the ostriches, falcons, hawks and eagles combined, Reginald was deeply troubled. There was no telling what they would do when led by Poe, but Reginald had a pretty clear idea of all the places where that kind of dark army could lead.

He had circled what was once Raven Territory several times already, but something told him to circle it once more. His gray, eagle eyes searched and zeroed in on the burnt-out land covering the bones of the demolished raven clan. He decided to descend. The closer Reginald got to the ground, the colder the air seemed to turn. Chills ran down his spine as his breath fogged on the freezing, night air.

The moment he landed, Reginald could hear the crunch of ice and hardened snow beneath his taloned feet. Never before had Ice been in their territory — only Fire. Reginald's pupils dilated to the size of tiny pins. He suddenly understood.

"*Eagle…*"

The unfamiliar voice surrounded him all at once, as if the air were kissing Reginald in soft breaths as the cold continue to chill him.

"You do not belong here."

The air around him grew even colder.

"*Where can I go when I have no sea to call my own…*"

"There are others to claim. Land beyond our own. Both the lion prince and Poe have seen it."

"*So did your king…Palimus…*"

Reginald's heart was beating rapidly as Ice continued to speak. "You helped us once before. You and the rest of the Creators, the Old Ones. You protected my queen. Now, you seek to destroy us."

"*Not true. I seek to rectify the destruction of the clans for all they have done, for all they have failed to do...*"

"My queen! The lion king! The other kings in the jungle and in the swamps and in the valley seek the same thing!"

"No, eagle. The lions despise your queen even though the king feels otherwise. He does not have many years left. And when he dies, what was once united will be severed once more. You know I speak the truth. You have seen it in the warriors' eyes..."

Reginald was trying to think fast, "Their eyes are no different than before. Change is hard but it happens!"

"Not this time. Your raven is smart enough to know."

"Then why was the lion prince allowed to awaken my queen? Why not let the clans perish on their own?"

The wind grew silent but remained cold. It was almost as if the question itself plagued Ice's heart as well. *"My sister..."* His voice was filled with deep anguish.

Reginald quickly looked to the ground and knelt down on one knee. He lowered his head and touched the cold, hardened soil. "Sister Earth, I beg of you...give us time. We can turn the tide. My queen...she will change it for all."

"She cannot hear you, eagle. She will not speak..." His voice seemed to catch. *"Your clan has always honored Fire. Only the raven seeks my help for what must be done. You eagles have never been able to summon anything."*

Something inside Reginald shifted and he slowly stood. He looked all around him as the snow slowly began to cover the ground. "That is because we have the light within, Ice. It is with us at all times — even in this one."

"Tok...tok...tok..."

Reginald's heart sank the moment he heard Poe's toggle. He looked out at the shadows before him and saw the crows, vultures and owls slowly emerge. They appeared from all sides, surrounding him, closing in on him the entire time Ice spoke. Poe's red, scarlet eyes illuminated in the darkness as he emerged from the shadows and stepped toward Reginald.

"You betrayed usss while we slumbered...you shared your thoughtsss with the enemy so that the lionsss would find a way back to our queen'sss heart..."

Reginald was outnumbered. Even if he were to vault into the sky, he knew he would not get far. He had aged while his brothers standing before him had kept their youth over time.

"There are no secrets, Poe — only lies. And they are the ones you tell."

Poe's eyes seemed to glow even more crimson. He tilted his large ebony head to the side, never taking his eyes from Reginald. *"You don't know pain. You have never watched those you love suffer...helplessss to ease their agony...to stop their tearsss and calm their criesss..."* He moved closer to the eagle captain. *"They're still crying..."*

"I know, Poe. I hear them too. But this is not the way!"

"Thisss is the only way!"

"To destroy the realm!"

"Yesss!!! To start over and begin again!"

Reginald's pupils were the size of pins. "There will be no one left!"

Poe lifted his head; the feathers on his crown stood straight up as he hissed, *"Wrong again."* Poe turned his back on Reginald and looked North. *"I have seen beyond our realm...there are othersss...for the first time, you do not see, eagle..."*

"Poe."

"Brothersss! Let usss show our once great captain what it meansss to suffer as we have suffered!"

The crows began to move in as Reginald shouted, "Our queen!"

At the mention of the queen, Poe spun around so quickly that Reginald had no time to react as the raven drove his dagger deep into Reginald's chest.

Poe was seething, *"Our queen is the reason I am here! With both of usss, we have always bowed to her will. Without you, she will now bow to mine!"*

Reginald was gasping for air. He grabbed Poe by the throat, refusing to go down. "Our queen does not live in the dark."

Poe ripped himself free of Reginald's grasp by driving his dagger deeper. *"She hasss no choice. The balance will shift the moment you die..."* He ripped his dagger from Reginald's body and watched as the eagle captain dropped to his knees.

Reginald lifted his large head and looked directly into Poe's eyes with the fiercest look Poe had ever seen. "Our queen..." He struggled to breathe. "Has Fire on her side!" Reginald pulled the sword from his sheath and forced himself to rise to standing. That was when the avenging birds moved in, and all that could be heard in the haunted forest was the sound of Reginald's cries.

XLIV

Rebekah jolted awake. Something was wrong. Nathan stirred awake, stroking her hair. "What is it?"

She listened closely, looking out over her balcony, but only heard an eerie silence. "I don't know." She stood up and moved toward the balcony. She looked down at the gardens below. Nothing moved. It was still night out, and there was something about the stillness that reminded her of one other night she had experienced before.

Nathan moved up alongside her and watched her face as she tried to decipher the feeling that had crept into her heart. Without looking at him, Rebekah grabbed Nathan's hand. "I don't hear them."

"Who?"

"The crows."

Nathan looked out across the darkened gardens.

"After I was poisoned, I could not hear the ravens. Somehow, as weak as I was, I managed to search the grounds for them. But I heard…nothing. Alexander found me in the fields and carried me back here. That was when he told me about what happened to them."

Nathan stared at her in silence.

"Now, I don't hear the crows, but it's not the same feeling as before." She tried to think, tapping her long finger against the edge of the marble parapet. "They're up to something…"

Nathan finally spoke, "When I arrived here, the wolf captain said to me, 'Watch for the shadows. It is there that darkness lies. And you will not find it in the jungle'."

Rebekah turned her head and looked at him. She laid her hand on top of his as she said, "Poe killed Marcus." Her eyes slowly began to dim. "He attacked the gorilla king. The eagles and Wolf Pack have been searching for him all night in order to capture him so he can incur the punishment for his crimes."

Nathan moved his hand away from Rebekah's. "Why didn't you tell me?"

"I had to find him first. That was the most important task. Reginald and I were out looking for him when he attacked the gorilla king." She turned back toward the garden. "The scavengers…they're with him." She looked out at the garden; her eyes grew even darker. "It's so dark tonight."

Nathan gripped the top of the parapet with his strong hands and looked down at the shadowed grounds below. "It never ends."

"It does today."

Nathan looked at her and saw the grave look on her face. "Evil never sleeps, Nathan." She looked at him. "I never imagined that it would be bred within my own clan, but I see where I have been blinded by optimism in the shroud of those who still weep and ride the winds of vengeance behind a shield of rage. And they do not want to rejoice with me in the dance of the living." She touched the engagement ring on her finger. "I have to fix the cracks in my own house before it completely crumbles." She looked up at him, "You must go. Protect the den. And if you see my raven and the crows, do what you have to do, and know that I will forgive you for it."

Nathan put his hand on her waist and pulled her close to him, kissing her one more time before he turned to go. She watched him move swiftly through the archway and into the hallway beyond. She walked the path he had just travelled and looked down the corridors. They were all empty. She continued walking down each hallway and only heard the echo of her footsteps. Her eyes grew darker and darker until she found her way back to her chambers. She rested her eyes on Palimus' portrait; his eyes stared back at her. That was when she heard a wolf howling in the distance.

Rebekah turned her head toward the sound, grabbed her cloak and headed on foot toward the Wolf Lair.

XLV

The moment Queen Rebekah entered the lair, she was met by three hyena warriors. "Queen…"

"Where is the king?"

"He collapsed." He lowered his large head. "He is dying, and the princess is nowhere to be found."

Rebekah's eyes went wide. She looked up toward Alexander's wing and raced up the stairs.

She burst through the doors and saw Alexander lying in his bed; his face was as pale as snow. His eyes were closed and his breathing was shallow. Hood stood beside him. Rebekah moved close to him and grabbed his hand. "Alexander…" He did not stir. "Wolf, can you hear me?" He still did not answer. She turned and looked at Hood, "What happened? Where is the princess?"

"In the den. She left with the lion prince early last night and has not returned." He shifted his large head to look at his king. "He did not know. When he found out she had gone to the other side of the realm, he shouted and fell to the ground. He has not awoken since."

Rebekah's heart was hammering inside her chest. "Has anyone gone to the den to summon Alexandra?"

"No one from the pack would dare cross into lion territory. Awake or not, queen, my kind has not ventured onto their lands in over fifty years."

"She must be told!"

Hood's eyes glowed as he growled the words, "She should not have gone, queen! *Lions* are not to be trusted!"

The moment he said the words, Rebekah's eyes swirled to sheer black. "You knew, didn't you? You watched as my raven killed the lion prince and you did nothing!"

"And what have you done, *queen*, but do as you please, as if your will were the one for all!"

Alexander suddenly stirred. Both Hood and Rebekah turned their attention back to the king. Rebekah touched his face, "Alexander…"

He slowly opened his eyes.

Byron was dressed in his royal best as he stood before the large mirror in his bedchamber. Minotauro and Sebastian walked inside, also dressed in their best.

"Do you think this will work?"

Byron turned to answer Sebastian, "We have to try. That's all we can do. If King Nathan is anywhere near how Queen Rebekah sees him, there's a chance."

Minotauro gritted his teeth. "If it doesn't work, it's your last day anyway."

"Thank you for that reminder." He adjusted his garments one last time.

"Let's go." They headed out the jungle and on towards the Lion's Den.

Daniel and Alexandra were sitting side by side on the hilltop in Bull Valley that overlooked Bird Kingdom. It was just before sunrise and they had been talking all night: about the past, the present, and the future — but more importantly, about the upcoming treaty.

Daniel was watching Alexandra's expression as she looked out toward the Great White Mountains. "What are you thinking?"

"I'm imagining. I'm thinking about what the realm will be like once the clans are united." She turned and looked at him, "Do you think your clan will throw another masquerade?"

Daniel laughed. "I don't know. If we did, I suppose I'd have to learn how to dance."

"You and me both." Alexandra looked out across the landscape. "You know, Daniel, this is the first time I've understood what it means to have hope."

She turned to look at him and saw his expression changing as he looked out across the landscape. "Daniel, what is it?"

He slowly stood. His eyes had slit to a cat. "It's the clouds. They're descending."

Alexandra looked up and saw the darkness moving toward them. "What is that?"

"Alexandra…" Daniel grabbed Alexandra's hands and pulled her back toward the den. *"RUN!!!"*

That was when the army of crows descended.

XLVI

Alexander slowly turned his head and looked at Rebekah. "Where is...Alexandra?" His mouth was dry and he had a hard time speaking. The left side of his face was completely paralyzed.

It was Hood who answered. "She's still with Prince Daniel."

He immediately started coughing, struggling to breathe. Alexander turned his head and looked at Hood. Even behind all the pain, he was seething. *"Go...get...her!"*

Hood did not know how to respond. He turned and looked at Rebekah instead. That was when all strength left Alexander. The wolf king looked at his captain in defeat, closing his eyes once more. He barely whispered the words, "Bird..."

She clasped his hand tightly.

He struggled to speak. "She...is the....cornerstone...of...my house!" Alexander coughed violently and opened his eyes; they bored into Rebekah's. "I can hear them...their voices..." He was struggling to breathe. "I...feel...death...I have heard...its voice... and am now kin to its call. I know that...of which...I speak." He closed his eyes.

His words hit Rebekah hard. "You cannot leave me, Alex. You cannot go. Not yet!" He did not move. *"Alex!"*

Alexander suddenly breathed in long and deep. He opened his eyes and looked at her. "Your raven is clever indeed. He has learned from the kings of old." He coughed loudly. "Now you listen to me, bird. My time is up. I have done all I was meant to do. Now, it is your turn. Turn the tide. Fix it! The way you wanted to so long ago. Build...your...house..." He grabbed her hand and squeezed it tight. "Build it up for your heirs!"

Rebekah's eyes were filled with tears. "Alex, I have no heirs."

His wolf eyes bored into hers as he growled, "Then you build it up for *mine!* Now go...get...my daughter." He gritted his teeth as he issued his last command. Rebekah felt his grip loosen as all life left the wolf king's body.

"Alexander..." His eyes remained fixed on her face — unmoving. *"Alex!"*

The wolf king was dead. Several moments passed by before she could move; she did not know what to do. She could feel the panic and the fear and the rage rising up in her body until she suddenly stood, shouting to the sky, *"POE!!!"* Her entire body racked as tears streamed down her face. Hood watched the queen as her eyes swirled to sheer black. The fur all over his body stood on end as he backed away from the queen. He watched as she moved to the balcony and whistled sharply to the sky.

The sun had not risen this day. The sky was completely shrouded in darkness as the clouds filled it.

"Queen..."

Rebekah did not even turn as Hood spoke to her. "Wolf, gather your pack. Go to the den. The moment you find your queen, bring her back here. There is no other command to follow. There is no other path to take. She is all that matters now."

Hood growled and nodded, racing through the doors as the wolves began to howl.

Rebekah searched the sky.

All she found was silence.

She whistled sharply again.

As she stood there, silent among the dead, she waited. It was the wind that answered her. It swirled all around her and moved out past her. Past the Wolf Liar. Past the forest and the lake. Past the fields that surrounded Bird Kingdom, until landing over Raven Territory.

The wind descended from the gray-colored sky and landed gently over Reginald's body. He was covered in blood as he lay there motionless. His breathing was almost nonexistent but he was still alive. Something within him kept him in the world of the living, refusing to allow him go out just yet.

It was the wind.

It swirled ever so softly over him, gently moving through his feathers. He could barely open his swollen eyelid as the wind continued to move all around him, almost as if trying to nudge him back into the world of the living, trying to get him to move.

But he didn't want to. He wanted to close his eyes and fall asleep forever, remaining exactly where he was.

And then he heard it.

Only she had ever called him in such a way. And she needed him. He knew she needed him. His clan needed him. But he couldn't find the strength to move.

She called for him again.

Reginald almost wept at that moment, feeling the pain shoot through his body as he tried to move a single limb. He was broken. He was torn. And yet, he knew he had to move. He had to get up. He shut his eyes as a single tear ran down his face. He couldn't do it. *Too much pain.* And yet he heard his queen calling for him. He was in agony knowing he could not help her.

That was when he felt it. Something underneath his mutilated body was stirring. His eyes opened as the earth began to move, swirling beneath him.

It was the sister.

Reginald, still unable to move, watched as a single rose emerged from the ground. Never before had Earth done anything for him. Just for the Critter Chief. Just for his queen. And finally for him. Overcome by that simple knowledge where he found that the world was giving him his miracle to have him do one last thing, he focused on the rose as it bloomed before him, focusing on it as he breathed in...and out.

Rebekah continued to stand alone on the balcony waiting. She could not hear a single bird. She could not see a single warrior in flight. Rebekah thought back to that night so long ago when the lion king had sent her a message, asking for her help as the realm sought to create a new treaty.

It was a moment of excitement.

It was an opportunity that gave her hope.

Yet she did not trust it.

It was Poe and Reginald she sought counsel with then. It was the two warriors — chiefs of their clans — who had given their opinions on what was they thought should be done with such an ask. The light and the dark, with her as queen to balance it out so that the path would be made clear.

But there was no light today.

There was only the dark.

And the path was now unknown to her, for she did not know what the night had wrought. As she continued to stand there calling for her eagle, her heart began to sink.

There would be no balance anymore.

Rebekah closed her eyes and wished for a different moment than the one today, for it seemed that this was the day that would turn the tide for her, for her clan, and most important...for those still living in the realm. She thought of her mother then, and her father. The loneliness she felt when they had died. She was all alone then, except for her birds. At least, that is how she felt until Ivan and Tatiana and Alexander surrounded her with the love she needed to feel alive in the world. And now...they were all gone. And here she was, standing alone once again with not even her birds to comfort her.

And then she heard it.

Rebekah moved toward the parapet and gripped the top of the

railing tight. She searched the sky for what she thought she had heard. She could barely breathe as she looked at the clouds. That was when they parted and her eagle descended.

Tears filled her eyes as she watched him struggling in flight as he made his way to her. A single ray of light lit his way as he flew toward her. A gentle wind filled the air. It was then that Rebekah saw Reginald faltering in the sky, only to be helped by the wind that carried him safely to her.

She stepped away from the balcony edge to make room for his descent. Even from where she stood, Rebekah could see how badly beaten Reginald was. She tried not to weep knowing how such infliction must have come to him and who must have dealt him blow after blow.

Reginald landed on the balcony, colliding onto it until his body skidded to a halt before her. Rebekah rushed toward him, wrapping her arms around him as he lay there, struggling to breathe; she held him tight. Her eyes darkened as they roamed the bloodied feathers. She saw the massive lashes and deep penetrating wounds that severed his broken body. Rebekah looked at his face; he was staring back at her with his one swollen eye and blackened other.

"My queen..." His voice was barely a whisper.

She could not speak. All she could do was hold him close as the tears continued streaming down her face as the light from above continued to shine down over him.

She touched her medallion, gritting her teeth in frustration as she clutched it in her hand. "It won't work on you. Only humans..."

"I know, my queen." He laid his talon over her hand. "It's all right."

She shook her head.

"No, my queen. It's all right." Reginald breathed deeply and looked into his queen's eyes. "You asked me once...to undertake the greatest honor of my life." He struggled to breathe. "You asked me...to be your remnant. You have always wanted your legacy to be that of the good, a reminder that there are champions in the unexpected; that words matter but that action behind them matters more. You have wanted us to be proud of that legacy rolling in on the coming of the tide. But what makes me most proud, my queen, is not the one you sought, but the one you have given me anyway." He closed his eyes and breathed in deeply once more. When he opened them, they were shining brightly, looking back at her with strength. It was then that Reginald, in all his pain, rose up.

"Reginald…"

He continued to push his broken and battered body up until he was kneeling before her. When he looked up at her, he gazed at her with a deep, resounding strength that seemed to rise up from inside his heart as if the emotion he felt could not be contained.

"It is not by what you have wanted that makes me proud to carry you on my wings…it is what you have done that makes me shine, my queen. The remnant you have born in this world is not an heir, but something far more powerful — *it is love.*

"My queen, you have loved when you didn't want to. You have given when most would not have shared. You have smiled when you wanted to weep, and you have cried when you wanted to laugh. The universe has seen your actions even if the world takes no notice. But know that I have. Know that that is what kept me going all these years. Know that's what has kept me alive through today, for this time, to carry you on my wings once more." He slowly stood. "Leave the legacy you always wanted, my queen. And together, our clan will shine on."

Rebekah looked up at her eagle as he stood, shaking as he tried to stand tall. The darkness in her eyes lightened until they were their shining gray. Not once did the queen or her captain look away from one another. The sun continued to brighten until both of them were consumed in the light.

Rebekah reached up and took his large eagle head in her hands, "You…have served this clan well, Reginald." He lowered his head to hers; they stood there resting their foreheads against one another's. This was the dawn of an extremely different day. She exhaled deeply as she said, "Take me to the den."

XLVII

T hey were flying past the Great White Mountains when something had caught Rebekah's attention. "Reginald, fly closer to the ground if you can."

He dove down slowly, still wavering as he attempted to fly with his broken wings. But whatever pain Reginald was in did not compare to the agony he felt the moment the landscape came into view.

Rebekah gasped the moment she saw them — her ostriches — they were slaughtered. Their bodies covered the grounds in large mounds all across the landscape. Reginald was beside himself, *"No..."*

Rebekah was deadly silent. Her eyes had swirled to dark, black pools as they flew past body after body of murdered warriors. It was then that Reginald saw Ume's body lying atop a massive heap of murdered warriors. He descended, landing beside him.

Rebekah dismounted and walked slowly toward the great ostrich chief and knelt down beside him. From the deep wounds along his neck and chest, she recognized the marks — they were claws. *Crows.*

"My queen, I don't understand this. Poe had Ume build a wall to protect the clan from outsiders. Why would he order the murder of our own kind? Why...would they do it?"

Rebekah stared at Ume's face, resting her hand gently over his heart. "Ume knew, Reginald. He knew what they were up to. He saw a wrong and aimed to set it right." She reached up and closed

Ume's eyes and rested her hand over his heart speaking a silent prayer. She looked out across the path of slain ostrich warriors and out toward the plains beyond. If this was any indication of what she was going to discover on her way to the den, Rebekah knew that this was going to be the darkest day of her life.

Reginald flew across the plains, through the gray-filled sky, carrying his queen on his back. Rebekah could feel his body trembling in pain as he flew across the remaining kingdoms toward the den. Looking at his blood-soaked feathers, something deep within her heart began to grow. It wasn't sadness. It wasn't anger. It was a confident strength filled with a sense of peace that Rebekah had never known before. Strange to feel that way when a rogue raven and an army of crows was reeking havoc on the realm in the name of the clan. She should have felt rage over what Poe and her warriors had done. She should have felt sorrow over the blow she had just received. But she only felt peace and a sense of focus regarding whatever scenario was coming her way to do whatever it was that must be done to put an end to this murderous mutiny.

The sky was filled with darkened clouds that seemed to dim even more the closer they came to the den. As they descended, the silence that had filled the landscape as they soared past Bull Valley was now consumed by a cacophony of thunderous shrills, roars and cries as the clouds parted and the den came into view.

And what Rebekah saw...was an absolute annihilation.

Crows, vultures, and owls pulverized the clans below. They outnumbered all the other clans twenty to one. She watched in horror as the crows dove in and out of the sky, swooping down upon the clans as they tore body parts limb from limb, carrying bodies in their beaks, plucking them up from the ground and careening them through the air until gravity pulled them below to their deaths. The lions were fighting alongside the gorilla, bull and amphibian clans as they fought the army of birds.

Crow after crow, she watched her warriors decimate what was left of the clans. That was when she saw Poe. Poe was fighting with Kenuen as the eagle attempted to protect and defend the other clans from the vicious attack by his brethren. Other hawks and falcons were battling it out with the crows and vultures as they fought to defend the other warriors as well.

She saw Alexandra down below fighting tooth and nail with the owls as they dove down to attack her. Hood and members of the Wolf Pack had surrounded her and were battling it out with the incoming birds from the ground. There was nowhere to run. The crows had burned the entrances to the den, trapping warriors inside while the remaining clan warriors came face to face with them outside the courtyard.

That was where Byron, Minotauro and Sebastian were. They fought side by side with their own kind to take out the birds as the crows continued to viciously attack. And she knew what she was seeing: should any one of the kings or the princess be killed, the rest of the clans would fall. Poe was shouting to the crows to double up and zero in on the kings…and the princess.

And then she saw Nathan.

He was fighting alongside Daniel, fighting ferociously to protect his grandson.

Reginald hovered in the sky as she took in all points of the battlefield watching this massacre upon the clans. Reginald looked up at Rebekah out of the corner of his eye, watching the emotions collide onto her face as she took it all in.

How do you want to be remembered?

She looked out at her birds reeking their bloodbath over the realm.

Better than this day.

She shifted her gaze to the remnants — the three kings — as they wielded their weapons against her crows.

Wiser than the others.

She looked at Daniel and Alexandra.

Kinder than the rest.

She looked at Reginald's wounds, feeling his body racking in pain beneath her body.

An eagle that soars rather than the scavenger who settles.

She looked up at the sky and saw only clouds.

To do something great.

She looked down at her engagement ring, touching the finely crafted rose.

To be someone unexpected.

She leveled her eyes at Poe as he moved in to attack Nathan.

To be different...than Palimus.

Her eyes finally shifted, reaching Reginald's. They held each other's stare; a silent communication passed between them. She nodded only once. He nodded in reply, completely in tune with what her will desired. "We will need the Thunderbirds..."

He moved across the sky and shouted the loudest shrill he had ever sounded. For a moment, it seemed that all activity stopped and the world went silent. And it had. All across the den, everyone looked up and saw Queen Rebekah and the great eagle captain hovering in the sky.

Kenuen shouted to the Thunderbirds, *"TO THE QUEEN!!!"*

Poe seethed as the Thunderbirds ascended, rising toward the queen. Seeing Reginald carrying her on his wings, he was beside himself in disbelief. But what chilled him to the bone was the look his queen was now giving him. She was angry; deadly angry. And she was looking at him. He watched as she ascended. In that moment, Rebekah's words came rushing back to him. He knew what it was she was about to do. He shouted to his army, *"SSSTOP HER!!!! SSSTOP THE QUEEN!"*

A legion of vultures, crows and owls rose up and shifted their position mid-sky, ascending toward their once-beloved queen. Poe rocketed into the sky and beelined straight for Reginald.

"POE!!!"

Poe turned his head and looked back, having heard the lion king's cry. He saw Nathan charge across the field down below, hacking away at each and every crow that attacked as he made his way forward, following Poe's path. Poe raged as Nathan continued to charge across the lands toward him, hacking away at his brethren as each of them moved in. He looked up and down between his queen and the king, tormented as to who he should follow. Finally, he descended.

Daniel spotted his grandfather racing across the fields, severing the limbs off of every crow in sight. He was about to follow him when he suddenly heard Alexandra scream. He turned and saw a dozen crows descend on her pack, ripping the wolves from the sky, leaving her exposed. *"ALEXANDRA!"*

He raced toward her.

Byron was wielding his scepter, Bane, using it as a hammer, a sword, and a spear. Minotauro and Sebastian were beside him. As they fought alongside their warriors, they made their way to Daniel and Alexandra.

United as one, they banded together to cover all sides of the battlefield as the crows continued to descend. The gorilla, bull, lion, wolf and amphibian warriors closed in around their kings and queen, creating a barrier against the birds to protect them at all costs. All of their lives depended on it.

Poe was in the dive gunning for Nathan down below. Nathan's eyes were slit to a cat; he kept charging forth until the lion king and the raven collided. Nathan swung his sword and connected. Poe shrieked as his forearm flew through the air. It had been hacked clean off. He spiraled in the air until finding his center. He halted, hovering in the sky as he zeroed in on Nathan. He pulled the dagger from its sheath and dove down once more.

Kenuen was beside his captain awaiting Reginald's command.

"We must protect our queen. I need to gain speed. I am heading for the sun."

Keneun slowly nodded, understanding what the great eagle captain was communicating to him without speaking another word. Kenuen turned and shouted to the Thunderbirds. He moved in front of Reginald as the rest of the eagles gathered in V-formation, surrounding the queen. They soared over the center of the valley, flying faster and faster, rising higher and higher into the clouds. As Reginald and Rebekah climbed their way higher into the sky, the vultures, owls and crows ascended, attacking the Thunderbirds on all sides. One by one, the eagles fell away as they battled it out with their brethren.

As they rose above the clouds, the sun finally came into view, shrouding them in light, Rebekah clasped both hands around Reginald. "Reginald…"

Reginald's voice was calm and steady, "Do not be not afraid, my queen…I am with you to the very end."

Rebekah closed her eyes and reached one hand up to the sun. She placed her other hand over her heart. A ray of light burst forth from the sun and…*SNAP!* A lightning bolt shot down through Rebekah's hand, down through her body, and into her heart.

All across the den, the birds stood straight up, suspended in midair. Their bodies hovered; they were paralyzed, held by an unseen force.

Byron and the rest of the group watched, stunned, as the battle immediately stopped…and all went silent. Daniel searched the sky, watching as the battalion of bird warriors hovered.

Alexandra shouted, pointing to the sky, *"LOOK!"*

Thunder rolled out across the sky…and lightning followed.

Poe was a few yards away from reaching Nathan when a bolt of lightning snapped down and ripped him back into the sky. Nathan watched his ascent as the clouds parted, pulling him toward a black hole filled with lightning. All around Nathan, birds were being ripped from the realm and up toward what looked like an electrified vortex.

That was when he saw her.

The world around him ceased to exist the moment the clouds parted...and Rebekah fell from the sky.

Daniel, Alexandra and the other kings saw the queen rocketing down to the ground below as the birds continued to be pulled beneath her, disappearing from the realm as the lightning continued to strike. It was Byron who understood what he was seeing. *"No...no, queen!"* Lightning bolts lit up the sky ripping bird after bird from it, pulling them back towards their queen and into the black hole. The vortex continued to draw all the birds in, swallowing them whole. Byron charged forward. Sebastian, Minotauro and the rest of the warriors followed closely behind.

Nathan raced across the plains making his way to the hilltop. He knew the path well; it was the same hilltop he stood upon for fifty years as he awaited for the queen to awaken.

It was a hill filled with sorrow, hope and regret. And as he raced up the hill one last time, he was not the king who had grown old over the years as he waited for her. He was the king who loved her the way he had done when he was young. He was the man who had vowed to live his life as if his queen were always beside.

And as Rebekah's body continued to spiral down from the sky, he ran even faster. He could see Reginald's body spiraling beneath her until Poe's body came into view. The three of them — the queen, the eagle and the raven — were joined as one, falling from the sky together.

He had to get there. He had to try. He refused to believe that the world would not allow him this…one…thing.

But he didn't make it.

Rebekah, Reginald and Poe smashed into the ground. Their collision caused the entire hillside to quake, throwing Nathan to the ground as the earth shifted upon impact. He could barely see in front of him as dust filled the hillside. He pushed himself up and ran toward the large hole in the ground. He slid down rapidly, trying to find his way toward her through the debris. And once the dust settled, he could not believe what he was seeing. Reginald was lying dead on the ground, his head was facing East while Poe's head was facing West. Rebekah's body was lying on top of them. No sign of any other bird existed save these two warriors. Nathan simply stood there, breathing hard, as he stared at Rebekah. He could see one of her hands resting against Reginald, and the other hand rested over her heart. She was wearing her ring.

The moment he saw the ring, all strength left Nathan; he fell to his knees. "No…" He looked up in rage and pain, shouting to the sky, *"WHY?!?!"* His cry of pain echoed across the valley. He was breathing hard, and it was getting even harder for Nathan to breathe as he lowered down beside her body, reaching for her hand. He touched her face, gently moving a piece of hair from her forehead. "You promised me…" He lowered his head and lifted her hand to his heart. He could not take it. He began to cry. He lowered down beside her, resting his head against her chest as he held her hand to his heart.

"The doors will not close this time without me."

Nathan closed his eyes.

Several moments passed where the realm was filled with an unnatural silence. Nothing seemed to move. Not even a tree seemed to be stirring.

Byron reached the top of the hill. He looked down and saw Rebekah and the lion king down below. He raced down the hillside until coming to a full stop at what he saw before him.

The gorilla king took in the sight of Rebekah lying dead between her warriors with the lion king beside her. He could still see the burns all over her skin; it pained him to know what she had done for him. And now she had done something more for them all. He stood there, unable to speak as Minotauro and Sebastian made their way beside him. They turned their heads the moment they heard Daniel, Alexandra, and Cheetah approach.

Daniel moved between them. The moment he saw his grandfather, he fell to his knees. "My king..." But Nathan did not stir.

For all the tragedy the great lion king had seen in his lifetime, with all the lives he had seen go before him, he had finally joined them.

Cheetah let out a mournful sound beside his prince. Alexandra knelt down and touched Daniel on the shoulder.

Daniel could not find the strength to lift his head.

Sebastian looked all around, seeing no other bird in sight. "What happened here today?"

Byron was still looking at Nathan and Rebekah's hands clasped in death when he said, "The realm was united as one."

ONE MONTH LATER

XLVIII

Byron stood on the other side of a glass coffin. Rebekah's body rested inside. Laying on her chest was her golden medallion with the carvings of the raven and the eagle. He stared down at her lifeless face, untouched by decay, still in shock of all that had happened in so short a time. Books and scrolls were scattered all across the floor. Minotauro took in the sight of the chaotic mess as he stepped up from behind. "The dead have always stayed that way."

Byron did not turn. "The world shines a little less brightly without her."

Minotauro stood beside him looking down at Rebekah as well. "It always does when one is as loved as this queen was. My bulls mourn her still."

"She was hope for so many things for me, my friend. I cannot stand to let her go. If I bury her in the ground, then I can no longer bear witness to her sacrifice. A carcass of dreams without meaning — and death will have truly won." The bull king took in Byron's face. "I have a jealousy with death, Minotauro, and it's not my time to go."

"No, it's not. You're not alone in this, my friend. I, too, am exhausted of pain and its arrow of sorrow aimed at our people. Not everything should be this hard. But without the struggle, there is no victory." He rested his hand on Byron's shoulder. "We shall conquer this threat of death. Despair and destruction shall not reign supreme."

Byron finally looked at him, grateful to have a friend like him.

"Don't get lost in the what-ifs and what-could-have-beens. It's the road of what can be that you must march upon...keep going."

"I thought bulls were supposed to be all brawn."

Minotauro slapped him on the shoulder. "We are...but we're only faking it."

Byron slowly smiled.

"Now for some news...my bulls have distributed the food to each of the clans. Each has been given a month's supply."

"And the crops in the northeast corner?"

Minotauro's smile faded. "Wilting."

Byron sat down on the top step, resting his head against the glass coffin. He looked out the never-ending gray sky, searching for the sun.

Minotauro lowered his head, "I'll send word to Daniel and Alexandra."

Byron picked up one of the books beside him, tossing it into the rest of the pile. "And send word that I cannot find anything in all of our history that points to land abundant with water."

"I think I'll leave that part out for now." The bull king turned toward the doors and shouted to a guard, "RAM!!!"

A ram warrior charged inside. Ram was over seven feet tall. He snorted and lowered his head to his king.

"Send one of your men to the lair. Go to the den. Tell the queen and king...the crops are dying."

Ram nodded gravely. He charged out the ballroom door. Minotauro turned back to Byron and took in his friend's face. "There is good news. Sebastian has broken ground at the dam."

Byron scoffed, "A dam for a sea without water." He shook his head, smiling at the irony.

"Nonsense. It sends a message to the universe...that we expect it to answer!"

Minotauro grinned and exited the door. Byron closed his eyes and breathed in long and deep. He had been trying to hold onto the last bit of hope; he still had it in his heart. But with each passing day, he could feel it slowly slipping away. "Ah, Rebekah...if only you could still send us the rain." He lowered his head. It was then that he saw his shadow on the ground in front of him. He turned his head and saw the sun shining down from above. It had been the first bit of sunlight he had seen in over a month; almost as if the sun itself were mourning the loss of the queen. Byron could feel his heart hammering inside his chest as the sun began to grow brighter and brighter until its rays moved along the floor and over toward Rebekah's coffin. Byron stood and waited as the light moved across the glass until stopping right on top of Rebekah's medallion.

The medallion...it suddenly began to glow. The sun beneath the head of the eagle and that of the raven was on fire but the medallion itself did not burn. Byron gripped the coffin and tried o pry open the lid. It would not budge. He used all the energy he could muster to pry it open.

"*Minotauro!!!! Minotauro!!!!*"

The bull king rammed through the door and turned on his heel like a buffalo as he charged toward Byron with three single steps that hurled him across the ballroom and next to his friend. He saw the medallion on fire and Byron struggling to open the coffin.

"HELP ME!"

He joined him as they struggled to open it together. "What...did you seal this with?!?"

Byron struggled, "Toad venom. Stop! I got it...move! *Move!*"

Minotauro backed away. Byron took his bone scepter from his side. "Forgive me, Rebekah."

He raised the scepter high above his head and slammed it down onto the coffin, shattering the glass.

"*The four main elements in this world are fire, ice, wind and earth...*"
The lion king Daniel sat behind a large desk reading through

various scrolls, maps, books and notes strewn all across it. He was a man on a mission. Cheetah stood on a ladder on the second level of the library searching for a book on one of the shelves. Daniel picked up an opened book reading through one of its passages.

"The balance between them maintains the thread of order amongst life and all forms of species. Without it, the natural order of what was intended would be thrown into chaos, shifting the balance of one element over all. The result would be what we are experiencing now…drought, famine, plague…all of which are a result of fire dominating that which was intended to be even-planed."

Daniel put the book down. Cheetah jumped down from the ladder onto the first floor.

"Marcus wrote an entire book describing the elements. And I have no idea what it means. The elements had nothing to do with the famine and drought. It was the birds who brought the rain and maintained the crops, not the dominance of fire."

He rubbed his eyes.

Cheetah cocked his large cathead to the side, "You look just like your uncle when you do that."

"A month of reading his handwriting is ruining me. What do you have there?"

Cheetah looked at the book resting on the desk, "His account of the events surrounding the year the peace treaty was signed between the kingdoms."

"Let me see."

Cheetah handed it to him. Cheetah looked through some of the maps.

"At least this one was put into press. I might actually be able to read it. What I don't get, Cheetah, is why he had so many maps of territories beyond the five kingdoms. How much land is out there?" He turned toward his guardian. "Did SinJin ever say anything to you about what they were looking for *specifically?* Anything other than food and water?"

Cheetah sighed, "Not that I know of, king."

Daniel exhaled deeply. "I can't seem to get used to that title yet. *King.* I miss them both." He turned his attention back to the massive amount of information on his desk. "These maps are mere footnotes in all this mess. If only Marcus had written how it all connects into one single book." He flipped through various scrolls on the desk. "And the frustrating thing is that I can't find one lone passage in all of this on how he thought to bring the rain."

Cheetah hissed, "How would you know if he did or not — you cannot read his writing."

Daniel looked up at Cheetah; a low growl rumbled in his chest. Cheetah lowered his head, bowing, and leaped back up to the second floor. The lion king stood and stretched. He looked out the window. "It's almost dawn."

"Just like your grandfather."

Daniel threw a cloak over his shoulders. "Watching the sun rise over Bird Kingdom seems like the right thing to do — especially now."

He and Cheetah exited the library and headed toward Bull Valley. The moment the library doors closed behind them, the large window Daniel was just looking through was forced open by the wind. The wind moved toward the scrolls and maps on the desk, blowing through them as if an invisible hand were sifting through them with a purpose. The wind stopped when one particular document came into view. The title of the passage read *The Poisoning of the Bird Queen.*

Alexandra stood at the banks of Wolf Lake. She was staring out at the still sheet of glass, weeping in the moonlight. As her tears cascaded down her face, she could not find the strength to fake a sense of hope. She could not find the energy to issue a command. Her world had been turned upside down in a single moment, leaving her stripped of her comfort as she became queen to a lair because of the devastating death of her father.

The moment Hood had told her her father was dead, she ran the fastest she had ever run in her life back to the lair. She could not believe it. It did not seem possible; any of it. She wasn't ready. She wasn't ready for any of this.

As the days passed, they seemed to flow into each other; they were all the same. She had no idea what she was supposed to do now. All she knew that every single person she called "family" was gone: her father, Reginald and Rebekah.

The entire realm was still reeling from the assault it had undertaken, continuing to put itself back together. She and the rest of the kings were attempting to get to know one another, knowing they would all need to work together to come up with a plan as to how to keep the keep their clans alive by keeping the crops in Bird Kingdom from dying.

It was all too much for her to bear. Alexandra had never felt so alone in her entire life. She looked up at the sky, willing herself to see Reginald flying over her lair. She looked toward Bird Kingdom, imagining walking into Rebekah's garden to talk. And then she looked to her own lair, hoping she could see her father sitting in his chair by the fire just one more time. But they were all gone.

"Oh, father..." She lowered her head and wept. If she had collected all the tears that had fallen over the last few weeks, they would fill the entirety of Wolf Lake. She wiped the tears from her eyes and looked out at the darkened waters. Something about the water...it was the same feeling she had when they had found Marcus' body — that someone was watching her.

She listened closely to the sound of the trees and the water before her, listening for someone. But she did not hear anyone. She did, however, see something. Alexandra narrowed her eyes and looked out toward the lake. There was something in the water. The moonlight was hitting whatever it was just right, causing the object to sparkle as it began making its way to shore. She did not even notice that her breath was fogging on the nighttime air.

Alexandra moved in closer and reached down into the icy water. She grabbed hold of the object and pulled it out of the lake. She gasped. Resting in her hands was a silver medallion in the shape of the moon; it also had what looked like a wave carved across it. It was beautiful. She looked up at the pale orb, feeling a sense of comfort, as if someone out there heard her cries.

But who? And where had the medallion come from?

Clasping the medallion around her neck, tucking it beneath her tunic, she made her way back to the Wolf Lair and entered her father's chambers. Alexandra sat down in her father's chair staring at the chessboard. It was dusted over; evidence of an unfinished game still covered the board. Hood entered the room carrying a plate of food in his hands. As he approached his queen, he took in the pale color of his queen's face and the dark circles beneath her eyes. He set the plate down beside her.

"You need to eat, my queen."

"An appetite escapes me."

"But you *must* eat!"

Alexandra leveled her eyes at him. "Do not think me a member of your pack, Hood! *I'm* the one who gives the commands in the lair now! I will eat...when I'm hungry."

Hood came around the chessboard and knelt before her, gripping the armrests of the chair. "But we *feel* it! The pack is weakened by your cries!"

She hit the chessboard, scattering the pieces across the floor rising from the chair. "Am I not allowed to mourn my father!"

"We *all* mourn our king! But not enough to grieve ourselves into the grave. You must think of *us* now, queen!"

Alexandra shouted in reply, "I know!" Tears streamed down Alexandra's face. "I just..."

More mournful howls sounded in the distance. Hood cringed when he heard the desperate cry of his brethren. He turned his large head and looked Alexandra dead in the eye, "You are strong, queen. Shed no more tears. Tears are for the forgotten ones. Our king is not forgotten. He is alive in you...now feed his memory. Eat something."

She turned her head to the balcony that overlooked the woods in the lair hearing the cry of her pack. Alexandra looked at Hood and saw his weakened state and the sadness behind his tired, wolf eyes. Hood rose and turned to leave the room.

She called after him, "Hood..."

He stopped. She looked at the scattered pieces on the floor.

"Do you know how to play? I need...a partner in order to play." Alexandra covered her eyes as tears streamed down her face. "I'm sorry. He was…my rock."

The wolf captain's eyes softened, "No, my queen…you were his."

Hood bent down and picked up the pieces.

XLIX

I *have dreamt of her face...*
And she danced before me in my dream, dressed in the color of the darkest night,
dancing in the moonlight. Shadows of large creatures danced beside her, moving and
gliding to the sound of a lone drum. They danced side by side, dancing as one, dancing
before the fire that blazed red like the sun. "Who are you?" I asked her.

She turned to face me, uttering the words with the softest of sounds, "The one that is
forgotten, the one who honored the Sun."

She faded then, in and out of my dream.

"Tok...tok...tok..."

Rising from the shadows on her right and on her left there came an eagle and a
raven, whose eyes glowed red, red like the sun. The bird warriors turned away from the
fire — one faced east while the other faced west. Upon their movement, the flames grew
higher as the woman swayed before the flames. She turned swiftly then, so that we were
eye to eye.

"Fire...wind...ice...earth..." She looked at the sky. "Protect my clan."
Rebekah raised her eyes to the sky. "Only a noble heart..."

Rebekah slammed her hands together in front of her and sent the light forth.
The lightning exploded from her castle and a massive shockwave burst forth
from her gates and out across the kingdoms.

Daniel's head snapped up. He looked around at the scrolls on the
desk, moving them around, searching frantically through them.

"Fire. Wind. Ice. Earth. The Elements."

He shoved more books off the desk.

The howl of a wolf sounding in the courtyard stopped him dead in his tracks. Alexandra and Hood entered the library.

"I don't believe it. I don't believe the news I heard today. Minotauro and Byron are wrong! It can't be happening this quickly!" Alexandra took her gloves off and picked up a book, sat down, and fervently searched through it. "With all this knowledge and history, there has to be an answer, Daniel!"

"It's a hidden stairway if there is, Alexandra." Daniel took in her forlorn form. "I've missed you."

She slowed her flipping but did not look up. She moved her head in Hood's direction. He bowed and left the room. Daniel moved toward her, crouching down in front of her, taking her hand. Alexandra threw the book down onto the pile on the floor. She stood and moved away from him and over toward the window looking up at the moon. She shook her head in anger. "You missed something. I know it!"

Daniel clenched his jaw in frustration and stood up. "I haven't seen you in days. You have no idea what I have or haven't done."

"My father would've found an answer."

Daniel struggled to swallow his anger at her retort. "You know, Alexandra, it's moments like these where I wish I *could* remember everything I ever learned. Where I regret not having paid closer attention...because maybe then I *would* have an answer for you and the entire realm!"

Tears streamed down her face; he saw that she was crying and that she was trying not to. He calmed down and walked over to her. "I'm sorry. I didn't mean to yell at you."

She wiped the tears from her face. He wrapped his arms around her waist and rested his chin on her shoulder.

"What can I do?"

"I know you've been looking for an answer...for all of us. I just miss him. I'm angry, Daniel. The blows just keep coming. I didn't expect the news today. I...I'm trying to see that autumn tint of gold..."

He followed her gaze and looked up at the moon. "What?"

"My father once told me that the tide would turn. It was a time when the days stretched like months and I couldn't bear the thought of putting forth the last of my energy into the idea of hope. And yet I felt more alive in my sadness. I clung to it as if melancholy itself was the life raft of that very same hope…it made no sense. Even now, I can picture the sun as we stood over his balcony…that sun with its autumn tint of gold. How I wanted those rays of light to fill me up with the same hope my father had in his eyes as he looked upon it. I wish for that same sun now."

She leaned back into Daniel's strong arms and closed her eyes. "Perhaps there is no answer to a question that was never intended to be asked."

"Or maybe it isn't the moon you should be looking at when trying to see your sun." He kissed her cheek.

Alexandra smiled.

"I wish I could bring you the hope you need. I don't like to see you cry." He lifted his head. "Wait a minute…"

Daniel looked over at the books and walked swiftly back toward his desk. He rapidly began his search again amidst all the books and scrolls. Alexandra watched him. "Daniel, what is it?"

"The sun. Fire. It dominated the kingdoms…"

He could not find what he was looking for. Daniel's eyes slit to cat as he roared, "*CHEETAH!!!!*"

Cheetah burst through the doors and leaped across the room and over to the desk.

"Where's that book! The book on the elements! The green one that Marcus wrote!"

Alexandra watched Cheetah leap to the second level of the library.

"Rebekah…she called upon them…in my dream…"

"What dream?"

Daniel sifted through more papers until his eyes fell upon the scroll on the poisoning of the queen. Cheetah leaped off the second floor and landed beside his king. He looked over Daniel's shoulder to see what he was reading; the book on the elements was in his claw. Daniel turned his head and saw the book. He looked up at Cheetah.

"The elements aren't just forces of nature, Cheetah."

Alexandra was confused, "Daniel, what are you talking about?"

Byron and Minotauro burst through the door. "Lion!" He was wearing Rebekah's golden medallion. "Something extraordinary has happened!"

Daniel took in the glow on the gorilla king's face. "Don't tell me…it's about the queen."

L

The Mariner Sea lied as still as glass. All around its banks, Sebastian worked alongside members of his clan: frogs, toads and salamanders as they carried a large tree on their shoulders and over toward the sea's banks.

"ON THREE! ONE…TWO…*THREE!*"

They hurled the tree down onto a growing pile of wood.

The frogs went into a frenzy of croaks. Off of his frogs' warning, Sebastian turned to see Byron, Minotauro, Alexandra, Daniel and a small guard of each of their warriors approaching.

Byron called out to his friend, "I thought you would've had the dam built by now, Sebastian! Perhaps I should send my gorillas to help you!"

He smiled the moment he saw the gorilla and bull kings. "As long as they don't attack us for chopping down their trees." They clasped hands. Sebastian nodded in acknowledgement to Daniel and Alexandra. "Quite the entourage here today. What did I do to deserve it?"

Byron answered, "There is a shadow in the mist and it lies with your clan. At least, I hope he does. It has to do with the night the Bird Queen was poisoned by one of the frog waiters."

The moment he said this, Sebastian's face turned to one of pure fury. All work around the dam stopped; logs dropped to the ground. The entire amphibian clan responded and the booming retort of frogs and toads ensued.

Sebastian was angry; he turned and shouted at Daniel, "*LIES!* My clan was the scapegoat to a greater plot by *yours!*"

Cheetah and members of the Lion Guard growled threateningly. Warriors of the amphibian clan gathered around their king. Byron and Minotauro moved toward Sebastian to calm him down.

Minotauro placed his hand on the amphibian king's shoulder, "Easy there, Sebastian. Hear the lion out."

He looked at his friends. The look in their eyes calmed him. He nodded to Daniel to continue. Behind him, Sebastian's amphibian warriors quieted their croaked retorts. Daniel motioned to Cheetah; he approached carrying the book on the elements in his one claw, while a metal chute draped across his shoulder and chest carried the scrolls and maps Daniel had been studying.

"My uncle kept a detailed record of the histories of the clans. He was obsessed by it; a servant to the recorded word." Cheetah took a scroll from the chute and handed it to Daniel. "This record states that although the queen was poisoned by a frog..." Daniel looked Sebastian dead in the eye. "An *innocent* frog...it was a toad of this clan who saved her."

The toad warriors looked at one another and croaked lowly in reply. Sebastian looked Daniel dead in the eye. "Not just *a* toad, lion...a *chief.* Netapheha." The toads' croaking grew louder at the sound of his name. "Quiet down, men."

Byron asked, "Is he still alive, my friend?"

Sebastian shrugged, "He was before my time. If he does, my toads would know. Why?"

Daniel unraveled the scroll and showed it to Sebastian. "The piece of the borax stone on Netapheha's headdress counteracted with the poison to save Queen Rebekah. It's that stone that Marcus believed had to have come from outside the realms of the seven kingdoms — there was never any stone like it."

Byron added, "We had hoped to ask the chief how it came into his possession."

Sebastian looked between Daniel and Byron. "I'm missing something here."

Minotauro answered, "Where there's one stone, there are others."

Daniel took the book on the elements from Cheetah. He tossed it to Sebastian. "Queen Rebekah called upon the four elements to protect her kingdom — at least, that's what I dreamt."

Sebastian's eyes narrowed, "The *elements?*"

Byron answered, "Fire, ice, wind and earth."

The frogs eyed one another knowingly. Alexandra caught their exchange.

Daniel added, "Marcus alluded to the same thing in his book. He tried for years to figure out how Queen Rebekah froze her kingdom in time."

Byron added, "Ice froze it."

Minotauro jumped in, "Earth guarded it."

Alexandra added, "Wind breathed down a shockwave that destroyed the dam."

Daniel finished with, "And fire avenged it. The sun heated this world into famine and drought."

Byron looked at Sebastian with a smile on his face. "That's our theory, anyway."

Minotauro pointed to himself and mouthed the words to Sebastian, "Mine."

Sebastian took it all in. "You want me to believe that a non-fact is fact…based on a dream."

Daniel shook his head. "No. All I know is that my uncle believed it. He tried to call upon the elements the way he thought Rebekah did — fire, wind and ice most of all…to see if that would bring the rain."

Byron defended their theory. "But, of course, he never figured out how to do it."

"What does this have to do with Netapheha and other stones?"

Minotauro answered, "Good old Marcus thought of another way it could possibly be done."

Daniel showed him the scroll on the poisoning of the queen. He began to read the section Daniel pointed to. "Marcus believed that if there was one stone that could bring life…"

Byron interjected, "Perhaps there was another stone that could bring the rain. That's what he was looking for all those years."

Daniel's face softened. "And that's what he was looking for when he entered the Lair before Poe killed him."

Sebastian took in the look on everyone's faces. "Stones? You're all serious."

Minotauro grinned widely. "The universe is answering."

LI

L ed by a maimed, gigantic toad warrior named Chango, Sebastian, Alexandra, Byron, Minotauro and their guards marched through the swamps. Chango led the group by torchlight, carrying the torch in his one remaining webbed hand. He stopped in front of a large gate made of cattails and bamboo.

Chango spoke in a raspy voice, "This is the gate to his sanctuary, my king."

Sebastian moved to the front of the group. He took in the size of the gate, feeling the bamboo all around it but it would not budge.

"There's no door. Minotauro..."

Minotauro nodded to Ram. Ram handed off his torch to Rod, a silverback warrior, and charged toward the gate. He careened off it, smashing back into the swamp. He barely made a dent in it. Byron looked up at how tall it reached. "Rod, see how high it goes."

Rod tossed the torch to an orangutan guard beside him. He climbed up the bamboo. While they waited, Sebastian looked at Ram on the ground. "I never thought about it before, but perhaps I should use the bamboo for the irrigation canals. If they can knock your guard senseless, Minotauro, they can carry massive amounts of water across the kingdoms."

Minotauro snorted in reply just as Rod slammed down onto the swampy grounds.

Rod surveyed the area. "I never reached the top, my king. It goes on for miles."

Alexandra sighed deeply. "Of course, it does."

Byron looked up and down, kicking at the base of the gate. "Sebastian, how strong is bamboo at its roots?"

"Depends on how deep the roots go."

Byron looked at him and then at Chango and the rest of the clan guards. His eyes moved to Sebastian. "What is a gate without a guard?"

Sebastian's eyes shifted the moment he realized the answer to the question. A small smile crept onto Byron's lips. "You *are* the Amphibian King, aren't you?"

Sebastian's eyes twinkled. "Out of the way, ape."

Byron moved to stand behind Sebastian. Sebastian looked down at the roots of the gate. He called to the swamp below. "Netapheha! CHIEF OF THE TOADS! YOUR KING IS AT YOUR GATES!"

Nothing happened.

Minotauro piped in, "Perhaps you should have said it louder. More from the diaphragm like us bulls."

"Shut up."

Suddenly, bubbles began rising to the surface from the murky waters below. Chango and other frog soldiers croaked in reply. The bamboo and cattail gate rattled and shook. It grew taller as the bamboo rose out of the water. More bubbles emerged until, from under the bamboo gate, twenty heads of toad warriors rose up from the swamps. The bamboo and cattail gate rested upon their heads as they ascended from the swampy waters below. The toad guards looked at Sebastian and bowed in unison, *"King."*

Sebastian was bewildered but tried to keep his cool. He stepped forward. "Open the gate."

The twenty guards split in half and the gate opened. Beyond its walls was a bridge leading across darkened waters. Spectral lights lining the pathway lighted the bridge. Sebastian led the group across the bridge. When they came to the end of it, he stepped in

front and gazed at the bridge. He could see that it continued along a walkway until disappearing under the murky water. Byron and Minotauro looked over Sebastian's shoulder.

Sebastian surveyed the situation. "It looks like we're going to have to swim the rest of the way." He turned and saw the look on Minotauro's face. "What...there's something bulls can't do?"

Minotauro's face turned green. "It's not one of our better talents."

Byron looked back at their entourage. "The guards will have to remain here. This passage isn't large enough for all of us."

The warriors in each of the clans erupted in protest. The lions roared, quieting the rest of the warriors.

Daniel commanded the group, "We are all remnants here! If we cannot trust each other, each relying upon the other to cross this bridge, we may as well take up arms and fight each other now!"

No one said a word. Alexandra touched Daniel's arm. "Daniel...my pack is right to protest. I don't know how to swim underwater. None of my wolves do."

Chango called to her. "Queen, you will be safe with me." He extended his one remaining webbed hand out to her. The Wolf Pack growled lowly.

Sebastian approached the wolf queen, "You're safe with my clan, Alexandra."

She shifted her wolf eyes to her pack. They quieted down. Daniel put his arms around Alexandra. "You don't have to go if you don't want to. I'll tell you everything that happens."

"It would dishonor the pack if I didn't go with you kings." She moved from Daniel's embrace and over toward Chango. "I trust you, warrior." Alexandra looked back at her pack. "Hood, I'll return soon. We have a game to finish."

He nodded to her as she placed her hand in Chango's.

Sebastian instructed her, "Breathe deep, Alexandra."

Sebastian dove down into the swamp. The moment Chango's hand clasped Alexandra's, he swiftly pulled her down with him into the cavern below. As Chango pulled her through the water, Alexandra could see Sebastian swimming up ahead following the lamps lit afire by clear-looking stones. Sebastian was completely in his element as he swam rapidly toward the caves at the bottom of the massive swamp.

Alexandra held her breath tightly, hoping they'd get to dry land soon. She could feel herself starting to panic as her lungs began to burn. Sensing her anxiety, Chango swam even faster.

Minotauro and Byron plunged down after them. Daniel was the last one to enter. Cheetah handed Daniel the metal chute with the maps inside. Daniel put the strap over his shoulder. "Good luck, my king."

Daniel patted him on the shoulder. Just as he was about to dive down into the swamp, a black paw stopped him — it was Hood. He spoke low. "My queen favors you. My king respected yours. Protect her."

"There is no need for you to fear…"

Hood's fangs protruded. He growled viciously; his large fangs sharp and menacing. "I do not fear, *king*! But I hear things beyond mere words. I see things beyond obvious action. She is not safe! Nor are you…I cannot tell where the danger is coming from but it is near. Its breath is cold on my neck. *Protect my queen.*"

Hood stepped away from the lion king and stood side by side with Cheetah and the rest of the Lion Guard, Wolf Pack, Amphibian and Gorilla Soldiers. Daniel took in the sight of all the clan warriors standing side by side. He burned the image into his mind as he dove down. He followed the bridge as it led to an underwater cave. He swam even deeper. As he continued on, frogs suddenly appeared all around him, swimming up alongside him. They kept a short distance, but their sudden appearance and blank stares were unnerving. Unsure of what they were up to, recognizing that he was all alone in the surrounding waters, Daniel swam even faster.

Up ahead he could see the bridge rising up to a small narrow opening between two rocks. Two frogs raced up next to him. Not all three would fit. Daniel raced between them. The frogs backed off as Daniel rose up to the opening. He reached the top of the water and was directly beside Minotauro, having caught up to him. The bull king did a double take at seeing Daniel suddenly appear.

"You're fast for a lion."

Byron was on the rock shore. "Not everyone's as slow as you, Minotauro."

"Muscle sinks faster, I'll have you know."

"Mine didn't." Byron grinned.

Byron helped Minotauro out of the water. Daniel turned around and saw about a dozen frogs in the pool watching him; their eyes resting just above the water. "The frogs…"

Byron's smile faded the moment he saw them.

Minotauro turned to his friend, "Sebastian…your warriors were supposed to stay behind with the rest of our guards."

One of the frogs spoke up, "We mean no harm, kings. We were merely curious as to how the lion swims as he does."

Sebastian turned to his warriors, "And how does the lion swim?"

The frog answered, "Like a shark warrior."

The kings turned their attention to Daniel. Sebastian asked, "How is that possible?"

"I'm part Mariner." Daniel turned away from the frogs and walked over to Alexandra.

Byron replied, "I'd forgotten that. Better yet, maybe you can give Minotauro some tips."

Minotauro slugged Byron in the back. Sebastian turned toward the cave up ahead. "Focus, people." He started walking toward a massive stone staircase.

As they climbed, Byron noticed the drawings on the cavern walls. There were pictures of old warriors, battles and kings. "I had no idea this place existed beneath your swamps."

Sebastian answered, "Neither did I."

Torches lit the spiral rock staircase all the way up to the top. Alexandra suddenly froze and looked rapidly around. Her eyes were wide.

Daniel grabbed her hand, "What is it?"

Alexandra was perfectly still. "Did you hear that?"

They all stopped and looked at the wolf queen.

Byron asked, "What did you hear?"

"I heard my…" But before she could finish her thought, she whirled around again. "*THERE!!! Did you hear him?*" Tears stung her wolf eyes as she looked at Daniel.

Daniel's eyes narrowed, "Who?"

"My father. I heard his voice, Daniel." Minotauro shook his head. Alexandra saw him. "Bull, I'm a *wolf.* I heard it."

Minotauro looked at her in pity, "The dead don't..."

"To hear the cry of one's people and desire to find a way to answer it...is a noble thing indeed."

The kings whirled around at the sound of the voice. Byron's eyes grew wide in recognition. *"Rebekah..."*

"You must learn that it isn't polite to barge into a room unannounced."

Daniel spun around as the voice traveled to the opposite end of the cave. "Marcus..."

"To come to my kingdom to turn the tide...I riot for such courage — it was once the passion of my own heart."

Everyone looked all around the cave as the voices traveled above them and all around them at the same time. Minotauro grabbed the hilt of his sword. "What's going on here!"

Chango answered the king, "The voices of the dead."

"And they speak the truth."

The moment the old toad's voice sounded, Chango bowed his head in respect. The kings and wolf queen looked upward toward the corral staircase from where the voice descended from. The group followed Chango toward it. He led them to a carved out corner of the cave filled with the furnishings of a small home. Seated at a rock table, quill in hand, writing fervently by candlelight sat the Toad Chief Netapheha. The Borax Stone rested on the crown on his head.

Marcus' voice sounded around the cavern once again, *"Royalty or not, civilization requires the simple act of knocking."*

The group looked past the toad chief but still could not find the source of the voice. Daniel smiled faintly as his uncle's words filled the caverns; it comforted him.

It was Sebastian who approached first, "Chief..."

"Come in, king, come in." He stopped writing and finally looked up at the group. "Humph..." Netapheha shuffled from around the desk and over toward Sebastian. He reached for his king's hand and stuck his tongue out to kiss it. It latched onto the king's emerald ring, and snapped back into his mouth. He looked up with his black glossy eyes. "Welcome, my king." He shuffled back toward his desk as the voices sounded all around the cave once more.

First came a high-pitched male voice, *"Four kings and a queen..."*

Followed by a low-pitched male voice, *"Searching for the Elements..."*

And finishing the sentence was a deep-baritone male voice, *"Beyond this realm..."*

To which Netapheha answered, "Yes, yes, yes." Netapheha started writing again.

Bewildered, Sebastian was still searching the cavern for the source of the voices when he asked, "Chief, what is that?"

"*Who* would be the appropriate term. That is my totem."

Suddenly, as if on command, a gigantic nine-foot-tall creature jumped out of the darkness in front of Netapheha's desk. He bowed to the kings and queen. As he rose, the group took in his appearance. The creature had the head of a snow owl, the arms of a bird — one arm was an eagle's, the other a raven's — and the torso of a wolf. Hanging around his neck was an emerald stone.

Alexandra cried out in shock, "A bird!"

"No, no, no. A totem, young queen. Not a bird."

The owl looked at Alexandra and lowered his large head to hers so that they were eye to eye. He spoke in Alexander's voice, *"She is the cornerstone of my house!"*

Alexandra's eyes grew wide.

Byron shook his head, "This is unbelievable."

The owl looked at Byron. His head turned to reveal another head, that of a barn owl. "Tick..." The head turned again to reveal a third head, that of a horned owl. "Tock..." The head spun again back to the barn owl. "If you please."

The whole time, Netapheha continued writing. "Tick-Tock..."

The head spun to look at the toad chief.

"Bring me the Tablet of Destinies."

Its emergence had not occurred in over fifty years. Not since the kings and queens of the seven kingdoms had met in the Lion's Den to discuss the new treaty — one that never saw light of day.

Tick-Tock's head swiveled to horned owl. He vaulted into the darkness using his wolf hind legs. The toad chief looked up and took in the appearance of his five visitors.

Sebastian, awe-struck, continued to ask, "How is it that your totem exists?"

Netapheha looked up and shifted his bulbous eyes to the wolf princess. "It's an old ritual mapped out centuries before you came into existence." Alexandra was unnerved by his look, unsure of why it was he was even looking at her when it was Sebastian who had asked the question. He lowered his head and continued writing, "Strange to see enemies stand together as friends. But only five where there were once seven. Strange indeed to live through such transition." He finished writing and looked up at the small band of royals. "Remnants, remnants...remnants of the past, of the present, of the future."

Tick-Tock emerged once again with the Tablet of Destinies. His head spun to a different head with each word he spoke. "Become...becoming...became...each of these in turn."

Netapheha took the tablet from him. "Yes, yes, yes."

Daniel continued to stare at Tick-Tock. "How does he do that?"

"As my totem, he can hear the dead — the voices of the past; he can speak in the present and foresee the future. But not all at once. His heads would spin right off if he didn't siphon the noise of the dimensions."

As the toad chief read through the tablets, Byron stepped closer to the totem and looked into Tick-Tock's eyes. They stared at one another taking each other in as if memorizing one another. Tick-Tock's head slowly turned from the snow owl to barn owl. "You can hear the voices too, king. They still speak to you."

Byron replied, "How?"

"Through the life they led."

Byron slowly stepped away from him.

Sebastian moved closer toward Netapheha. "Chief, we've come..."

"You seek an answer to a question that was never intended to be asked." He looked at Alexandra. "The universe is answering." His black eyes shifted to Minotauro. He continued to read the tablet with his stubby, web-like fingers. "Where did I get my stone that

263

brings life…life to a queen…life to a totem…a stone to bring life to the clans…"

The group looked at one another with hope and excitement. Byron moved closer to the chief and asked, "Does such a stone exist? A stone that can bring the rain?"

Netapheha studied the gorilla king's face. "You carry the Bird Queen with you. You wear her around your neck."

Tick-Tock's head shifted to the face of a snow owl — the voice of the past. He spoke in Byron's voice, "*I love your queen, Reginald.*"

"Interesting, indeed. May I see the medallion, young king?"

Byron took the necklace and handed it to him. Tick-Tock crouched down to it. The moment Netapheha dangled it before his glossy eyes, it ignited and Rebekah's voice could be heard coming from Tick-Tock's beak, "*Fire. Wind. Ice. Earth. Protect my clan.*"

Tick-Tock looked at the five remnants and repeated her words again in her voice. "*Fire. Wind. Ice. Earth. Protect my clan.*"

Daniel let out a deep breath. "It's true then. She did call upon the Elements. It wasn't just in my dream." Encouraged, he reached inside his chute and pulled out the book that Marcus wrote.

Minotauro shook his head in disbelief, "And they answered."

"Yes, yes, yes. Fire most of all. Rebekah's father honored the sun every morning he watched it rise over the Wolf Lair, knowing that it was the sun that would make his crops grow. The sun is offspring to fire. Fire answered the bird queen by giving her this medallion."

Alexandra cocked her head to one side, "You speak of fire as if he were a man."

"He is a man. And so are his brothers — Ice and Wind."

Byron was shocked, "Brothers…"

"Rahelio, Rhodes and Zephyrus. Yes, yes, yes. It was their sister earth…Agoura…who gave me the Borax stone. It was her vines that guarded the Bird Queen's gates. It was Rhodes who froze the queen and her kingdom and Zephyrus sent out the shockwave. Only inside the queen's gates was the land untouched — left to grow until the noble of heart awakened her once more."

He lowered the necklace and looked directly at Daniel.

Minotauro looked confused. "I thought the birds brought the

rain."

"With the help of the Elements. They would fly to the sun and call to Rahelio. He would rouse his brothers. Rhodes brought the ice, the sun's fire melted it, and Zephyrus would blow the mist across the seven kingdoms on the wings of the bird clan. All very simple. Yes, so simple."

Daniel extended his scrolls to the toad chief, "My uncle...he has books, maps, journals of lands beyond the kingdoms."

Netapheha waved his hand, dismissing the maps and scrolls. "Lands to seek stones. But stones only the Elements have to give. No, no, no...impossible to find. They are gifts."

Tick-Tock's head spun to the horned owl — the voice of the future. "One gift. A violet stone. One of rain. One of pain."

Netapheha looked at him.

Tick-Tock tilted his head to the side, "Embrace it or race it...it is she."

They look at Alexandra in unison. Her eyes narrowed. Tick-Tock's head spun to the barn owl — the voice of the present. Sebastian turned to Daniel. "You were right, lion. There is a stone to bring rain."

"Yes, king...a stone, indeed."

Sebastian looked at Minotauro and Byron. "There is a way. Our clans will not perish!"

Alexandra placed her hands on her hips, "You aren't listening, king. It is not so easily done." She looked at Netapheha. "Queen Rebekah knew she could call upon the Elements to protect her clan — the sun most of all — because her clan honored them. The Creators..."

Byron looked at the sun medallion on Netapheha's desk.

Alexandra continued, "I have never even heard of them. I never knew that the Elements existed. None of us did. Why would these same Elements that we have never honored just suddenly decide to give us this gift, this stone, if we've never sought them out? How can this be done?"

Netapheha eyed her closely. He looked back down at the Tablet of Destinies. "Only four may go. You are ready."

Sebastian looked at everyone in the group. "There are five of us."

266

Tick-Tock swiveled his head, "Three kings for three brothers. One queen for one sister."

"Decide...decide..." Netapheha went back to writing.

Minotauro put his hand up. "Um, I missed the part of where we're going."

Daniel touched the metal chute at his side. "To the lands outside the kingdoms."

Minotauro turned back to Netapheha. "Excuse me, chief, but instead of leaving our clans, can't we call upon the Elements right where we stand?"

Netapheha stopped writing and looked up. "And where *do* you stand, bull king?"

"I don't understand the question."

"That is why you must go. Two left. Decide, decide."

Minotauro turned back to the group in utter confusion.

Byron shrugged helplessly. "My clan is in charge of maintaining the crop. They do it every day; they don't need me here. The bulls are in charge of distributing it."

"And they can do it in their sleep — *literally*. Besides, I have nothing better to do."

Byron looked at the wolf queen, "Alexandra has no choice but to go if the toad says she must. Daniel has the maps to what lay beyond the kingdoms."

"And I know them well."

Byron nodded. He, Daniel, Alexandra and Minotauro turned to Sebastian. Sebastian was looking at Daniel when he realized everyone was looking at him. "Oh, come on!"

Minotauro was unconcerned. "It makes sense. The dam needs to be ready should we succeed in obtaining the stone."

Byron placed his strong hand on Sebastian's shoulder. "I'm sorry, my friend. We need you to stay and add to the most important piece in this equation."

He nodded in disappointment. "Yeah. All right."

Daniel approached Netapheha. "Chief, I have all these maps, but I don't know which way to go."

Tick-Tock eyed him. "It is you."

"He's right. You are your own compass. Pay attention to the

direction of your feet and you will know which way to go. One foot in front of the other. Yes, yes…"

Daniel was at a loss.

Netapheha sighed in impatience as he explained it another way. "You are the captain of your own ship. You are the writer of your own story. You are the lone journeyman of your path, lion king."

Tick-Tock added, "Created. Creating. Creator." His head swiveled to the snow owl and spoke in Rebekah's voice, "*You are noble indeed, to come to my kingdom to turn the tide, young lion…I am glad it was you who was worthy.*"

Minotauro crossed his arms. "He really freaks me out when he does that."

Netapheha's eyes bored into Daniel's. "Never forget the queen's words. They are your brand. The Elements will see you coming. Yes…yes…"

Daniel nodded. "Do they mean harm?"

A shadow seemed to cast itself across the old toad chief's face, but he did not answer. Instead, he turned his attention to his totem, "Tick-Tock…"

The totem's head spun to barn owl as it answered, "Become."

Netapheha nodded. Tick-Tock jumped over the desk and stood next to the remnants. He bowed to them. "Take my totem with you."

Sebastian nodded in gratitude. "Thank you, chief."

Netapheha nodded in respect, "My king." He went back to writing as the others head down the staircase once again. Byron was the last in the group to leave.

"Gorilla King…"

Byron turned.

"Your medallion."

Byron walked over to retrieve it.

"She wanted you to have it for a reason. A gift for a season."

Byron took the necklace, but Netapheha did not fully let go. "Your father was a brute; a man of ruthless action. You have the voice of a true king. It causes a reaction in others…especially nature. Call to the earth…for it is the sister…who is the most powerful element of all."

Netapheha let go of the necklace and resumed his writing. Byron touched the top of the staircase and charged down the stairs to the swamp below. The vines on the staircase moved gently in reply. A rose blossomed where Byron had touched it; it was a lavender rose. It went from full bloom to a wilted flower. All the while, Netapheha watched it, never conveying any emotion as he observed the message being communicated to him. Instead, he simply lowered his head and continued writing.

LII

Daniel was re-reading the emerald book on the elements, continuing to devour the mythology and legends behind the Creators. It still bewildered him how little he knew, yet it excited him that he was still learning.

Brothers. A sister.

What did that even mean? What did being immortal even mean? And why had these beings not revealed themselves to him or anybody else the entire time the realm had been in existence? How had the clans even know to seek them out? How had Rebekah known. So many questions...

He placed the book down on the desk beside him and stood, moving toward a large mirror. He adjusted his cloak as he looked at his reflection in the mirror when Cheetah knocked on the door.

"Come in."

Cheetah entered the room. The moment he saw his king dressed in his royal garments, he was overcome with a deep sense of pride. Cheetah's chest rumbled in a low purr as he knelt before his king. "My king...it is time."

Daniel exhaled deeply. He opened a small drawer and pulled out the tiny compass that Marcus had left him. It seemed so long ago when Marcus was killed yet it was only a month ago. He clenched his fingers around the small compass and placed it inside his pocket. He grabbed the book on the elements, tucked it inside his cloak, and turned to walk through the large doors. He walked down the long corridors that led out toward the main courtyard. He moved toward the staircase that led up to his throne. As it wound around, the rest of the den came into view. Gathered in the courtyard were all the clans of the five kingdoms. Seated on their own thrones laid out all around in circular formation were the rest of the kings and queen.

The Lion's Den warriors roared upon seeing their king. It was a sight to behold as Daniel took in the warriors filling his courtyard, standing side by side as one.

Daniel looked over at Alexandra. He could clearly see the nervousness written all over her face. He smiled encouragingly at her before shifting his gaze to Byron. The gorilla king was seated on his throne in between Minotauro and Sebastian. He nodded to each of the kings in acknowledgement and respect.

No throne was higher than the other — something Daniel purposely tried to rectify from former generations. This was a new era and a new day where all needed to be united as one. And this day was no ordinary day. As he and the rest of the kings — along with the wolf queen — had planned the day's events, none of them was completely sure of how the day would go.

Daniel stood and looked out at the five kingdoms gathered in his den. Feeling the compass in his pocket and the book against his chest, his voice was filled with the confidence of a king as he spoke, "When I was a young boy, my uncle, Prince Marcus…"

The lions erupted at the sound of Marcus' name.

Daniel smiled and continued, "He told me that some people shape their own course in life, while others are shaped because of it. My uncle was a man who forged his own way. He stepped outside the realm of collective thought, need and desire and relied on his own reason, logic and vision to find an answer to end the horrors and fears that haunt our lives to this day. He sought a means to end famine. He set a value on each of our lives in order to find an absolute."

Daniel touched the book in his cloak. "And he did it by walking down the path of a road less traveled. He wrote it down by going through a different door than the one all others were walking through. He did it by creating his own. Without his individual motivation and drive to merge his desire to become a man who sought a means to harvest the rain and bring life back to the kingdoms, I would not be standing before you today. Your kings and queen would not be joined alongside me in the den if not for the power of one single thought from one man's mind to bring about a miracle to the collective group of all gathered here." He paused before continuing. "Because of my uncle, the forging of his path has shaped my course. And I aim to be the change he wished to see by marching upon the path he cleared for me...and for you. Everyone gathered here is the receiver of my uncle's gift...because he did find the answer. He found a way to bring the rain."

The clans reacted to this revelation. The lion's den roared and erupted in pride once again.

"At month's end, the bull and gorilla king, and wolf princess and I will set out to obtain the means to accomplish this goal. The Amphibian King will remain here with you and rule over all of you in our stead. He will oversee the completion of the dam so that it can be filled once again with the rain that the rest of us kings and queen...will bring."

The clans' murmurs grew louder.

"Until that time, each clan will be responsible for building their side of the dam."

Daniel looked down, trying to gather the courage to convey the message he longed to share; the one he hoped would be understood by all. "I know that there is still distrust amongst the clans. The pain and suffering that each of us has born witness to has scarred us, numbed us, tainted us and shaped us." He looked up and out at all the faces staring back at him. "But there is no reason to fear anymore. There is no need to hunt and prey upon one another any longer. We are meant to live free and pursue each of our own means of happiness. So I say to you...decide. Put the value on your life and those around you. And decide...what is your absolute? Do you wish to hold onto the shadows and the scars, or do you let go of them and live free to pursue your happiness?"

He looked out at all five kingdoms, taking in the appearance of all the warriors.

"We are, by nature, meant to be different…living in our own territories that fit our natures by design and accentuate our skills and gifts. We are where we are supposed to be — each living in one of the five kingdoms. I can't imagine being a lion living in the sea. Or a bull living in the swamps. If we all acted the same way, marching through the same door, thinking the same ideas, my uncle would never have given us the hope that we have so desired…so that in our uniqueness, we can come together as one for one common goal for one common purpose. It is upon these grounds that I say to you bulls, wolves, gorillas, amphibians and lions…make your choice from your own hearts and minds. Build the dam for your side or not. For in building up one side, you build it up for all."

Daniel looked out at the den. All were silent until Byron rose up. "My clan decided before we arrived today. We will build our side of the dam."

Sebastian rose. "We've already begun ours…"

Alexandra looked at her pack. Hood and the rest of the pack barked their reply. She stood up with the other kings, "My pack will begin building theirs."

Minotauro remained seated. He looked over at his herd. They stomped their hooves and snorted, butting heads in angst to their king.

Ram, a Black Angus warrior, grunted loudly, "We will build it, king!"

He rammed his head into another warrior beside him. Minotauro turned to Daniel and nodded. Daniel turned to his lions, "And what say you, keepers of the den!"

They roared in reply. As they did so, the entire courtyard seemed to quake.

Chester, captain of the lion guard, shouted, "King! Our prince has led the den down this road…we will march upon it and honor him!"

Daniel nodded, feeling the pride of this moment rising up in his heart. "Then let the journey begin…and let the rain come!"

The entire courtyard erupted; they had done it. They had brought the realm together for a common purpose and goal — and all were on board. Daniel could not help but look up at the sky and wonder if Nathan, Marcus and Rebekah were looking down at this moment with a sense of peace and a sense of pride. A pang of sorrow eclipsed Daniel's heart at that moment, as he realized that sometimes what you want in life, what you hope for, you may never see. You may never experience. You may never know. Realizing that he was the one to enjoy this moment for them all gave Daniel a deep sense of humility as he stood amongst the clans united as one. And as the sun shone down over them all, Daniel could not help but feel that even Fire himself had given his blessing over their next endeavor. He stepped down from his throne and joined the rest of the kings and the queen as they stood amongst their rallied troops.

From the shadowed corner in the courtyard, Tick-Tock stood. He watched each moment in solitude, standing away from the warriors and their kings as the message was conveyed and received. He moved along the shadows, shifting through the corridors unheard and unseen, until he came to large gate that led out from the Lion's Den and out toward the realm beyond. He pushed through the gates and made his way to the hilltop in Bull Valley that overlooked Bird Kingdom. That was when his head swiveled from barnyard to horned owl — the present to the future.

Vines rose up from the ground and wound around his feet. Tick-Tock looked down at them and tilted his large head to the side. He watched as the roses bloomed and wilted to a dark brown until they turned to ash. A soft wind blew past him, blowing the decay away and out across the land beyond. Tick-Tock lifted his eyes to the sun and whispered, "Whoever control the sea, rules the realm." He lowered his head and stared out toward the Wolf Lair. "Embrace it or race it...it is she."

Tick-Tock felt the air all around him turn cold. The Wolf Princess was right; this was not going to be so easily done. He looked North, out past Bird Kingdom, glimpsing the large element fortress that lay beyond. And as Tick-Tock swiveled his head from horned owl to snow owl, he listened to the voices of the dead, zeroing in on Feyedor's — the wolf king from the Old War — as the land before him turned from green to brown to snow.

Hundreds of miles away, atop the Element Fortress, the wind began to blow harder and faster as the rumbling inside the enormous mountain began to moan and quake. All along its sides, snow began to formulate around its base until it sprouted up all around the mountain as it covered the monolith all the way to its peak. Rising up from the snow-filled cap, Ice himself emerged. He stood and looked out past the forest below and out toward the realm of the five kingdoms beyond. The look on his face was lethal.

"Brothers, they are coming."

The wind whipped all around the mountaintop, spiraling down to the ground below where Rhodes shifted his gaze, following his brother's path. There, he saw several pairs of eyes staring back at him, their growls rumbling along with the tune of the mountain. And then he saw it: a single rose. Rhodes' turquoise-colored eyes stared at the flower, watching as it wilted before him. The fierce and determined look he had on his face melted into one of pure grief. He gently picked up the flower, holding it in the palm of his hand as tears filled his eyes.

"Sister...I'm sorry."

A soft breeze carried the flower away petal by petal until all that was left was a thorn-covered vine. The Lord of the Sea clenched his fist tight as the thorns burrowed deep inside his flesh. His entire body shook with rage as he pounded his fist into the rock, over and over again, until the sound of his fist echoed like a drum as the cold wind blew and the sky turned dark. Even the growls below stilled at the drumbeat of pain that sounded all around the fortress. Rhodes slowly stopped his hammering upon the rock and glared out at the realm beyond. "Mercy...does not live here."

And from the mountain beneath him, Fire spoke the words, *"It is in the suffering that we become."*

Rhodes tilted his head to the side, glaring at the realm beyond as he replied, "Then suffering it will be, brother."

ABOUT THE AUTHOR

Corina Marie Zurcher is the author of the children's books *Growing Up Claus*, the Christmas book *Snow Falls* and the fantasy trilogy that includes: *Archangels*, *The Father of Lights*, and *Legacy*. She is also an actress, screenwriter, producer and the owner of RowanMeir Films. *Nobility* is the second book in The Legacy Trilogy and is the novelization of the screenplay. For all other information, visit: www.corinamariezurcher.com.

ABOUT THE ILLUSTRATOR

Scott Edward is a freelance illustrator specializing in concept art and storybook illustrations. Trained in traditional art techniques, Scott converted his skillset to digital art and uses Adobe Illustrator, Photoshop, Artrage, and Sketchbook Pro to bring his original style and artwork to life. Scott illustrates novels, graphic novels, and storyboards. He is currently working on various children's books including the series *Hailey the Courageous*.

Freelance and aspiring writers are encouraged to contact Scott to conceptualize their projects at www.scott-edward.deviantart.com.

www.ingramcontent.com/pod-product-compliance
Lightning Source LLC
Chambersburg PA
CBHW021219250626
47155CB00008B/2881